A Coal Country Novel

# Copper Creek

## Hillary DeVisser

*Hillary DeVisser*

# Acknowledgements

Thank you to my family for cheering me on and enduring long-winded conversations about characters and plot details that matter so much to me. Thank you to Angie Clifton, Charli Franks, Tiffany Garnett, and Amy Gibbs for racing through early drafts. Your input, enthusiasm, and encouragement is very appreciated and went a long way towards making this story shine.

To those that provided details about areas I know nothing about: coal mining, military life, and all things emergency medicine, I can't thank you enough and hope I did the details justice. Thank you so much for your time and patience with all of my questions: Sam Bohnert, Chad Brown, Jessi Dugan, Lindsay Dunn, Brian Murphy, Lisa Pogue, Kathy Ragan, Amy Tongay, Marshall Watkins and Bob Williams.

I am especially thankful to Sarah West with Three Owls Editing for her editing services and to Cassy Roop with Pink Ink Designs for her formatting and cover design services. Thank you for helping this story put its best foot forward.

# Copper Creek

# One

SHE KNEW SHE SHOULD SAY something. People didn't just sit side by side for hours without speaking. Anna risked a glance over at Travis as he helped get the bags out of the trunk. He looked lost in thought, a semi-frown on his face. Anna didn't know if it was the strain of the past week showing on his face or worse, maybe he was planning when he would pack his things and move out. How long does a person wait to leave their fiancée after her father's funeral?

*Fine*, she thought. Maybe she was over-exaggerating, but he had ridden from the airport to their townhouse with his hand clenched in a fist. That had become such a usual gesture for him that she had looked about twenty times to see if he was still doing it over the thirty-minute drive home. Anna had to hand it to Travis though, despite whatever inner conflict he was fighting, he had certainly been helpful and kind over the last few weeks. He had been her rock through the funeral and hadn't seemed to mind staying several days afterward to make sure Anna's mother was okay.

They had woken up last Saturday to a shocking call, learning that her father had suffered a heart attack. The call had come from Levi, her sister's fiancé. She shook her head at that word. *About time*, Anna said under her breath as she unlocked the garage door.

"Did you say something?" Travis asked, taking the heavy suitcase from her hand and stepping into the mudroom of the townhouse.

"No, just thinking about Jesse and Levi. It's so good to see them together again," she said, her voice sounding as small as she felt.

"Yeah, he seems like a nice guy," he said, walking through to the kitchen. "I'll go ahead and unload the suitcases into the laundry if you want to just go up." Anna walked over to him then and gave him a tight hug.

"Thank you so much for everything you've done. We couldn't have made it without you there to stand by me and to help out with Mom" she said, her eyes filling up with tears. "You were so strong for us and I appreciate it. I don't know what I would have done if you hadn't been there for me," she said, her voice hitching at the end. Travis held her for a minute, then pulled out of her hug.

He walked to the fridge to pull out a beer and looked back at her over his shoulder. "Anna, Walt was a good man. He was always good to me," he said, lifting his shoulder a little, like he had only done a little favor instead of helped to guide her through the death and burial of her father.

To Anna, the few feet between them seemed to stretch to the size of the Grand Canyon. When it was clear he wasn't going to say anything else, she walked through the living room to the stairs. She wondered if he'd come to their bedroom or sleep in the guest room like he'd been doing before they got the call.

Since the day her father died, Anna's dreams had haunted her, replaying the worst day of her life. Her phone rang a little after 8:00 AM that Saturday. She knew it had to be something terrible before she even answered. Eadie and Jesse never called that early; they knew about her Saturday morning routine. She let herself think back for the hundredth time at her surprise to see it was an unfamiliar number with the area code from her hometown. When she heard Levi's voice on the other end, her heart lodged in her throat. Her dad, Walt, had suffered a very serious heart attack. She heard her own voice loud and shrill as she asked Levi to repeat himself several times while trying to wake up enough to take in the horrible news. Within minutes of hanging up she had managed to purchase two seats on the next flight to St. Louis.

Her voice had woken up Travis down the hall. He ran into their room and packed for them both while Anna frantically dressed and called a friend to come pick up and look after Harry, her Standard Poodle, while they were gone. Harry was probably sick without her for a week. She couldn't wait to pick him up in the morning. He was such a big, sweet baby. *Surely Travis didn't plan to take Harry when he left. He couldn't be that heartless*, she thought to herself, her eyes welling with tears at the thought of it. She remembered the day they adopted him from the area Poodle Rescue. A mother Poodle had lost her owner right before delivering puppies. When they walked into the room and saw the precious little puppies, all black except for one silver gray fellow, she knew which one was hers. She and Travis treated that dog better than some people treated their children, a fact she knew all too well as a teacher.

Anna quickly showered and changed into pajamas, avoiding looking at her own face in the mirror as she brushed her teeth and put on her moisturizer. She didn't want to see her own wan face and puffy eyes until she had slept for a very long time. She dried and brushed her long, straight, copper colored hair and flicked off the bathroom light. Her room looked like it had been ransacked. Her bed was still unmade from her frantic departure. Dresser drawers were pulled out, and her closet doors were thrown open with discarded items laying in the floor. Normally those things would have driven her absolutely crazy, but tonight she was just too tired to care. Anna turned off her light and closed her eyes on a terribly painful week.

Her dreams repeated again, the way they had every night since her dad had died. She got there too late to say goodbye to him. She ran into the hospital room to see her mother Eadie leaned over her father, sobbing. Her sister

Jesse stood behind her mother, one hand on her shoulder, another pressing a tissue to her mouth to hold in her own sobs. The moment Jesse turned and saw Anna, a grieving sound escaped from Jesse's lips that made Anna crumble from the weight of it. She had never heard a sound like that ever in her life, and she never wanted to again as long as she lived. Anna hadn't made it in time. Her daddy had already passed, and she hadn't been there to say one more I love you. She doubted she'd ever recover from that particular hurt.

Her dreams were repeated snippets of that day. She remembered frantically driving from the airport to her hometown, Travis dropping her off at the door of the Emergency Room before parking the car, running through the doors where some lady she recognized waved her through. "Your family is in room four, honey," the woman said. Anna stopped then, frowning at the woman's words. *She should have said your father is in room four*, she thought, breaking into a run to the room. The same scenes played through her mind over and over, wrecking any chance she'd have at a restful sleep. She was so exhausted from lack of sleep and caring for her mom that she had very dark circles under her eyes. Her time since the funeral had been spent graciously accepting (and shooing away after enough time) the well-intentioned visitors that seemed to flock to her parents' house. She was grateful that her parents had so many sweet friends, but my goodness, Eadie needed her rest.

Anna woke late the next morning, thankful for uninterrupted sleep. She padded down the stairs after brushing her teeth to find Travis in the living room, his two suitcases and a backpack waiting at the front door. He didn't look like he had slept at all, and Anna was perversely happy to see it.

She stared at him hard for a minute without speaking, then turned to walk into the kitchen. With shaking hands she poured a cup of coffee, forming her face into a detached mask. How strange that he should stay awake all night packing his bags and preparing to leave her, yet still take the time to make coffee the next morning and drink none of it. For a hateful second she visualized him falling asleep at the wheel then driving over some guardrail, coasting down a mountain. How dare he leave her! She cringed at her own awful, detestable line of thinking, took a very deep breath then carried her mug of coffee to the couch where she sat down facing him as he stood awkwardly in the corner of the room closest the door. Without saying a word, she crossed her legs and waited. *Let him be the one to speak first*, she thought.

"Anna," he said, standing then shifting strangely from leg to leg like one of her Kindergarteners requesting a bathroom break. "Anna," he started again, fiddling with the keys he had pulled out of his pocket. Just then it struck her how many times she had seen him do the exact same gesture, and how it wore on her last frigging nerve. "I hinted around about this the night before your dad…" his words hung awkwardly in the air. "Before Walt passed" he said, clearing his throat and looking at her with eyes slightly bugged out. She took another sip of the coffee, so very thankful to have something to busy her hands. "And we haven't talked about it since, because it just wasn't a good time," he said, staring, as she made a very unladylike scoffing sound.

"Sorry, please go on," she said, nodding and sipping her coffee.

He frowned at her then, seeming to finally perceive that she was watching him as if she was at a play that she hadn't wanted to attend in the first place. "Anna, we aren't in a good place. It's all gone wrong somehow, and we both know it wasn't working," he said, seeming to wait for her to argue.

For a minute she was conflicted. She did want to argue. After three years together, including an engagement and a shared townhouse for at least a full year she had completely thought it was working. Anna was so bone-deep exhausted that she didn't know whether to laugh or cry, but she was certain she was tired of crying.

"Travis, I'm just not sure what you need me to say. I love you. I don't understand why this is happening, and truthfully, I think you've lost your mind." At this, he gave her a stern look like he was going to interrupt. She held up her hand to silence him and continued. "I hate this. I really do, but I will not argue it. I won't beg you to stay. I don't understand any of this, but I absolutely will not beg you to stay," she said, taking another sip of her coffee.

He looked at her with a wild mix of confusion, apparently unable to understand that she didn't feel the same way, and relieved that she wasn't going to argue. "Anna, I'm going to go now," he said, picking up his suitcase after opening the front door.

"Goodbye, Travis," she said, not getting up from the couch. And he went, locking the deadbolt with his key from outside like he had done every weekday for a year when he left early in the morning for work. Simple as that, as if he were just heading to the office instead of leaving his fiancée a week after her father died.

Anna didn't move from the spot for a full two hours except to refill her coffee cup and sit right back down. She didn't turn on the television or read or pick up her phone to text her sister. She sat quietly and processed the fact that Travis was gone. At noon her stomach growled, reminding her of her humanity, despite her annoyance. She couldn't quite call it anger, or sadness or shock. Annoyance seemed to almost fit. She fixed a quick frozen meal and called Gail, the friend and neighbor watching Harry.

As she walked the block through the neighborhood, she heard him before she saw him, peeking excitedly through the front window of Gail's townhouse living room. Sharp barking and wild shaking of the tail ensued as Anna knocked on Gail's door. As soon as the front door swung open, Harry pounced on Anna, his usual manners out the proverbial window. As Anna hugged her furry baby the tears she had blinked back over the past few hours poured down her cheeks. None the wiser, Gail was sure the tears were from Anna's grief alone and she got down on her knees and hugged Anna and Harry both.

"Honey, I'm so sorry for your loss," Gail said, grabbing Anna in a hard hug. Tears welled up in Anna's eyes before she could stop them.  As it turned out, she really, really needed a hug.

"I'm so happy to have been able to keep Harry. He was just a perfect baby doll while you were away," Gail said, loosening her hold on Anna, but keeping her hands on her shoulders. Anna was so choked with the emotion bubbling up all she could do was frantically nod in reply. She and Gail were close, but Anna wasn't anywhere near ready to talk about what had happened. She wasn't quite sure how to put it into words.

Swallowing her tears, she took a deep breath and stepped back from her friend, allowing Harry to jump up as she stooped to hug her sweet pup close. "Thank you, Gail. It was such a relief to know he was with you," she said, getting control over her voice and her mind. She managed a tiny bit of small talk and gathered Harry's things, thankful that Gail didn't insist on too much conversation. She walked him back to her townhouse, gathered her mail from the mailbox, and bit back the furious scream that almost erupted when she saw the key Travis had placed there. He was really gone.

# *Two*

ANNA GLANCED AT HER CALENDAR as she planned lessons for the upcoming week. She was once again amazed at how quickly time passes and that life actually does go on despite whatever is thrown at a person. She couldn't help but think that time never really holds still long enough the way it should when a person experiences a loss. She knew her experience was no different. The months passed, and she found herself growing used to the stillness at home. Anna realized during the first few weeks after Travis left that he hadn't really been making much of a footprint in her life. Her schedule had barely changed without him at home. She rose early to exercise at home then poured all her energy into teaching her Kindergarteners and preparing for the upcoming day. At night she walked Harry around her neighborhood and to the nearby dog park for his daily adventures. The only thing she really missed was the security of knowing there was another person in the house during the night. After a while, Anna realized that if that was the only reason she missed Travis, it was better that he had left. She missed occasional sex, but hadn't really worked up the nerve to try to meet someone.

Her weekends were mainly comprised of relaxing with Harry and surfing the web for fun project ideas for her class. Like clockwork, she made Saturday morning calls to her mother, Eadie, to find out how she was doing. Later, she'd call Jesse to find out if their mother really was okay. Anna hated being so far from them, but she had made her home in Denver. She had followed Travis here for a job opportunity that he couldn't turn down several years ago and found she really liked it. She took advantage of her westward facing back deck every evening that the weather allowed. She liked to watch the sunset paint the sky with deep blues and purples before the dark set in at night.

That's where she was one Friday evening in late-March, winding down with the chilled air, staring into her fire pit while enjoying a glass of red wine. Her phone rang and she jumped, startled by the sound of it. Anna grabbed her phone and thumbed the 'answer' key, nervously expecting the worst. After the loss of her father, anytime her phone rang at an unexpected time, she assumed it was bad news. Her heart relaxed a bit at the relaxed tone of Jesse's voice.

"Hey, Sis, are you busy?"

Anna tried to calm her heart rate. "I jumped like I was

shot when the phone rang. Think we'll ever stop doing that now?" she asked, taking a large gulp out of her glass.

"I don't know, Sis, it'll take some time."

"Part of it, I guess. What's up, Jess?"

Anna heard the pause in Jesse's voice as loudly as if she had spoken. "Spit it out, Jessie. What's up?"

"Well, now that I've called to ask, it makes me sound like a presumptuous horse's ass. For all I know, you could be running around naked with somebody, making your own big plans," her sister said, catching Anna off guard as she tried to not spit her wine out on her coat.

"Jesse, what the heck are you talking about? No naked planning here, I'm sitting outside trying to drink a glass of wine!" She laughed.

"I'm being stupid, I know. I was wondering if you'd want to come stay with us over Spring Break if you don't have any other plans," Jesse said, clearly wishing she hadn't assumed Anna didn't have any plans. Now that the words were out of her mouth, she realized that Anna was young, beautiful, successful and might very well have plans to jet off to Jamaica or some other exciting location for her Spring Break.

Anna laughed; her plans for Spring Break hadn't gone beyond ensuring she had enough coffee, eggs, apples and dog food to get her through the week without any unplanned shopping trips. "Jess, I don't have a thing planned. I figured I'd just hole up here with Harry, slap on some sweatpants and watch as many old movies as I want. I'd be happy to come for a visit." At that, Anna felt her stomach give a little flip.

She had sort of accepted her fate as an Old Maid, and the thought of doing something unexpected practically thrilled her. "Should I plan on staying at your house or Mom's?"

"Might be easier to stay at Mom's since my office is in my spare bedroom. You're getting a little long in the tooth to crash on the couch," Jesse said, trying to imagine Anna getting any sleep with her boys roaming around.

"Yeah, and I certainly can't sleep in your bed with you. There might be a big, hairy man in there!" she crowed, smiling at the thought of crawling in bed to find Levi there instead of Jesse. "How's it going with Levi, anyway?" she asked, picturing how content Jesse had seemed by his side.

"Pretty good! And engaged or not, he isn't sleeping over, at least while the boys are home. Now when they're not home, that's another story. I'd forgotten how much I liked sex. Thank God for that man," Jesse said, cackling into the phone.

"Okay, okay, too much information!" Anna said. "I'll plan on staying at Mom's. She could probably use the company anyway. Aunt Ruthie won't be there, will she?" she asked guiltily. She was so thankful that her aunt was able to come stay with her mom after her dad had passed; however, Aunt Ruthie was best handled in small doses. Ruthie's home was in the neighboring town just a few minutes away, but she had spent most of her days from sunup to sundown with Anna's mother. Ruthie was really loving, and really, really loud. Anna was a Kindergarten teacher, used to shockingly high decibels of sound – but a person had their limits.

Jesse laughed. "Yes, the coast is clear. Mom said that Aunt Ruthie is going to visit Jake that week, so you're safe."

"Whew, then count me in. It's getting chilly, Jess. I'm going to get this fire out and take my stuff in for the night. I'll take a look at my calendar and tell you what day I'll drive in," she said, wrapping her coat more tightly around herself.

"Drive? Good grief, Anna. Are you sure you don't want to fly?"

"Nah, I don't mind the drive," she said. "Plus, I don't want to leave Harry. We'll be fine."

"Okay, Sis. It'll be good to have you home," Jesse said, feeling so relieved. She hated not being able to comfort Anna about her breakup. *Travis had always been a smug little jerk*, Jesse thought. It figures he'd have the world's worst timing in breaking up with her sister.

"Jess, I'm glad you called. I could use a change of scenery," she said, surprised at her own admission. She had been doing her best to block out her feelings and not waste time thinking about Travis and how he practically vanished from her life after three whole years together.

"See you soon. Love you."

"Love you, too. Night," Anna said, hanging up the phone and going back into her townhouse, locking the door against the big, pale moon and winter chill.

# Three

AFTER A FEW HOURS OF SETTLING into her room and talking to Eadie and Aunt Ruthie, Anna needed some air. *God I love my family, but what happened to Jesse promising me that Aunt Ruthie would be away for the week,* Anna thought to herself with exasperation. Despite the extra guest and non-stop chatter, the house felt so empty without her dad there. Walt had been a quiet man, but his presence was always known whether he said a word or not. He had emanated strength, intelligence and calmness. Being the only man in a house full of women had limited his ability to fit a word in edgewise, even if he did have something to say. He had always seemed content to be in the room, watching the news and absorbing more of their conversation than they ever imagined.

Now, the house was still full of chatter, and every room

looked the same. Walt's empty recliner in the living room was as all-consuming as a black hole. It pulled like a magnet at the heavy weight that Anna still wore on her chest. She held it there with invisible arms. She hadn't been there when he took his final breath in the hospital. The last thing she was going to do was give up the incessant weight that comes with losing a parent. She wasn't ready to face the emptiness inside her.

Anna went into her bedroom, leaving Eadie and Aunt Ruthie to the latest reality show that had them hooked. They bantered around so much while watching those crazy shows, it was no wonder they had the volume cranked up high. If they didn't talk over the TV the entire time, they wouldn't have to have it up so loud. Anna half smiled to herself at the memory of her dad rolling his eyes when she'd walk into a room. He used to get so tickled at how Eadie would ramble around, not content to just sit and watch a show. She was in constant motion, getting up to stir a pot on the stove, fuss with another basket of laundry, or just get up to tidy something.

She changed out of her pajamas into jeans, brown boots, and a dark green sweater. Late March might technically be Spring, but it was still cold, even for a Denver transplant. She stopped by the bathroom to take a brush to her long red hair. It was straight as a stick, no matter what she did to it. Thankfully, it had a healthy shine and a few streaks of a lighter, almost strawberry blonde hue. The money she saved on hair color was staggering. Her friends from work loved to give her trouble about the unfairness of it all. Anna picked up her purse and walked back to the living room, anticipating shock and awe from her mother and aunt that she'd consider going out 'at this hour'.

"Mom, I'm going to run out for a bit and meet Sorcha for a drink." She smiled, bracing herself.

"Anna, good Lord! At this time of night?" Eadie declared, shock on her face. She scrambled for her watch. "Eight PM! Won't Sorcha be home with her family?" she said, eyes wild with judgment. Eadie operated under the assumption that leaving the house after dark was scandalous.

"Her husband is putting her daughter to bed," she said, pulling her keys out of her purse and giving both her mom and Aunt Ruthie a kiss on the cheek. "Love you," she said, pulling the door closed behind her. Outside, Anna leaned against the door, letting the cold, crisp air fill her lungs. She hated that the house she had always loved was suffocating her.

Anna felt a little guilty lying about meeting Sorcha. She had called her best friend as soon as she had made plans to come home and visit the family over break, but didn't think she could bother her that late at night. Sorcha was probably busy tucking in her little one, reading stories and snuggling in for the night. Anna's stomach tightened at the thought, and she tamped down those sad feelings that washed over her from time to time. Had things worked out as planned, she'd be busy preparing for her wedding in April. Maybe she'd be ready to plan for a baby soon after. She wasn't getting any younger, and she did want to be a mom someday. Instead, she was home, alone, driving to the local hole-in-the-wall bar. *Who cares?* she asked herself. She was thirty years old, she could go out for a drink alone if she wanted.

THE PLACE HADN'T changed a bit, she thought as she walked into the Hawk's Nest. The bar still reeked of cigarette smoke, even though the state outlawed smoking in restaurants and bars a few years back. Anna picked a seat at the bar, hung her purse on the little under-bar hook and ordered a bourbon and ginger ale from the bartender. She accepted her drink and took a decent gulp, feeling the liquid slide down her throat, warming her nicely. She closed her eyes in quiet appreciation of a good, strong drink. Just as she was trying to remember when the last time was when she had actually had any alcohol stronger than wine she felt, rather than saw, someone walk up to stand beside her chair, and she shivered as goosebumps rose along her body.

Anna tilted her head back and looked up into the whiskey colored eyes of Aidan Doherty, Sorcha's incredibly sexy older brother. She felt her mouth go completely dry and her heart kick up to a frantic pace. Anna knew she was making a weird face but seemed to only have control enough over her body to take another deep drink from her glass.

Aidan quirked an eyebrow, no doubt shocked at her lack of words. He hadn't seen her in years, but he remembered her well. A little too well, actually. Anna and Sorcha had been inseparable as kids. Back then, they had been a pain in his ass, always so noisy and loud and right in the middle of whatever he and his friends had been trying to do. As a teenager though, she had been someone he couldn't ever quite shake out of his head. He was two years older than Sorcha, his wisplike, viciously funny little sister. Sorcha had a caustic wit and could never resist a well-placed barb. Anna had been her shadow, pulling courage from her funny friend and harnessing her own kind of quiet power. Where Sorcha was very small with a wild mass of wavy, auburn hair and bright blue eyes, Anna was taller, willowy and had hair the color of strawberries and sunshine with green, cat-like eyes. It was all he could do to keep from reaching out to feel that silky curtain of hair. He wondered what it would feel like now, draped over him, her pale skin glowing in the moonlight.

His memory flashed back to the night he had seen her exactly like that, several years ago. He was on leave from the Marines, transitioning from training to his next placement. His parents were called away to his grandparents' house out of town, and like true deviants, he and Sorcha had invited a few friends over to enjoy the night. He only had a few left around town back then; most had gone away to college. Sorcha, however, had friends aplenty.

Aidan remembered watching Anna all night, pretending to drink Jungle Juice for hours and laughing her way around the house. He had thought she was sexy as hell. He hadn't failed to notice that she barely sipped from her cup, and never refilled it. He had never been much of a drinker either, and remembered at that stage in life, the pressure to fit in seemed to require tremendous alcohol intake.

She always conjured up such conflicting feelings in him. He had remembered Anna as the annoying younger sister-type before he left for the Marines. That night at the party though, he noticed how beautiful she had become. She wasn't gangly, freckled, and incredibly loud. She was grace in motion. A quiet, fiery confidence teemed beneath the surface of her face. Her eyes smiled as if she knew the punchline to a joke that no one else was quick enough to figure out. Those same eyes had been glancing his way through the night, holding his gaze for just a few seconds before looking back to a friend, a pink flush on her cheeks.

All these years later, Aidan still got turned on thinking about what had happened that night. After watching her throughout the evening at the party, he finally found her not surrounded by a gaggle of friends. He remembered smiling down at her and holding out his hand. She looked right into his eyes and placed her hand in his, then followed as he led her to the backyard. The sound of her quiet laugh was as fresh in his mind then as it had been all those years ago. He had led her to the treehouse where she and Sorcha used to play Pilgrims as little girls. The dilapidated wood playset still held, however, and he had coaxed her up the platforms to the top.

He still remembered when he sat down on the floor, pulling her to him. He smiled down at her, expecting to take the lead and had been utterly and completely shocked when she charged him. Anna had straddled him, pushing her lips into his so hard that he bumped his head on the wall behind him. She laughed then, wrapping his head in her arms, giving him perfect access to her breasts. They fumbled and stripped down in near silence, the only noises were the pants and gasps only known by the truly horny.

Anna's pale skin had glimmered in the moonlight, her hair cascading down her body and tickling his chest. Her mostly well-behaved personality had never hinted that under her clothes, she might be hiding seriously tiny scraps of midnight blue silk. They had explored each other in a frenzy, using kisses to swallow gasps and moans, not wanting to attract attention from the other friends who might be roaming around outside.

AIDAN WAS JOLTED back to reality when he realized she had said something. "What?" he asked, embarrassed to have slipped out of the moment.

Anna pasted a fake smile on her face. "I said, 'Hey, Aidan,'" she said, frowning up at him a little. "I wasn't expecting to see you here tonight," she said, hoping she was at least sounding casual. She felt the flush rise up in her face and cursed her pale complexion, willing her cheeks to cool.

He settled himself down in the seat next to her and raised a finger to the bartender, gesturing that he'd take another drink as well. Aidan could tell that he had unnerved her, and he liked that immensely.

"So, what are you doing now? I thought you lived in Idaho or something?" he said, taking a gulp from his beer. Anna wasn't sure she wanted to shoot the breeze with him. *What was he drinking anyway*, she wondered? Squinting at his beer. *Light beer*, she snickered. *So much for a tough guy*, she thought, taking another big drink from her bourbon. She changed her mind on that when she looked again at the muscles on his arms. He was still as hot as he ever was. She had always had a thing for him, even as far back as middle school. He was two years older and Sorcha's oldest brother, so he had always been off limits. *Well mostly off limits*, she thought to herself, her mind flitting to that night in his backyard. That memory was never far away, not a bad one to play over on long, lonely nights.

Aidan had always been a total smart ass. He had been bossy and relentlessly teased her when she was younger. As much as she hated how she clammed up around him, she had loved every minute of his attention. It didn't seem like she was doing a better job talking to him now than she had as a teenager. He was tall, with sandy brown hair and hazel eyes. He had been out of the service for a while but apparently still worked out. He was basically a walking wet dream. It was all she could do not to put her hand on his shirt to see just how hard his muscles were now. She certainly remembered how they had felt years ago. There had been only one night she had worked up the courage to pounce on him, and that had mainly been because he was only home for a short leave. Anna had wanted him for years.

She realized that night how very timid she had been living and how very short life really was. Anna had been in awe of him, and his courage to put himself at risk for his country. He had wanted a chance to get out and see the world. Anna still remembered the maps that papered his side of the room that he shared with his two younger brothers. Anna had loved hanging out at Sorcha's house. She had only one sister herself, where Sorcha's house seemed to be swarming with kids. Devout Catholics to the letter, Sorcha's parents had five children.

Aidan was staring at her expectantly, and she chuckled to realize they were both completely communication-challenged. She mumbled as much and realized she might be a little tipsy when her words didn't come out as clearly as she had liked. "Spring break," she said louder and hopefully more clearly, trying to answer his question and avoid sounding like an idiot. "Well, as much as you can call this Spring Break. I don't remember it being so danged overcast here all the time. And it's Denver, Colorado, not Idaho," she answered, still facing forward.

"Denver's nice," he said, leaning in to her profile a bit, "a few nice sights to see there." He laughed. "But do they have all this?" he said, turning and circling his arms wide to encompass the spectacle of humanity in the seedy little bar. She turned around to take in the room and laughed at him and he grinned, watching her pretty cheeks flush. Her thoughts were so easy to read on her face with that beautifully translucent skin. Unable to stop himself, he couldn't help but wonder what she'd look like when she came. Would that flush of blood color her chest as well as her face? He certainly hoped to find out.

Still watching her, he saw her eyes widen in panic and darted a look at the door. A man was heading straight for Anna, and she looked like she couldn't move from the shock of it. There was only one thing to do, Aidan thought, come to her rescue. Without being obvious, and feeling not even a little threatened by the size of Travis, he stood and gave Travis his back.

As Travis closed in on them, Anna was stunned when Aidan stood, blocking her view of Travis. Suddenly, his big hand tilted back her face, and her eyes closed when his warm lips met hers. It was like a bolt of electricity shot through her, and she instinctively swayed on her barstool, pressing toward him. For a moment it seemed like they were the only ones in that crowded, noisy little bar.

Aidan couldn't believe the sensation rolling through his body, both hot and cold at once. He had intended only to shock the runty little bastard stalking toward Anna like he owned her, but the kiss felt so good, along with her body melting into his, that he hated to stop the kiss. When Runt Man cleared his throat again, Aidan heard the hoots and hollers coming from the other patrons of the bar. He put his hands to her shoulders and stepped back. Anna had the most incredibly dazed expression on her face. She must've felt the power of their kiss, too.

"Sunsets," she said, blinking up at him.

"What?" he asked, silencing Runt Man with a 'just a minute' gesture, very much not appreciated.

"Sunsets," she said again. "You asked me that night in your backyard which I preferred, sunrises or sunsets," she finished, her line of thought much clearer to her than him. "I didn't know how to answer back then; I hadn't seen a sunrise."

Her answer hit him like a brick wall. He couldn't believe she remembered that night, too. "Okay, Anna. Sunsets it is," he said. He put his arm around her and turned them toward a very red-faced, angry looking man.

"Jesus, Anna. Didn't take you long to pick up someone in a bar, did it?" he asked, wearing a mousy little sneer on his face.

She frowned at him, irritation burning off the fog from Aidan's surprise kiss. "Travis, what in the living hell are you doing here? I thought you had dropped off the face of the earth, for God's sake." She took a deep breath and decided she wasn't done. In a flash she was up and off the barstool. With a step toward him, her teacher-pointer-finger popped out and aimed right at his chest. "I haven't heard from you in months, and you suddenly show up here uninvited, somehow put-out that I'm not home, mourning the loss of our crappy little engagement?" she asked, her color rising as fast as her hackles.

At that, Travis looked from Anna up to Aidan and smartly adjusted his expression and took a step back. Aidan looked down at Travis without expression on his face. He had perfected a look of disinterest that could be withering to self-important little assholes. Aidan had plenty of opportunity during his time in the military to mask his expression and still somehow completely unnerve a lesser man.

"To think I was coming here to get you back. To tell you I was wrong," Travis said to Anna. "I wasn't wrong about anything. You're always going to be the same, Anna. So freaking predictable," he said, his words slurring together. "The only thing different about you is what man you're letting in your bed," he said, turning his face just in time to be smashed in the jaw by Aidan.

Before the bartender even made it around the bar, Aidan was leaning down over Travis, his mouth so near to Travis' ear that nobody else could hear what he said.

"You're going to apologize to her for that one day," he said calmly and quietly, further outraging Travis.

Aidan stood, put his hands in the air in a mock surrender gesture toward the bartender, then bent and picked up the barstool that Travis knocked over on his fall to the floor. He put his arm out to Anna, who tossed a ten-dollar bill on the bar to pay for her drink. She allowed Aidan to drape his arm over her shoulders, and stepped over Travis on her way to the door.

They walked in silence to her car in the parking lot, her body trembling with either nerves or rage. Aidan held his hand out and she dropped her keys in his hand. As he reached past her to open the passenger side door, she wrapped her arms around his neck and pressed her lips to his. Shocked, he circled his arms around her, wrapping her close to his body as she pressed against him. Her breathing was ragged, and her hands gripped his neck, pulling him down to her.

Anna knew it was crazy to stand there kissing Aidan in the parking lot, but she felt like she was drowning and he was the life raft that would save her. Her heart raced, but her arms held him tight, as if he wasn't every bit as into this kiss as she was. She could tell that he was--he felt like liquid fire, slipping his tongue into her mouth, tasting her.

He released her only when they heard the door of the bar opening. The last thing he wanted was to have another run-in with Anna's ex. If he lost control of his temper, he could really hurt Travis. He didn't need any trouble like that in his life. Aidan's experience had been that people who didn't know him well expected him to be wracked with PTSD from his time in the Marines, and acted half afraid of him. He tucked Anna into the passenger side of her car and shut the door. He took a glance at his old Chevy in the parking lot of the bar and hoped that little jerk wouldn't mess with his truck. It wasn't worth much, but it held lots of sentiment.

Aidan slipped behind the wheel of Anna's Jeep and fired up the engine, adjusting her seat back to accommodate his height. He looked over to her, her green eyes were locked on his. He lifted his eyebrows, she nodded, and he turned her car toward the direction of his house. He tried and failed to not smile, and she tried and failed not to smile back.

# Four

A FEW MINUTES LATER, HE CUT the engine in front of a small Craftsman-style house in a neighborhood full of houses that looked mostly alike. He looked over at Anna, who wore a funny expression on her face.

"Ready?" he asked, giving her the first opportunity to change her mind. He knew she had had a drink or two at the bar, and he wanted to be sure her head was in this decision.

"I am," she said, and opened the door. Aidan couldn't help himself from appreciating the way her butt looked in her jeans. *How is it that some people just get sexier over time,* he wondered?

He took her hand in his and walked her to the front door. He fiddled with the lock, opened the door, and flicked on the light switch. Anna wasn't certain exactly what she had expected, but it hadn't been to see how neat and tidy Aidan's house was. There wasn't a thing out of place that she could see from the entryway. She put her coat and purse down on the chair and turned as he put his arms around her. He kissed her gently and pulled away.

"Would you like some water?" She shook her head no. "Okay, a tour?" he asked.

"Definitely a tour," she said, looking around in absolute puzzlement how a man could keep a house so clean. She wasn't quite as Type A as her sister Jesse, but even she was surprised by how neat a housekeeper Aidan was.

"You keep a very neat house...that blows my mind a little," she said, grinning up at him as he walked her past the kitchen and down a hallway.

"Ah, picked up on that, huh? Yeah. Guilty. Total neat freak," he said, pulling her toward him at the doorway to his bedroom. "A few years in the Marines will do that to a guy," he said, causing a shiver to run down her spine.

She couldn't help but ask herself why it was that Marines were so collectively hot? Anna had in her mind that they were the best of the best, the roughest, toughest of men. Aidan threw his head back and laughed.

"Chalk it up to good marketing," he said, flooding Anna's face with a blush. She had muttered the words aloud. She was going to have to be more careful with that habit. She was so used to being alone that she caught herself talking aloud to herself all the time.

He walked her into his bedroom, flicked a side table light on, and turned Anna to him, resting his hands on her shoulders.

"Anna, I want to be with you tonight, but I need to know this is what you want, too," he said, looking down into her pretty eyes. She turned her face up to him, put her hands on the button of his flannel shirt and answered.

"Yes, I want to be with you," she said, as she put one hand up to his neck, feeling the scratchy day-old growth there. Everything about him screamed virile, rugged man. A night with him was exactly what she needed.

"Thank God," he said, practically pushing them both down on the bed. She laughed and he smiled, pulling the hem of her shirt up over her head. He let out a huge whistle, and a laugh.

"Look who has a few little secrets!" he said, reaching across her to flick on the light on the other bedside table.

"Ah, you like those, huh?" she said, looking down at her own side, decorated with a tattoo of a compass, large but surprisingly dainty at the same time. The lines were thin and the detail light, but the contrast of the dark ink against her milk white skin was stunning.

"It's beautiful," he said, running his fingers over the design, dipping his head to kiss her skin. She arched her back in response, the sensation an incredible mix of pleasure and surprise at the scratchiness of his chin.

"What else have we here?" he said, rising over her, straddling her, an absolutely delighted smile on his face. He looked like a kid on an Easter egg hunt.

"And this, this is nice," he said, his fingers tracing a pink and green lotus blossom, done in watercolor style.

The colors softly splashed over the flower, gorgeous and feminine, nestled there on her side, no bigger than the palm of his hand. He cupped her flower with his hand for a second before moving his hand to her breast, covered by the prettiest green bra he had ever seen.

"Not to be outdone, these are a work of art, too," he said, feeling the weight of her in his hands, freeing her from the bra with the expertise of a man who was no stranger to lingerie. She raised up to give his fingers room to work the lace free, as his gaze moved over her. Anna knew she should be embarrassed by the amount of light in the room, but something about the way Aidan looked at her made her feel almost exquisite.

Anna felt thrilled that Aidan appreciated her tattoos. They had been gifts to herself as she came to grips with her failed relationship. Travis had hated tattoos on women and Anna let that stifle and influence her choices while they were together. She had been wanting to get a few for several years and it was one of the first steps towards finding herself after their relationship floundered.

Anna sighed with the pleasure of Aidan's lips on her skin as he took his time tasting her. She already knew he was going to be incredible. As she uncovered the delicious expanse of his chest, undoing his shirt one button at a time, her other hand traced his skin. She took her time with this chore, savoring the look of torture on his face.

"You're killing me," he said, ripping the shirt up and over his head before she got to all the buttons. She laughed as he grabbed her and pulled her to him, skin to skin. She closed her eyes and dipped her head back, enjoying the feeling of him against her. His skin was so warm, hard muscles covering his chest, stomach and arms.

She moved her arm down his, appreciating the feel of him against her, finding his own art decorating his body. The United States Marine Corp insignia--the Eagle, Globe and Anchor--rested on his chest above his heart. She turned him slightly, finding Semper Fi on his bicep. His very big bicep.

"Very nice, yourself," she said, running her fingers over the designs, feeling her pulse quicken when her eyes met his. He hooked his finger in her jeans, toying with the button.

"Any more surprises?" he asked, his gaze hooded. "Anything else you'd like to show me?"

She nodded and stepped off the bed, turning around as she pulled off her jeans, moving her long hair over one shoulder, revealing a mandala flower design between her shoulder blades. The whole gesture was too much for him. He pulled her back to the bed, down on her back and was over her, his body covering hers as he kissed her lips. She arched against him, wrapping her legs around him, wanting so badly to have him right where she wanted to feel him most. His lips trailed a path from her mouth to her neck, down to her collarbone in that perfect, kissable spot. His fingers traced her body, alternating between light and heavy touches, his warm breath on her skin only fanning her flames.

He moved his hand between them, making Anna feel a wild mix of desire and desperation. She broke away from him and removed the last barrier between them. He moaned and leaned across her to pull a condom out of the bedside table. He made quick work of it and was moving against her in under a minute.

Anna hadn't been with anyone since she and Travis had broken up. She was completely out of practice, but didn't even pause to consider it. Aidan had her body nearly screaming with desire; just the feel of him against her alone was enough to blow her mind. She worked to match him, thrust for thrust. Her hands roamed over his body, feeling him strain against her, his hand adjusting her leg in a slight way that brought him deeper inside her.

He worked her body like he was born for the task. In no time she cried out with her release. Aidan gave her a minute, his hands roaming over her back. Finally, though, he exceeded his own patience. He pushed into her, drawing himself in and out until he was spent. He fell against her, clutching her like she was the most precious, valuable thing in his world. He rolled to the side, pulling her close against him. They lay entwined as their pulses calmed and their breathing returned to normal.

Anna must've fallen asleep in his arms, because she jumped when he tried to leave the bed. He looked down at her and made no attempt to hide his perusal of her still-naked body lying comfortably in his bed.

"I didn't mean to wake you, I just have to take care of something," he said on his way to the bathroom. Anna looked at her watch and sucked in a gust of air, not realizing it was so late. She bolted out of bed and started dressing quickly.

"What's wrong?" he asked. "You're not leaving, are you?" he said, walking back in the room, looking like heaven in a pair of pajama pants and no shirt. She could look at him without a shirt for an eternity and never get bored. He looked like something off a novel cover, all hard angles and scruff.

"Yessir, I have to. I'm staying at Mom's house, and while I'm not 18, I still don't want to freak her out by staying out all night." She smoothed her shirt down and walked to his mirror, fussing with her hair and running her fingertips under her eyes to clean up the sleep smudged eye liner.

"Oh," he said, sounding just a little disappointed. "I kind of hoped you'd stay over. Can I do anything to change your mind?" he asked, moving to stand behind her while she faced the mirror. He moved her long hair away from her neck and pressed a kiss to the tender skin there.

"Not this time," she said, then blushed, wondering if it was safe to assume there would be a next time. She had been with Travis for three years, long enough to feel far removed from the dating scene. *Was this just a one-night stand*, she wondered?

She looked down again at her watch and adjusted it. Aidan grabbed her wrist, moving the thick band of her watch to the side and discovered a thin little arrow hidden beneath it.

"Girl, you are full of surprises," he said, dipping his head down to kiss the arrow on the inside of her wrist.

She smiled up at him in a way that made him wonder why what he said made her so happy. She reached up and kissed him once more. Just as he moved his hands down to the waist of her jeans, dipping lower, she pulled back.

"Walk me out?" she asked, stepping out to the hallway, walking toward the front door.

"Of course," he said, wondering what kind of jerk she'd dealt with to make her even have to ask. "Give me a minute and I'll put on my clothes. I can drive you home and walk back," he said, starting to walk back toward his bedroom.

"That's okay, I'm a big girl," she said, grabbing his hand. "I was just hoping for another kiss." She grinned.

He shook his head, grabbed his coat, and slipped on his shoes. "Have it your way, hardhead," he said, smiling down at the bark of laughter that escaped her.

"Hardhead? God, you used to call me that all the time," she said, rolling her eyes at him.

"I can't believe you remember," he said, smiling down at her, his hand on her neck, thumb beneath her jaw, tilting her lips up for another kiss.

"There's a lot I remember about you," she said, placing a smile on his face that he knew would be there for days.

"Can I call you tomorrow?" he asked, wondering at the nervous feeling he had in the pit of his stomach.

"Yes, but..." she said, leaving him wondering what she was going to say. "One catch, you have to get my number from Sorcha." When his eyes bugged out, she laughed. "That's right! You get to be the one to tell her about this," she said, opening the door and sitting down. "That's more than I can take on," Anna said, smiling as she shut her car door.

Aidan stood in the driveway, smiling at her headlights until she backed out into the street and drove away, a small wave thrown into the air as she made her way home.

"Oh God, Sorcha's going to kill me," he said aloud, smiling to himself as he walked back into the house and threw the lock. Sorcha was a force to be reckoned with. He had seen true battle, however even a tough guy like him dreaded the fight at hand when his sister found out he had a thing for her best friend.

# *Five*

ANNA WOKE UP IN HER CHILDHOOD room, stretching in the sunlight filtering through her window. She loved her job, but she was really starting to enjoy getting to sleep in. School breaks always seemed to go by so much faster than the regular part of the school year. She only had a week and hoped to make the best of it. She smiled, scenes from the night before playing through her mind. As she picked up her things on her way to the shower, she hummed to herself, taking in the scent of coffee and bacon in the air.

Harry heard her walking around and charged into the bathroom, pushing the door open with his big paws. She fussed over him appropriately, judging by the light in his eyes that Eadie or Aunt Ruthie had probably slipped him some bites of bacon or pancakes. He was irresistible. After a good ear scratch and belly rub, he abruptly turned and ran back down the hallway.

Anna climbed into the shower and let the warm water pour down on her head and shoulders. She felt almost giddy, remembering the feel of Aidan moving over her, and into her. All those years of being attracted to him, that one evening so many years ago where they made out. They probably would've gone further that night had they not been interrupted. Sorcha never knew Anna had been gone from the party, let alone naked with Aidan.

She laughed out loud, picturing Aidan squirming over the process of telling Sorcha about his interest in her lifelong best friend. Though they told each other everything back then, Anna hadn't wanted to tell Sorcha about nearly being with Aidan. Not because she didn't want to listen to the fit Sorcha no doubt would've thrown, but because it was special to her. She had wanted him for so many years at that time, she had the chance to go for what she wanted and took it. Risk didn't come easily to Anna. Her sister Jesse had been the brave one. Anna had been more reserved, content to observe, take things in, and quietly work toward getting what she wanted. She still remembered the feeling that washed over her when she saw Aidan watching her so long ago. She had felt a rush of power, and she liked it. Anna had always considered herself pretty enough, but not someone that shined. Sorcha was always the brightest--and loudest-- light in the room. Anna had always been comfortable being around the fire – Sorcha was more comfortable being the flame. When Aidan had looked at her back then like she was sexy, desirable, she felt something well up in her, and she liked it.

Of course, that night was many years ago, and she had matured and grown more comfortable in her own skin. Anna even liked the way she looked now. She had long ago accepted that she wouldn't have a curvy figure. She was long and straight as a stick. She worked out on a regular basis to keep her body strong and eventually accepted that she wasn't inheriting 'the family boobs'. Once she became an avid runner, Anna was thankful that she didn't have to spend big money on the fancy sports bras that Jesse had to invest in. She was pleased with her hair, a task that took a bit longer than her acceptance of a small but adequate chest. She had never hated being a ginger as a kid because Sorcha's hair was as red as a sunset, and nobody was going to give her any trouble about it. Anna's copper blonde hair fell in a long curtain around her, as smooth and shiny as Sorcha's was curly and wild. She loved her friend so much that she felt Sorcha was almost as much of a sister as Jesse was to her.

Anna might have been happy to keep her secret with Aidan from long ago, but she wasn't about to be anybody's secret now. She wanted to say that she wasn't going to be anybody's hookup, but it was a little late for that, she thought wryly.

If Aidan wanted to see her again, he'd have to fess up and break the news to his sister. If not, she'd enjoy her week, and spend her time with her family and dear friend. Anna liked being back home. Except for the time she had spent when her father had passed, she hadn't been home for any length of time in years. When they'd come in for a visit, Travis would be polite, but he always seemed ill at ease. He was from a town just a few miles away, but his family relations were really strained. When they'd travel home, he wouldn't even tell his family that he was coming for a visit. He'd hole up at Walt and Eadie's house with his computer, as content as Travis allowed himself to be. Anna couldn't judge him for that. His upbringing had been horrible, and he had wanted to escape to a city, really any city, and leave the past behind him.

As she dressed in her workout clothes, laced her running shoes and combed her hair into a ponytail, she replayed the moment when Travis walked into the bar. He had been so cut and dry, so impersonal, when they broke up. It had been like he disappeared completely. No calls, no texts. He was just gone. After he left, Anna had been numb for a while. It was completely surreal. She was full of so many questions. Who just walks away from an engagement without a full explanation? When he resurfaced, why did it have to be while she was home? Why had he been home? Surely he hadn't been visiting his family, finally. Anna realized she couldn't wait another second to talk to Eadie. She had to have told him where she was going, right?

Anna rounded the corner to see Aunt Ruthie slipping Harry another bite.

"Morning," she said, giving both her mother and aunt a kiss on the cheek.

"Morning," they answered.

"Anna, it's so good to have you home again," Eadie said. "I've missed having both my girls nearby."

"I know, Mom, it's good to be here," she said, filling a plate with the breakfast leftovers. "Thanks for letting me sleep," she said.

"Aunt Ruthie?"

"What, honey?" Ruthie answered

"Have you ever cleaned up Standard Poodle diarrhea?" Anna asked, not looking up from her plate. Eadie gasped and Ruthie's eyes were huge, dropping the piece of pancake that she was getting ready to feed Harry into her napkin.

"Got it, smartass," she said, taking her napkin to the trashcan. Eadie walked by Anna, pinching her with her thumbnail like she used to do when her girls were young and naughty in public.

Anna winked up at her mother, patting her knee to get Harry's attention. He had been stalking Ruthie and now that he knew she'd sneak him bites, he wouldn't be leaving her anytime soon.

"Mom, I ran into Travis last night. Had you talked to him?" she asked as nonchalantly as she could.

"I was hoping you were going to bring that up. I didn't know if I should ask about it or not," she said, fussing over the coffee pot.

"He called last night just a few minutes after you left. Apparently he had tried calling you but you didn't pick up," she said, leaving it hanging there, expecting Anna to fill in the reason why she hadn't answered.

"I didn't hear the phone, but honestly, I wouldn't have answered," she said, pulling her phone out of her pocket. No missed calls. She held the phone up to her mom, useless, since Eadie and technology didn't mix.

"No missed calls. He probably knew I wouldn't answer." She shrugged.

"Sorry, Anna. This is just such an awkward situation. I didn't know if it was important or not, and didn't know when you'd be home, so I told him you were going to the Hawk's Nest with Sorcha. Did he go there?" she asked.

"Oh yeah. He showed up and we didn't talk much. He was with his friends and seemed pretty drunk, which was out of character," she said, not looking up. "I was talking with Aidan when he came in. Mom, do you remember him?"

Eadie nodded. "That's one of Sorcha's brothers, right? Is he around here now?" she asked. "I always thought he was so handsome!"

"Now, Eadie, you know he lives here now! We were just talking about him, ooph!" Ruthie grunted, rubbing her knee, apparently having received a sharp under-the-table kick from Eadie.

Anna looked at the pair of them, not sure where to start.

"Anyway, Travis got kind of lippy with me, and Aidan knocked him on his butt when he got rude with me."

Ruthie hooted. "God, I love a good roughneck man," she cackled, not flinching at all under Eadie's wilting glare.

"Well, that's too bad, dear. What did he say to make Aidan so upset? I can't believe he'd be rude to you after you had been together for so long," she said, shaking her head. "I can't help but think you narrowly escaped a mess with that boy." Anna wasn't going to touch that statement with a ten-foot pole. Eadie had known that Travis had trouble with his family, and she made no secret that she worried over what baggage Travis might be bringing into their eventual marriage.

Anna chose her words carefully, "I was sitting at the bar, talking to Aidan--" she tiptoed around the fact that Travis saw Aidan stick his tongue down her throat. "He apparently didn't like it," she said, deciding to leave it at that.

"But why would he care if you were talking to Sorcha's brother?" she asked. "Didn't he see Sorcha there? My God, you can't be in the same building with that kid without knowing she's in there!" Eadie said, eyes bulging, a laugh about to escape her lips. Eadie had always loved Sorcha, in all her wild and wooly madness. It's like she knew that Anna's relaxed and timid-natured spirit needed that little fireball to round her out, to make her life even more eventful and fun. Eadie had expected obedience and respect above all, but she also had been really open-minded, especially for her generation, about letting her children go out and experience life.

Anna decided to come clean, or at least mostly clean. Sorcha was going to be around, and she wasn't about to weave a web of lies to get tangled in later. "I have to fess up. I didn't call Sorcha. She was probably busy getting her daughter to bed, and honestly, I just needed to get out of the house," she said, her words hitching at the end. Without warning, her eyes filled with tears, and she got a big lump in her throat. In a flash, Eadie's arms were wrapped around her daughter.

"I know, baby," she said, hugging her as she had a million times, as only a mother can. "I miss him so much I can't hardly breathe," Eadie said, patting Anna.

They held each other standing next to the table, Ruthie dabbing her eyes with a tissue. Walt was still everywhere in the house, every corner filled with his quiet presence. It was comforting and disconcerting all at the same time.

After a bit, Eadie pulled back from Anna. "We're going to be okay, Sweet Pea," she said, her voice thick with emotion. Walt had always called Anna by the name of Sweet Pea and Jesse had been Peanut. Anna nodded through the tears streaming down her face.

"I'm going to go for a quick run, just down to the track and back," she said, grabbing Harry's leash from the hook by the door. As he pranced around in the way only a 70-pound Poodle can, she wrangled him out the door. She would've loved to go run at the high school track, retracing steps from long ago, but she knew there was a no dog policy, so a jaunt down to the track would have to do, instead.

Her run with Harry was just what she needed--she loosened her muscles, worked up her heart rate and let her mind go to that 'just breathe' place that she loved so much. Anna wasn't wired in a way that mindlessness came easily. Her mind was always racing, which meant teaching

Kindergarten was a perfect fit for her. No matter what she was in the middle of doing, there were ten distractions. Her little kiddos were the highlight of her life, but Lord, were they a busy bunch of kids.

Anna had known she wanted to teach from the time she was a little girl. Her mom and Jesse had told her countless stories of discovering her as a kid with her stuffed animals and baby dolls all lined up at the kitchen table, or in rows in her bedroom, each with a blank piece of paper and crayons, with Anna yammering away at them.

One of Jesse's favorite stories to tell on Anna was when the girls were 15 and 10 years old. Two boys that Jesse had had a crush on had 'just happened' to walk by their house while they were outside. Jesse had been standing out front, nervously talking to the boys when Anna ran up, unfazed by the burgeoning hormonal tide, and asked the boys if they wanted to go play school in the treehouse. Jesse had been mortified, and it took mere seconds for the boys to go far, far away from their house.

Though break was nice so far, Anna's mind was on her students as she got back to her house. Untangling Harry from his leash, she went over the faces of her high risk students in her mind, praying they were being well-fed and loved over break, home with their families instead of at school, with the guarantee of attention, affection and meals and snacks. How adults could bring precious children into the world and not lavish them with love and at least the bare necessities, was beyond Anna's comprehension. But, year after year, she saw an increase in need. She did all she could to fill in the gaps, buying snacks with her own money, slipping food into their bags at the end of the day, with a few extras for the weekends. What warmed her heart the most was that she wasn't the only one. She had a few friends at the school, especially those lovely ladies in the office, who also snuck into the room at the end of the day on Fridays, nonchalantly slipping brown bags into the backpacks of the kids that needed it most. Anna unconsciously winced, thinking that those poor children would barely get to eat on the weekends without those supplies. Times were hard all over, and she prayed daily for more resources to do more good.

Anna had just made it back to her neighborhood when a car slowed and parked on the street. She turned and cringed when she realized Travis was driving the car. On the opposite side of the emotional spectrum, Harry was delighted to see Travis and barked and pranced as he walked up.

"Look, I'm not going to stand here and listen to you talk ugly to me, Travis."

His hands were up in the air immediately. "I'm not going to say anything rude, Anna. I actually want to apologize," he answered. Having momentarily stunned her, Travis took this as his opportunity to get out what it was he had to say.

"I went by our place this week,"

"My place," she corrected. She saw a muscle in his jaw tick at her interruption.

"Your place," he conceded. "I wanted to tell you that I

made a huge mistake in leaving you." At this he stopped, waiting for her to fill in the gaps. She didn't say a word.

"It just felt like the right thing to do, you know?" he asked, but still she said nothing. "I was ready for something new. We were in a rut, a routine... I needed something that wasn't a drag every day."

At that, Anna had heard enough. She slapped her leg to get Harry's attention and started walking again.

"Wait, I didn't mean it like that," he said. "What I mean, is that I got bored and I left, and I'm sorry. When you didn't answer, I went to Gail's to see if she knew where you were. She mentioned you had gone home, so I just assumed it was because you were sad. I followed. I certainly didn't expect to see you there with some guy," he said with a near sneer, absentmindedly rubbing his jaw.

Anna drew up short and turned on him. "Travis?"

"Yeah?"

"I was going to spend my life with you. You got bored, left without much of an explanation and practically vanished into thin air. I moved on and think you should do the same."

He stared at her for a moment and she didn't so much as blink.

"Fine," he said. "I'm sorry it went down the way it did. You've never been much on change, I figured you'd want to get back together."

"I've learned a lot about change over the past several months. I've learned to lean in," she said. "Goodbye, Travis."

"Bye, Anna," he answered, turning back toward the direction of his car.

ANNA WALKED BACK home, deciding she was just going to block that conversation out of her mind. To think that she had nearly wound up spending her life with someone who could just grow bored and check out. She felt fortunate to have gotten out of that mess when she did.

Back at the house, she unleashed Harry and headed toward her bedroom. On her way to change clothes, Anna heard Eadie call from the kitchen. "Anna, Sorcha dropped by to see you. She asked that you give her a call when you get a minute."

Rolling her eyes and bracing for the impact, Anna answered, "Okay, Mom. Thanks!" After dressing, she lay down on her bed, dragging her phone from the little holder she wrapped around her arm during her run. Three missed calls and six texts. Some were from Sorcha, and a few from an unfamiliar number. She didn't have to work very hard to figure out who that number belonged to. She skipped the voicemails and went straight to the texts.

*"Call me, you dirty little skank"* – Sorcha

*"You know I'm joking, right?"* – Sorcha

*"Dude."* – Sorcha

*"Anna, I'm stalking you now. I'm at your house. I'm under your bed."* – Sorcha

*"For reals. Call me."* – Sorcha

*"It wasn't quite the lead balloon I was expecting. Call me. A.* – Unknown number

With a smile on her face, Anna added Aidan to her

contacts, then thumbed her phone to her favorites. A high school picture of Sorcha with overalls and a baby-T-shirt popped up when she clicked on Sorcha's number.

"It's about time you called me back," she said in place of a hello. "I thought you and Harry had been kidnapped or something."

"Nope, just went for a run. Okay, let me have it," Anna said, wondering what was about to happen.

"Let you have it? Are you serious?" Sorcha said, incredulous. "This is the best thing I've ever heard!" she crowed into the phone.

"You aren't mad?" Anna asked, truly surprised.

"No way, Anna. You're my best friend in the world. Aidan is my big brother, and next best friend. I've been hoping you two would hit it off for years. Especially after you two got naked in my backyard," Sorcha said, letting that sentence drop like a bomb.

"Ahhhhhhh. You knew about that? How did you know about that?" Anna asked, feeling the color drain from her face.

"I saw you walk out of the room after him, so I did what anyone would do. I followed you. When I saw you both climb up into the tree house, I ran back to my room and peeked out the window. Remember it faced the tree house? When I saw the clothes flying off, I got as far away from the window as I could, locked the door from the inside and shut it so none of the other perverts could watch."

Anna shut her eyes, not sure if she wanted to laugh

or cry. She had guarded that secret like it was a matter of national security, and Sorcha had known the whole time.

"Anna, are you there?" she asked into the phone, her smile evident in her voice.

"Dang it, Sorcha, I've never been able to keep anything from you *except* that. I can't believe you never let on that you knew."

Sorcha exhaled and a pause hung in the air. "Anna, I had hoped you'd get together back then, but Aidan was going back to his base in California, and you were in school. I wanted it to turn into something, but it didn't seem to fit.

Of course then you met that rat bastard, Travis. You all seemed so happy, and Aidan was off doing God knows what for Uncle Sam. I figured that ship had sailed," she said.

Anna couldn't help but shrug; everything Sorcha had said was true. She heard Sorcha's voice muffled as she coaxed Clara out of whatever mess the little stinker had managed to find.

"Sorcha, can I come over tonight? I want to see you and squeeze Clara," she said, feeling the little tug in her heart again, wishing she had her own baby girl to care for and love.

"Absolutely! We're having spaghetti. Bring some wine, and a tarp if you're going to be anywhere near this little hot mess. She's the grossest eater I've ever seen, but she has a fine time of it."

"Okay. Five alright?"

"Yeah, Evan will be home by then. See you then!" she said, already talking to Clara before she ended the call.

Anna looked at her phone again, debating calling Aidan or making him wait a bit. She wasn't a game player, but she didn't want to seem overeager. It had been years since she had dealt with this. Things with Travis had been so easy. They'd known who each other was in high school, but they had been from rival towns. What a silly thing, Anna thought, tidying up her room. All these little towns in her neck of the woods were vicious rivals in sports, thereby dividing up into even tinier segments. She probably would've met some great friends when she was younger, but God forbid you cross over and date someone from another town! It just wasn't done. At least not until college when everyone suddenly realized most of the things they were preoccupied with in high school regarding social class and labels didn't matter.

After killing as much time as she could stand, Anna called Aidan. Just about everyone she knew preferred texting over talking, but she was a voice to voice girl. Even a letter girl, a hopeless romantic, she guessed. He answered on the first ring. Anna smiled, liking the idea of him anticipating her call.

"Hello?"

"Hey, Aidan, it's Anna," she said, good manners foregoing the fact that he knew who it was since he had her number in his phone.

"Anna. Good news. She didn't try to kill me," he said, a laugh in his voice. "I think the doughnuts helped pave the way. The way to Sorcha's heart is definitely through her stomach," Aidan said.

Anna agreed, Sorcha was a doughnut fiend. "So you bribed her, huh?" she asked, pacing nervously around her room, trying to calm her nerves.

"Yeah, it actually wasn't bad at all. I skipped the part about the awesome sex, but I let her know I ran into you at the Hawk's Nest. Oh, and that I punched that Lipless Wonder of an ex-fiancé. She liked that part. She actually clapped."

A loud guffaw escaped Anna as she clasped her hand over her own mouth and scrunched up her eyes. "Lipless Wonder?"

"Fitting, am I right?" he asked, proud of that little insult.

"Definitely, but I didn't say that. I'm a classy gal who doesn't badmouth her exes," she said, her anxiousness gone.

"I wish you could've been there this morning, I walked in with a big box of doughnuts around 8:30.. Clara was already climbing the walls, and Sorcha was sucking down coffee as fast as she could while already picking up a huge mess. She was making pancakes and Clara ran in, grabbed the bowl she was mixing it in and dumped it all in the floor. I walked in like some kind of knight in shining armor and got to save the day," he said.

"At first she looked overjoyed to see me, then she asked what I did," Aidan said, intentionally leaving out the vulgarities. Sorcha had a mouth on her when Clara wasn't in the room. "I called Clara in, got her settled at the table with a doughnut and glass of milk, and used the little monkey as my shield. You know how she gets," he said. Anna answering with a nod of her head.

"Oh yeah. I don't know how she's managed not to teach Clara any bad words yet. She's the kid I envision dropping the F-bomb in church," Anna said, barely holding back her laughter.

"Tell me about it," he said. "I don't know what we're going to do when Clara learns to spell. I basically told her we ran into each other last night, told her about Travis, then let her know I liked you and wanted your number," he said, leaving her tongue-tied.

"Anna?" he said, waiting for her to say something. Anything.

"Hmm," she said. "So you like me, huh?" Anna asked, enjoying the moment. "Like me or like me, like me?" she teased, drawing a small sigh from him.

"Like you, like you, I think. Want to go out tonight? On an actual date?" he asked.

Anna's heart jumped in her throat at his invitation. She couldn't help but feel excited about the idea of going out with him again. There was just something about him. "I can't, I'm sorry. I already have plans," she said, letting the comment dangle for a minute.

"Oh," he said, sounding a little disappointed, "well, I start seconds tomorrow, so that's out."

"Seconds?" Anna asked, "Where do you work? I can't believe we didn't cover that. I mean, I saw you naked, but don't know where you work. That seems a little backwards, don't you think?"

Aidan laughed, surprised at her honesty. "Agreed, that's

why I was asking you out for an official date. So we could talk without our tongues in the other's mouth. And I work at the coal mine, by the way."

"Good idea on the date," she agreed. "Very adult-y. I'll let you in on a secret...my big plans are to go over to Sorcha's. I need to get a Clara fix. I hope to spend a lot of time over there, actually. It's been too long since we've been able to visit. Do you think she'd mind if you came over, too?" Anna said. "I'd like to see you, too," she added, rubbing her palm on her forehead. This was all very awkward, Anna thought. She was extremely out of practice with flirting. Are people supposed to be frank? Play hard to get? God, what a waste of time.

"Good, I was hoping you'd say that. I'll be there. See you tonight," he said.

"See you later," she said. Anna hung up the phone, relieved to have that over with. Now to find something to keep her busy until it was time to get ready. She wasn't going to waste time thinking about what she was going to wear. Or say. Or how she'd act the minute she saw him. Or how she was going to keep her calm when Sorcha saw her face and knew she had bumped uglies with her brother the night before. She just wasn't.

## Six

ANNA DIDN'T HAVE TO LOOK FAR for a distraction. On her way to the kitchen, she was nearly knocked to the ground by Harry who was running full force through the house. Right behind him was the strangest looking puppy that Anna had ever seen. A boy, yes, definitely a boy, she laughed, scooping up the little bundle. He was white with black ears, spots, and the biggest paws she had ever seen on a dog. Not far behind him was Jesse.

"There he is! The little pain in the butt," Jesse said, wrapping one arm around the pup and one around Anna. "I'm so glad you're home! I was going to try and give you more time, but I couldn't stand it!"

"I've missed you, Jess." Anna took the puppy out of Jesse's arms, "Now tell me about this guy," she said, turning to walk back toward her bedroom where they could talk undeterred by Eadie and Aunt Ruthie.

"His official name is Mom-Gave-In, but we're calling him Oscar." Jesse laughed, walking into Anna's room, sitting on the bed. "The boys have been after me to get a dog since we got in the house."

"Ah, Mom-Gave-In doesn't quite roll off the tongue. I like Oscar, though," Anna said, sitting across from Jesse with the puppy between them.

"He's a Great Dane, so he will be the size of a truck in a few months, but for now he's pretty cute," she said, scratching behind his ears while Anna rubbed his belly. Harry inched his way in the room, sniffing at Oscar on the bed. Harry deemed the little beasty not much of a threat, and plopped at Anna's feet.

"Well, that's got to be a good sign," Jesse said, looking down at Anna's gentle giant of a pet. "If yours isn't going to try and eat mine, how about we leave them here with Mom and Aunt Ruthie and go exploring?" she said, looking hopefully at Anna.

"Exploring? What have you got in mind?" she asked, raising up gently so as not to wake the sleeping Oscar.

"The boys are at school and I took a day off. Want to go on a hike? I know you go a few times a week with your Denver health nut friends, I figured you were due for a fix," she said, scooping up Oscar, who stretched and yawned in her arms.

"I would love that!" Anna said. "I went for a run this

morning, but it's been years since I've been to Copper Creek. Can we hike there?"

"Perfect. I'll alert the babysitters," Jesse said, heading to the kitchen with Harry on her heels. He wasn't about to miss anything Oscar the Intruder was going to be doing.

Anna looked through the clothes she had packed and pulled out a long sleeve shirt and a light jacket to throw on. Content with her outfit, she walked to the back door to find her mom and aunt fussing over the dogs. Anna decided to ask Jesse if she thought they should get her mother a dog when it was time for Anna to go home. Eadie had always had a house pet, and after their last dog had passed a few years ago, she hadn't been able to get another. Now that Walt was gone, however, it might do her good to have the company in the house. She'd have to think more about that.

Jesse and Anna hopped in Jesse's SUV and turned toward the southeast end of town. Anna greedily took in the scenery as it changed from small town to fields, and eventually to gentle, rolling hills. They were quiet for a while, and Anna could practically hear Jesse's gears turning, trying to find the right way to ask about how Anna was doing. Anna could've remedied the silence and put her sister out of her misery, but she was enjoying the quiet so much she chose to just sit there, soaking it all in as they covered the miles. The sun was shining, the air was clear, and the humidity was not quite cranked up like it usually was in Southern Illinois. Anna almost missed it. Though she had enjoyed living in Colorado over the last few years, to her, sunny days, especially summer days were supposed to hit you with a wall of humidity and melt the makeup right off your face. Sure, the dry climate made it easier to enjoy the outdoors, especially on hikes and runs, but it just wasn't home.

Jesse reached over and patted her sister's knee. "I'm just so glad you're here. I've missed you something awful," she said, pulling up to the parking lot nestled into one of the roads of the National Forest. The girls got out, walking toward the path map, and Anna put her arm around Jesse.

"I've missed you, too. Thanks for taking such good care of Mom."

Jesse shrugged, giving Anna a small smile. "She's doing a bit better than I expected, thank God. I think having Aunt Ruthie in the house, making racket and helping with cooking has been a tremendous help. I was afraid it would make Mom nervous, but I think it's been good medicine."

"Yeah, by the way, I thought Ruthie was going to be visiting her kids this week," she said, trying to pin Jesse with a look.

"I know, sorry about that! I think something's going on with Jake and his wife and it wasn't a good time for her to visit. Mom didn't tell me much about it, but I think they're having some trouble," she said, swapping a sad glance with Anna.

"Shoot, I hate to hear it. What's with all the bad luck? Is it contagious or something? Family curse?" she said, wrinkling her nose at her sister. Jesse laughed and shrugged. "Is Jake still a police officer? I didn't get to talk with him at the funeral, and honestly, it's been a little while since I paid attention to who was doing what outside of our little immediate family bubble."

"Yes, he is. He's leaving Chicago! Ruthie is thrilled. Jake just recently got hired with our town's department. He's in the process of buying a house on the southwest end of town. By the sound of it, he's going to be living in it alone."

"Wow, that's going to be a serious adjustment. I imagine it's just a little different being a cop in Chicago and being a cop in Mayberry."

"Yeah, I bet so, too. I'm sure there will be enough to keep him busy. Our little town has its challenges," Jesse said with a shrug.

"Can I tell you something?" Anna asked, eyes sparkling at Jesse's nod. She whispered conspiratorially, "I never did like his wife."

Jesse leaned in. "I never did, either. He can do better. He needs someone more fun. His wife could suck the fun out of an amusement park."

Anna smiled, not really sure what to say. They looked at the map posted at the trailhead and made sure they were choosing the right one. They walked for a little while in silence, and then Anna finally decided to throw Jesse a bone.

"I'm doing okay, you know," she said, looking over at her sister who was carefully picking out her steps on the path.

Jesse stopped and pulled Anna into a hug. "I'm so glad, kiddo. I've been trying to figure out how to jump into the interrogation," she said, giving Anna a weak smile.

"I figured as much," she said, earning a playful slap on the arm. "Let 'er rip, Jess."

Giving her sister a dirty look, she shook her head. "I still can't believe Travis left. Has he ever explained what the heck happened?" she asked, as they continued down the path.

"Not a word," Anna said, shaking her head. "At first, I couldn't decide how to feel. I didn't know if I was more hurt by that, or angry," she paused, picking her way along the path. The climb was getting a little higher, and the tree roots were thick on the ground.

"He just sort of disappeared on me. Then after a few weeks, it was almost like he'd never been there to begin with. The townhouse felt empty, but not uncomfortable. Heck, Jesse. Harry is better company than Travis was, most days," she smiled, enjoying Jesse's expression. Jesse had never been a big fan of Travis, but like Eadie, Jesse was not prone to meddling. If anything, Jesse understood what it was like to choose to be with someone not everyone liked. Jesse's ex-husband Drake had been one of the most arrogant son of a guns that Anna had ever met. He had seemed to love Jesse so much in the beginning, everyone had hoped it would work out anyway. Nobody in their family was the type to gloat with a big "I told you so" when a relationship foundered. Jesse and Anna had both dreamed of finding a love like their parents had shared, and so far, they were 0 for 2. Except now, Jesse had Levi.

"How are things going with Levi?" Anna asked, eager to find out the details. To her surprise, Jesse blushed.

"What? You're blushing? I don't think I've ever seen that," she said, ducking away from a playful swat.

"Shut up, I know. It's embarrassing," she said, looking down at her feet. When she looked up at Anna, her smile was bright, her eyes were clear.

"He's wonderful," she said. "So different than Drake, although I try not to compare them constantly. It's hard though. You get used to a certain way of being treated, whether you thought you would or not," she said, meeting Anna's furrowed brow with her hands raised in mock surrender. "I know, I didn't ever dream it would change so much. The early years were different. Something changed in him over time. I don't know if it was work, bad genes, or what, but it's like something sort of poisoned him from the inside out, I guess." At that, Jesse was quiet, carefully choosing what she wanted to share. Anna waited, not wanting to rush through this conversation. It had been so long since they'd had time to visit without the kids, or their mother, nearby. It was almost like a luxury to just be together without distraction or interruption.

"I hate that I let it get as bad as I did. I should have left years ago, but it's hard, ya know?" she said, continuing on the path. "I wanted to be sure I was doing the right thing for the boys as well as myself, and I had to be prepared financially to take care of us. That takes time," she said with a shrug.

"With Levi, it's just a night and day difference. His primary focus is and will always be his kids, and I commend that. That's a language I can speak. He's an excellent father, and those kids, Anna. They are incredible," Jesse said with a quick swipe of her hand to catch the tear gathering in her eyes. "They've been through so much with Emma's death. They all work together like a unit, including Stanley and Myrtle. They rally together to help the children feel secure, but still give them so many chances to talk about and remember Emma. Levi put together a scrapbook of her pictures, from her childhood all the way to the end. Her mother sent a big box and Levi worked to have them made into a photo book. He even had several copies made, and has them tucked away to give to the kids when they're bigger because the one he has out gets a lot of action. The kids look through it all the time, and he tells them stories to go with the pictures. Man. I just love him so much," she said, causing Anna to stop worrying.

"That's what I was waiting to hear," she said, patting her sister's arm. "I'm so happy for you, Jesse. Is he doing great with the boys?" she asked, hopeful.

"Oh yes." She smiled, the joy evident in her eyes. "The kids were a little standoffish at first, but we've taken our time and aren't rushing it. Levi comes over occasionally with the kids and we cook out. Sometimes we go on dates, but typically that's when the boys are at Drake's. I'm not about to leave them on my weekends with them."

Anna nodded. She couldn't imagine how hard it must be to have to share your children with a spouse, even one you trusted to be a good father at all times. Anna relaxed, enjoying the sound of Jesse's voice as she explained how Drake had mellowed a bit over the last few months, especially during the kids' visits, according to Michael, Jesse's oldest son. At first, Drake was hell bent on constant power struggles, but it seemed like he was adjusting more to the changes. It was clear that he was happy the marriage had ended, but he didn't like that Jesse had moved the boys to her hometown in Southern Illinois. He worked more than he was home, so it wasn't that he was necessarily missing family time, however it galled him to think she did something without his liking it. Thankfully, the boys' visits to his house were going well, and communication had opened up more between him and Jesse. She said the phone calls weren't nearly as hostile as they had been initially. Anna was relieved to hear it; her sister didn't need the additional stress. She loved her boys fiercely, and Anna could only imagine how much Jesse worried when the boys were away from her.

After about an hour, they came to Copper Creek. It was a gorgeous, wide creek, with a small waterfall feeding into it. Anna and Jesse were silent, almost reverently taking in the scenery. They had played in the creek so many times as kids, this was a favorite family spot for Sunday drives when they were small. On sunny summer days, light filtered in through the trees, shading the water that was always incredibly cold. The canopy of trees was so thick in places, they hadn't even been able to swim comfortably in the pools of water that gathered in the deep parts of the creek, but Eadie had let them stand under the falls on the days she remembered to pack an extra change of clothes and towels for the kids.

Usually, they were content to walk barefoot in the cool water, picking up stones, splashing, and as always, keeping an eye out for snakes.

"I haven't brought the kids here yet, they're going to flip," Jesse said to Anna. They milled around, stepping on rocks, avoiding the icy water. Anna couldn't stand it any longer, she was ready to spill the beans.

She sat on a big rock and watched Jesse as she ducked down, looking at some bulb sprouts that were poking up out of the greenery. Her sister had always had a green thumb, a trait that had skipped Anna completely.

"So, do you remember Sorcha's brother Aidan?" she asked, halfway holding her breath.

"Yes, of course," Jesse answered, giving Anna a weird look. In a town the size they grew up in, it was virtually impossible not to know someone a few years around your age. Especially someone as notably sexy as Aidan.

"Right." *That was probably a dumb way to start out,* she muttered to herself.

"Quit mumbling, Anna. You sound like Mom," she said, throwing a pebble at her sister's shoe as she sat down beside her. "Spill."

"Well, last night we met up at the Hawk's Nest, had a few drinks and…" she paused, working up her courage. "We slept together."

"Woohoo!" Jesse hooted, shocking Anna and probably terrifying anyone within earshot.

"Jesse!" she scolded, looking around although there was nobody to see.

"I'm serious, Anna. I'm absolutely glad to hear it," Jesse said, grabbing Anna by the shoulders. "Aidan is gorgeous, a good guy, and we've practically known him all our lives."

"Don't get ahead of yourself, I mean, he is a good guy. And really, really good," she said, waggling her eyebrows at her laughing sister, "but I'm leaving in a few days, so this is just a fling." Anna nodded her head as she said the words, as if she were trying to convince herself as well as Jesse.

"A fling," Jesse answered, slowly nodding her head. "I had my first fling ever this year, as you well know." She glared, thinking back to what a spectacular failure that had turned out to be. Be careful, those things can get intense. And screwed up," she said, eyes full of big sisterly love for Anna. "Guard your heart, kiddo. But have a heck of a good time in the meantime!" she said as she rose from the rock they had been sitting on.

"So, tell me more," Jesse said as she held her hand out for Anna to grab. "Aidan's just so sexy. I can't believe nobody around here has snapped him up."

"Tell me about it!" Anna answered. "There must be some personality quirk that hasn't popped up yet. It's not like we've been around each other long. Just a few hours. And that wasn't spent talking." She grinned, laughing as Jesse shook her head. Jesse was just five years older than Anna, but she alternated between sister and mother mode where Anna was concerned.

"Are you going to see him again?"

"Tonight. We're meeting at Sorcha's for dinner," Anna answered.

Jesse groaned. "Oh my word. Sorcha. How is she going to take this? Are you going to tell her?" Jesse asked, outwardly anxious for her sister.

"She already knows," she said, laughing when Jesse's eyes bugged out. "She is thrilled and practically has us married with children."

"Wow! That is not what I was expecting," Jesse said. "Thank goodness. It would be brutal, otherwise. Does she still have much of a temper, or did motherhood mellow her out?"

"She's every bit as vocal as she ever was, but I think she's changed a little. I'm not sure I'd ever call Sorcha mellow," she answered, a laugh escaping her lips. "She's relaxed a tiny bit though, maybe not as quick to snap, but if she does, be thankful you're not on the receiving end."

Anna and Jesse started back down the trail, their pace slow. They talked about Jesse's sons, Anna's close friends in Denver and debated the merits of surprising Eadie with a dog at some point. Anna couldn't remember the last time that she and Jesse had enjoyed an uninterrupted conversation for this length of time. She was going to make a mental note to start calling Jesse more. She had nearly forgotten how grounded and easy it was to talk to Jesse. Anna admired the guts it took Jesse to move the boys home and start a new life.

Before she knew it, the afternoon was gone and it was time to get ready to go to Sorcha's. Anna had big plans of wallowing around on the floor with Clara, so comfort was the order of the day. Not to mention Sorcha was cooking spaghetti. That required stretchy pants – that girl could cook. Anna settled on black leggings and a soft gray sweater tunic. She swept her hair up in a ponytail and threw on her boots. When Anna went to check on Harry before she left, she had to laugh. Instead of relaxing in his big dog bed in the living room floor, he was seated on the couch between Eadie and Aunt Ruthie. A red bandana had been tied around his neck, Wild West bandit-style. He spared her a wag of his tail then put his sweet dog head in Eadie's lap, where he would receive maximum petting. She was starting to get a little anxious about how Harry would fare when it was time to leave. Anna was an affectionate, attentive dog mom, but how could she compete with both her mother and her aunt? After bidding goodbyes, Anna slyly slipped in that she might stay over at Sorcha's house. She wasn't sure what the night would hold, but she didn't want to think of her sweet mother worrying over when she'd get home. Some things didn't change, and she knew Eadie would still listen for the door, despite Anna being 30 years old.

# Seven

WHEN SHE TAPPED ON THE DOOR, Sorcha answered with a squirming Clara on her hip. Sorcha looked a bit exhausted while Clara positively bounced with energy. Anna did a one-armed exchange with Sorcha, handing over her purse and a bag containing two bottles of red wine in exchange for the gorgeous strawberry blonde bundle. As she hugged and whispered to Clara, she let her eyes drink in the surroundings. Walking into Sorcha's house was like entering a comfortable nest. Their place was relatively small, but it seemed like every surface called out to be touched. Anna decorated her own home in cool blues and whites; Sorcha preferred golds, browns and reds. Anna couldn't help but feel that when she walked into Sorcha and Evan's home, she was being pulled into a cozy haven where snuggling down to hearth and home was the rule of the day.

The smell in the air was amazing. Her friend was a skilled cook and had been hard at it all day between bouts of playing with Clara. Baby dolls and toy cars were scattered on the floor. Plastic food and a toy baby bottle were lined neatly on the table; apparently one of Clara's babies would be sharing the meal with her parents, Anna, and hopefully her Uncle Aidan.

Right on cue, a low pitched voice called out a hello as Aidan stepped through the door. He smiled across the room at Anna and bent low just in time to catch Clara as she catapulted into his arms. He whisked the little monkey up high into the air. Anna's stomach did a little flip as she saw him there with a curly headed, giggling little girl in his arms. Anna intentionally averted her eyes and turned toward the kitchen to see Sorcha smiling at her over a glass of wine. Anna stretched out her hands in a 'gimmie gimmie' gesture, and Sorcha laughed out loud, pouring a glass for her idiotic friend.

When Aidan made it into the kitchen, having dispelled Clara, who now rode in on Evan's back around the living room, he walked up to Anna, and wrapped an arm around her waist.

"Hello, Anna," he said, ducking his lips in close to her ear. She nearly melted into the floor, but didn't want to give Eagle Eye Sorcha any more pleasure than she was already getting out of this rather awkward experience.

"Hey," she said, feeling uncharacteristically shy. She smiled up at him, and they turned together toward the squeals of delight coming from the living room.

"She ought to sleep well tonight," said Sorcha, turning back toward her spaghetti sauce. "Thank God, because she's been a little beast the last few nights. I never dreamed how little sleep I would get after having a kid. It makes me hate these people who brag about how their baby sleeps through the night after a few weeks," she practically spit the words.

Anna went over and hugged her friend. "I'm sorry, lady. I bet it's tough. I have an idea, if you don't mind a last minute houseguest. I'm without a curfew tonight." she laughed, waggling her eyes at her friend. "Imagine that, at thirty! Anyway, why don't I stay on the couch tonight and get up with Clara when she wakes up. You can get some sleep," she suggested.

"I would love that!" Sorcha answered. "Hell, I might even shave my legs and give Evan the green light," she crowed, dancing around the kitchen.

Anna laughed and looked at Aidan in time to see him cringe. It didn't matter that Evan was his best friend, he still couldn't handle the mental imagery that Sorcha loved to shoot at him like arrows.

"I'm out of here," he said, quickly escaping to the living room, where Evan now had Clara situated on his lap reading her a story.

Sorcha pointed to the pot and handed Anna the spoon. "Keep stirring this please," she said, making her way to the cutting board to get the veggies ready for the salad. They were quiet for a few minutes, a rare experience which let Anna know Sorcha was getting ready to dive into uncomfortable waters.

"So, this could be awesome," Sorcha said, a true smile on her face. "I've always kind of thought there was a spark between you two, especially after, you know, the tree house incident." Anna visibly squirmed.

"Maybe," Anna answered, not sure where Sorcha was going with this.

"Or," she continued, "It could be an absolute train wreck," she said, her voice sort of trailing off. Anna's head jerked up to meet the bright blue eyes of her lifelong friend.

"Train wreck?" she questioned, the hurt filling her face before she could stop it.

Sorcha threw her hands up in a 'wait a minute' gesture, and wrapped her arms around her friend.

"Anna, you're family to me. Aidan's my big brother. I just want whatever this is to be a good thing, and not an awkward thing. I love you both and I could never choose. I just want to be clear right out of the gate. I won't choose between you if whatever this is goes belly up at some point. You're both my family."

Anna returned the hug and nodded. "I get it, Sorch. I wouldn't ask you to choose, or talk negatively about him to you. I'm not even sure what this is yet. It's only about a day old, anyway. Unless of course you count the tree house episode years ago," she said, laughing at herself. How weird. How flat out weird to be back home, revisiting a fling that had left her all tingly inside for over a decade. The man had game. He was hands down the best kiss she'd ever tasted. And to mention hands, Anna sighed and blushed. She forced herself to stop the train of thought she was on. She didn't need to get overheated tonight, or at least not this early in the evening.

Clara walked toward Anna with her arms outstretched, and Sorcha took back the stirring spoon. Evan followed behind her, wrapping his arms around Sorcha.

"Hey, Evan," Anna said, patting his shoulder. "Nice to see you," she said, stepping into a hug.

"You too, Anna." He smiled. "Even nicer since I heard you're staying overnight. Thanks for pulling thirds, we need a break," he said, his lips finding Sorcha's neck.

"Enough, mister. You'll get yours later. Now stir," she said, handing the stirring spoon off once again.

Anna laughed and walked into the living room. Aidan was standing by the dining room table setting the plates and napkins for the dinner. Score a few extra points. There's nothing sexier in the world than a helpful man that does what's needed without having to be asked.


AIDAN FIT INTO Sorcha's little family like a comfortable piece of well-loved furniture. Anna watched him beneath lowered lashes, in awe of his place in a family she dearly loved while trying to be attentive but not too attentive. While she worked to divvy her interest up among everyone at the table, it was clear she was reacting to Aidan, if only at a chemical level. Sorcha snuck glances her way with an all-knowing half-smile on her lips.

After Clara was sufficiently coated with marinara sauce with crumpled pieces of bread squashed in her fat little fists, Sorcha deemed it bath and bedtime. Hands and faces were wiped, and Aidan and Anna stood to clear the dishes while Sorcha and Evan happily held Clara out for bedtime kisses and walked her to the bathroom to enjoy giving her a bath together instead of worrying over spreading out responsibilities of cleaning the kitchen for the evening.

Aidan cleared the table while Anna loaded the dishwasher and set the pans to soak. She plugged her phone into the speaker in the kitchen, and music that she loved filled the room while they worked. Soft and sultry sounds of Fink poured into the room amidst familiar and memory infused Dave Matthews Band songs. Aidan carried the last of the plates in from the dining room while leaning against Anna at the sink. He reached his arm around her to grab the dishrag, running it under warm water while the other arm came around to grab the dish soap. Such a simple mundane gesture seemed incredibly intimate while snuggled in close to her. His lips found the spot on her neck between her ear and shoulder and she shuddered, her back arching against his breath and proximity. She brushed against him, causing him to stir against her, holding still but burning down all at the same time. She cocked her head to the side and planted a kiss at his jawbone, enough to suffice.

Soft murmurings were coming in from the hall, signaling bedtime for sweet Clara, and the quiet beginning of a private evening for Evan and Sorcha, who so deserved a little quiet time alone. Sorcha's parents were all too glad to take little Clara so that the young couple could go on dates or have time alone, however their deep adoration for their daughter made it a tough time letting go for even an evening. Having Clara safe and sound under their roof while they had some much anticipated alone time was perfect for Sorcha and her man. Evan adored Sorcha, Anna thought as Aidan took the soapy cloth to the table to wipe it down. She was so happy her friend had found an almost fairytale kind of love in a world that seemed hell bent on destroying it. She was absolutely crazy about Evan, and he loved her like she was a princess and an answered prayer. Sorcha was a ball of fire, but Anna knew in her heart she was as loving and tender as she was fierce. Her heart felt happy thinking about how in love her sweet friend was with her life.

Anna flicked off the kitchen light as Aidan brought in the dish cloth to rinse and wring out at the sink. She leaned her head against his back as he washed and dried his hands, her belly starting to fill with butterflies at the thought of having him alone again for the night. He took her hand in his and led her back to the living room as Sorcha tiptoed into the room.

"She's out like a light," she said, grinning at her best friend and brother. "We are so thankful for this, you guys," she said, wrapping Anna in a hug and patting Aidan on the arm. "I love that kid to pieces but she's wearing me out waking up all the time. I'm sure it's a phase, but it feels like my short term memory is starting to take a hit from being so tired all the time. Part of the territory, I guess," she said with a shrug.

Anna nodded at her friend, "We're glad to help. Dinner was great, Sorcha, and everything's all tidied up. The coffee pot is set to start at 8:00 AM if by some miracle we're all still asleep. At least we'll wake up to coffee," she said, knowing full well that Clara usually woke up around 6:30 AM ready to take on the world.

"If I'm still in bed at 8:00 AM, you'd better skip the pleasantries and call the coroner," she said rolling her eyes. "But seriously, there are extra blankets and pillows in the linen closet in the hallway. Gobs of food and wine in the kitchen, and an extra set of toothbrushes under the bathroom counter. Unopened, even. We're fancy here," she said with a laugh.

"Got it, Sis. Pillows, blankets, wine, clean teeth, now go to sleep, or, um, whatever," he said with visible discomfort. At that, she smiled and walked quietly back to her bedroom where Evan was standing in the doorway. A quick wave to Aidan and Anna and they quietly clicked the door closed, leaving the room lit only by a soft night light in the hallway.

"How about I grab the linens and get started on the pallet?" he asked her.

"Sounds good. I'm going to run and change," Anna answered, grabbing the clothes that Sorcha had set out for her and walked quietly into the bathroom. When she came out in her t-shirt and pajama pants, she saw that Aidan had layered blankets and pillows and stoked the fire. He wandered in from the kitchen with two glasses of red wine and a pretty confident smile on his face.

"Easy there, tiger," she said, stepping into his arms after he placed the glasses on the side table. "Don't forget we're on Clara Duty tonight." Unable to stop herself, her fingers curled against the hair at his neck. She'd always had a thing for short cuts, and while his hair was longer on top, it was soft and nice to the touch against her fingers.

He dipped his lips down to hers and then to her neck and whispered, "I know, it's just hard to resist when I've got you here with soft blankets, a fire…" Aidan said, his fingers tracing the v-neck of her t-shirt. "Sorcha's really pulling out all the stops tonight, huh?" he laughed sarcastically, looking down at the ratty college t-shirt and shorts that Anna was wearing.

"Well, we're lucky she didn't leave out some crazy lingerie, she'd have had to pack you off to therapy." She laughed, then clamped her hand over her mouth, praying that she didn't wake up Clara.

"Shh!" he whispered, his finger going to his own lips. "The little nut just fell asleep. If she wakes up I'll never get to make out with you all night," he said, smiling as Anna's eyes bugged out.

"Making out sounds nice, but no funny business. I'm on kid duty, and I take that very seriously," she said, delivering the words with her quiet but stern teacher voice.

"Yes, ma'am, you've got it," he said, sitting down on the blankets and holding his hand out in invitation for her to do the same.

She plopped down next to him and rested her head on

his shoulder, staring at the crackling, blazing fire. "There's something so hypnotic about a fire, isn't there?"

"Yes, very relaxing," he said. "And sexy." He grinned as he reached over to pull her into his lap. She tilted her head back and enjoyed the press of his lips, and her fingers grazed his scruffy cheek. He had been clean-shaven when he came by for dinner but already the stubble was rough against her fingertips. His fingers traced the column of her spine, from her ponytail down her back. With his hands on her bottom he pulled her against his arousal and a sigh escaped her lips.

Her resolve about keeping the evening babysitter-appropriate started to weaken as his hands moved over her body, exploring her curves. She couldn't remember the last time before Aidan that she had felt that blissed out just from kissing and touching. There they were, making out like a couple of teenagers in Sorcha's living room.

A memory bubbled up and her body jerked with a silent laugh, interrupting Aidan's interrogation of her lips. "What's funny?" he asked, a grin pulling at the corner of his mouth.

Anna readjusted, pulling away from his lap a tiny bit to put some space between them while she cooled down. "I just remembered the morning after the Tree House Incident." She smiled, feeling his hands move up and down her sides.

"Ah, the Tree House Incident," Aidan said, closing his eyes, relishing the mental images. "I've thought of that night a hundred times at least" he said, wolfish eyes daring to gobble her up on the spot.

"Me, too," she said, shuddering as he brushed the hair

back from her neck. "I remember trying to creep out of the house the next morning without waking everyone up and heard something going on in the backyard. Do you remember?" she asked, wondering if he had played that weekend back over and over in his mind like she had over the years.

"Oh yeah," he answered, nodding his head. "I was hoping to find the jewelry that you lost when we were fooling around up there the night before." He grinned. "How I found that earring in pea gravel, I'll never know."

She smiled, remembering how mortified she had been to face him after they had made out. She had almost hoped she'd never see him again after that; her bravado had faded considerably with the rising of the sun. She recalled walking over to him as he bent to pick something up. He smiled down at her. "Found it!" he said, earning a reproachful shush from her. Anna had hoped to escape without Sorcha noticing anything weird was going on. With a face that showed every emotion, she knew she'd never stand a chance against Sorcha. Thinking back on it, what a waste of energy, since Sorcha had known all along.

Anna rose to check on Clara, tiptoeing through the hallway, and stood at her bed with Aidan close on her heels. For a minute she just looked down at the sleeping girl, all innocence and sweetness. Her curls fanned out on her pillow and her little hand up to her cheek. Anna smoothed her hair from her forehead with the lightest of touches and pressed a little kiss to the top of her head. Aidan's heart caught in his throat at the motherly gesture, and for a minute he fantasized that this was his house, his wife and his sleeping child. He had always wanted a large family and the chaos that went with it. He tamped those feelings back down and walled them off for now. He wasn't a fan of heartbreak and he didn't want to get his hopes up on Anna if she was going to be leaving to go back to Colorado in a few short days. He had to admit his timing seemed to suck. He held his hand out to her and flicked off the little bedside table lamp, leaving only the soft glow of a night light.

They made their way back through the house and settled down onto a pallet of pillows and blankets on the floor. Anna sighed as Aidan pulled her in close. He smiled at the sound she made and enjoyed the feel of her against his body. He'd never been much of a cuddler, but he suspected he'd do anything if it meant she'd be tucked in close to him like they were right then.

The night passed easily and Anna blinked at the light streaming in through the windows. She blinked harder when she realized she was being watched very closely by Clara. The little midge had arranged an armful of stuffed animals all in a line and sat inches from Anna's face. A surprised laugh escaped her and Aidan shot up at the sound. "Uncky Aidan!" Clara bellowed, launching herself across Anna to land in Aidan's arms. He pulled her in close and tucked her right against him.

"Look who's awake!" he said, tickling her and smiling at her squeals of delight. Anna watched the little scene and soaked up all the joy in it. Just then she heard the bedroom door open and Sorcha and Evan came in with sleepy smiles.

"Please tell me she woke you up 800 times and you understand why I'm so danged tired all the time," Sorcha said on her trek to get coffee.

"Should we lie or tell her the truth?" Aidan whispered, immediately catching Sorcha's attention as she came back with two steaming cups, Evan behind her with two more.

Her eyebrows were up to the sky and Anna said, "I think we've kept enough secrets..." she said, smiling at Aidan. "Sorry, Sorch, she didn't make a peep the whole night," she said, pulling Clara into her lap.

"That figures. Little stinker could've at least made you earn your dinner," she said, holding her arms out to Clara and enveloping her little body as only a mother can do.

They sipped coffee and gathered breakfast, enjoying the morning for a while until Anna realized she ought to get home to relieve Eadie of Harry. Anna gathered her things while Aidan packed up their blankets and pillows.

"Well, thanks again for letting us stay, it was nice to spend time here," she said, giving Sorcha a smooch on the cheek. "I'm going to go take Harry off Mom's hands and get him out for a run." Aidan stood to walk her to her car, handing Clara off to Sorcha. Picking up his own bag, he gave Sorcha and Clara a kiss and nod to Evan.

"See you guys later," he said. "See you later, Clare-Bear!"

"Bye bye! Love you!" she yelled, standing at the screen door watching Aidan and Anna walk to their cars. Sorcha took her little hand and led her off to have a grand adventure beating pans with wooden spoons while she cleaned up the kitchen.

"Well, that was our first official sleepover," he said. "Next one at my house, tonight?" he asked, putting her things into her car and watching her optimistically.

Anna weighed his question for a moment. She was loving every moment she got to spend with Aidan and couldn't decide if she should just jump in and enjoy this while she was here, or brace herself to not get attached since she was leaving in a few days. That second, Travis's words from the bar rang in her ear, "*You're always going to be the same, Anna, so freaking predictable.*" Shaking his words from her mind she decided to enjoy Aidan while she was with him.

"Tonight sounds good," she said. "What time should I come over?"

"Ugh, one issue. I start second shift tonight. I won't be home till 2AM. Can I give you my key? You can come on over whenever you like and make yourself at home," he said, then he winced. "Is that weird? Too early?" he asked, looking a touch anxious.

"That would be great. It'll give me time to snoop," she said, eyes going wide to scare him.

"Snoop away!" He laughed, fishing in his pocket for his keys. "I've got nothing to hide. Here, take this one, I've got another hidden at home," he said, pressing the key into her palm. "Shift ends at 2AM, I'll shower and be home right after," he said, leaning in to kiss her, his hand cradling the back of her head.

Even the simplest touch sent a thrill down her spine. It did feel a little weird to have his key in her hand. It felt like they had skipped about a million steps, but with a week to be together, there wasn't much time for social propriety, she guessed. She kind of threw that out the window once they slept together, she realized and chuckled to herself. They separated and got in their cars. Neither would've been surprised to know that Sorcha had been peeping out the window through the curtains, smiling to herself at the budding romance as she went to conquer life as a domestic goddess and mother supreme.

# Eight

ANNA RUSTLED TO THE DOOR with an overnight bag and paused to kiss Eadie on the cheek.

"Staying over, tonight," Eadie said, trying to play it cool. Anna flinched, trying to remember that she was in her thirties, had been engaged and even lived with her fiancé.

She nodded her answer. "Yes, he's working late tonight so I'm going to throw some dinner together and…" she paused, not knowing what to say next.

Eadie laughed at her daughter's discomfort. "Oh hell, honey. Go. Enjoy. You're only young once and the time flies, believe me," she said.

Anna couldn't help but laugh in response, thinking to herself she never thought she'd hear that from her mother. She knew Aidan wouldn't be home for hours, but she couldn't help but glow with anticipation. It felt a little like she was playing house, which she had done with Travis, but it hadn't ever been goosebump inducing. She was sure he would've eaten during his shift, but she had planned to run by the grocery store and put together a fruit pizza, one of her favorite snacks. Chances were fairly good that he was going to need his energy after work. Anna took her time at the grocery store and picked up a bottle of Riesling for herself to enjoy as she made the treat.

She let herself into his house while balancing the grocery bags on her hip. When Aidan's door swung open, she felt so excited to be there on her own for a little while. She put the groceries on the counter and tried to decide where to prowl first. She wasn't joking when she said she was going to snoop. Anna wandered around his living room, picking up the few framed pictures settled on the hearth. Faces she loved most in the world smiled back at her. Sorcha, Clara, Evan, Aidan and their parents stood arranged in front of a Christmas tree. Little Clara smiled her gummy little baby smile from a few years ago in another. She wandered into the kitchen. On Aidan's fridge were a few magnets from local shops and one picture: four close-shaved men in BDUs. This must've been his closest group of friends. His unit? His Platoon? Anna wasn't sure of the terminology, but she could tell by the looks on their faces they were brothers. They were dirty and sweaty but had wide smiles on their faces.

Just looking at his picture made a shudder pass through her. Anna had never dated a military man before. The thought that he had been brave enough to sacrifice his own well being to serve his country made her heart swell with respect. She already knew Aidan was a wonderful man, and that he was incredible in bed. Combine that with the kind of machismo required of a Marine and it was almost too much to take in at once. She didn't know yet what his job had required, but was in awe of his service no matter what he'd been through.

She walked around the rest of his home noticing how tidy things were, and in a perverse way was kind of tempted to move things around to see if he'd notice. In his bedroom, things were consistent. Nothing out of place. Anna turned the bed down, in anticipation of things to come. She walked through the rest of his place, looking through closets and medicine cabinets without finding a single thing to send her running for the hills, so she set about the making of her fruit pizza treat and drank a glass or two of wine.

Anna made herself comfortable, accepting easily that she wasn't needed to clean up Aidan's place. Travis's own domestic ineptitude had taught her to appreciate a man that could take care of his own mess. Instead, she tucked her treat into his fridge, brushed her teeth and decided to cash it in for the night. Anna ran a brush through her hair and went to sleep in a navy blue chemise that skimmed her thighs.

She was barely aware of the stirring in the room when she registered that Aidan was near. His presence was usually one like the sun, burning hot and impossible to ignore. When she awoke at that moment, he felt cool and empty, like a black hole instead of a sun. She instinctively rose up in bed, her arms reaching out to him. He pulled her down on his lap in the chair in the corner of his bedroom. Aidan buried his face into her neck, breathing her in as if she were the very air he needed to survive.

"Aidan, what is it?" she asked, her voice choked without even knowing what it was that had him so upset.

"Benji," he said, his voice nearly a whisper. She sat up, trying to enfold him as he crumpled. When he could, he spoke. "Benji, the youngest in our fireteam. He stayed in when we separated; he went career. He was hit by an IED in Afghanistan. He's gone," he said.

"Oh, Aidan. I'm sorry," she said. He shifted and she stood, pulling him with her to the bed. He melted against her as she threw her leg over him, trying to access as much of him as she could. "Aidan, I'm so sorry," she repeated, dumbstruck by the moment. "You poor baby," she said, pulling him to her body.

He held her close, his eyes pressed tight as he tried to halt the emotion rushing over him. Aidan's hands roamed over Anna's body, finding her naked beneath the chemise. In a second it was up and over her head, and he was out of his jeans and shirt and against her, skin to skin. He was so warm and hard; all she could think of was making him better. Aidan poured himself into her, pressing his lips against her mouth, clutching at her back, and pulling her legs up around his waist. He was there, inside her in an instant, her body aching to make him feel comforted. Anna made love to him with her very soul, wanting to console and heal him.

WHEN HER EYES fluttered open, Anna wasn't surprised to see Aidan sitting on the edge of the bed looking out the window. He had had a restless night, grief pulling at his mind. She placed her hand on his arm and gave him a squeeze, her heart breaking over his attempted smile. She wondered how in the world she was ever going to go back to the real world in a few days knowing this kind of man was at her fingertips. It seemed such a shame to get a taste of that kind of happiness and then just let it slip away. Long distance relationships were a little much to consider at her age, she figured. She had her teaching job that she loved, though it was really the only tie holding her in Colorado. Aidan had a good job at the mines, and his family was all in the area. He had a great little house and was settled. She could never imagine him pulling up all his roots to move out West. None of it really mattered, she thought. She knew what she was getting into when they got involved. For now, she needed to cram in time with her family as well as be with him as much as she could and then back to reality she'd go. For now, giving him comfort was about as far ahead as she could think.

"Want me to make us some coffee?" she asked, wrapping her arms around his shoulders.

He nodded in answer, rubbing his face with his hands. "That would be great, thanks," he said, leaning to give her a kiss. "I'm going to hop in the shower and try to wake up a little."

She watched him walk to the bathroom and her heart broke for him all over again. She made her way to the kitchen to start coffee and stared at the picture while it brewed. Aidan had said Benji was the youngest in their fire squad, but all four in the picture looked no more than 21 years old at the time. Their name patches weren't showing in the picture, so she just continued to look them over after fixing herself a cup. She started praying for Aidan and Benji's family, as well as the other men in the picture. She was so lost in thought that she didn't hear Aidan walk up behind her.

"He's this one," he said, pointing to the handsome, dark-headed guy in the photo with the biggest smile. "We were celebrating. Benji had the funniest, most inappropriate sense of humor." Aidan took the photo from her while draping his arms around her in a loose hug. "It was impossible to stay pissed at him...for long anyway," Aidan said, giving her a squeeze then putting the picture back on the refrigerator.

Anna suddenly felt awkward. She didn't know if she was supposed to stay over and have breakfast, stick around to talk with him or go on home. It struck her suddenly how strange it was to be sleeping over at the house of a man she didn't even really know. What was Aidan like when he was upset? Did he want to be loved on or left alone? Finally she decided to square her shoulders and ask.

"Aidan, I want to comfort you, but I don't know what you like." He stopped and looked at her, unsure what she was asking. She shook her head. "What I mean is, I just realized how little we really know each other. Do you like to talk when you're upset? Will I make it worse if I ask questions?" she said, walking over and wrapping her arms around his shoulders. "Are you okay with me staying for a bit longer, or do you want me to go?" she said, looking into his gorgeous brown eyes.

"I'd love if you'd stay for a while, and I don't mind talking about him. He was one of my best friends. I don't know what it's going to be like without checking in with him every few weeks," he said, his voice getting rough with emotion.

Anna could do nothing but hold him close. They stayed like that in his kitchen, the smell of coffee permeating the air, the sunlight streaming in through the window. The phone in his pocket buzzed and he pulled it out to answer, stepping back from her and toward the counter where she had set out a cup for him. She picked hers up and went into the living room to give him at least a semblance of privacy.

She heard him talking quietly into the phone, answering his understanding and making notes on the notepad on the table. When he said his goodbyes, she went back into the kitchen.

"That was Davis, with the details on Benji's services. It's going to be in Austin next Tuesday," Aidan said, moving to look at his calendar. Looking at his shifts, he exhaled. "I've got to call and get off work, figure out flight and hotel arrangements," he said, looking flustered and apologetic.

"It's okay, I can get out of your hair for now while you sort out the details," she said, leaning over to give him a kiss. "I'll gather up my stuff and head out. You can call me later on if you'd like," she said, giving him a forced smile. Anna wasn't used to not knowing protocol in situations.

"If I'd like?" he asked, standing up to walk with her into the bedroom. "Yes, I'd like that, Miss Fraser." Aidan grinned.

"Okay," she said, bugging her eyes out. "I haven't exactly had a lot of experience at this kind of thing, so give me a break, alright?" she asked, pulling a face at him.

"Me either, but I like it. I liked seeing you in my bed this morning when I woke up," he said, causing a shiver to run down her spine. She liked being in his bed when she woke up.

"I'm going to go to Jesse's for a while, then spend the rest of the day at Mom's house. I leave for Denver tomorrow afternoon." At that, it was Aidan's turn to bug out his eyes. "Tomorrow afternoon? Already?" he asked, his disappointment obvious.

"Yes," she said, wrinkling her nose. "I know we didn't get much time," she said, eyes on the floor. He pulled her into his embrace and held her close. His cheek rested against the top of her head and she felt his heart pounding in his chest.

He stood still for a moment like that and then said, "Anna, how am I going to let you go?" What could she say to something like that? She kissed his lips and left him in the kitchen while she gathered her things. Within minutes she was back in the kitchen and had gathered her things. Aidan pulled her in again, wrapping her in his arms. With his lips in her hair, he said softly, "I'm going to miss you. Doesn't hardly seem fair, does it?"

Anna didn't trust herself to speak, so she stepped back from him, shrugging up one shoulder and smiling with tears in her eyes. He walked her to the door and followed her out to his driveway. Taking her bag and placing it in the backseat of her car, he kissed her once more.

"How soon can I call you?" he asked, his eyes shadowed with the loss of his friend.

"I ought to be home by late tomorrow evening, but you'll be..."

"Underground," he answered, trying to plan it out when his schedule and hers would align.

"Listen, I know we'll talk. This has been – special –" she answered, feeling foolish with each word that came out of her mouth. It was more than special, it was like finding a feeling of home, belonging and excitement all intermingled. But, Anna had to be realistic. She belonged in her classroom in Denver, and Aidan had his family and life in Southern Illinois. She could kick herself for falling for him in a matter of days. She got into the car, gave him a small wave and backed out of the drive as she argued with herself.

"Not days, you idiot. Years. Years and years," she said aloud, pointing her car toward her sister's house. Jesse was about the only person she could stand to let see her cry, and the tears were going to come.

# Nine

THE MONDAY AFTER SPRING Break was always brutal, but Anna was never quite prepared despite her years of experience. At drop off the parents looked haggard and the children were either bouncing off the walls at the prospect of being back at school, or clutching their exhausted parents, not ready to jump back into the routine. To make it even worse, a school board meeting had been scheduled for 6:00 PM that evening. Anna usually went to the meetings to maintain a certain visibility and to stay aware of what was going on the district. More than anything she wanted to go home and put on her pajamas and curl up on the couch with Harry, but instead, she rushed home to let him out, fix a quick sandwich and then hurry back to the meeting at school. She filed into the library where the meeting was held and grabbed a seat next to a few of her friends. The meeting was packed, which gave Anna a sense of foreboding. She flipped through the agenda that was in the middle of the table and saw district funding as the first item to be discussed.

She listened to the proceedings with a heavy weight in her stomach. As the president of the school board listed her name among ten other teachers in her primary school as RIF'd – reduction in force due to low funding in the district. With a lump in her throat and tears streaming down her face, Anna listened as if she were in a fog as they discussed next the cuts that would come from the elementary, middle and high schools in her district. She was patted by well-meaning fellow teachers, touched hands and hugged with several others who were being laid off and nodded as mentions were made at the potential for rehire once the budget issues were fixed, but only one thing was on her mind. Escape. She had to get out of that building, out of that city. Out of all of it.

This was the last straw – the last thing she had going well in her life had now officially gone to hell in a handbasket. Anna decided as she made her way to her car that she would finish out the remaining eight weeks of her school year, turn in the keys to her townhouse and get out of dodge. Travis was gone. Her job and the security it afforded her was now gone. Her trust in the district was gone. Soon she would be, too.

She got in her car, locked the doors, dialed Jesse and switched the phone to the speaker setting as she started her drive back to her place.

"Hello?" Jesse answered on the second ring.

"Sis? I'm moving home," she said, a half-smile fixing itself on her face as Jesse hooted out a loud yell at her announcement. Anna filled her in on the details as she drove.

ANNA WASN'T ONE to let the grass grow under her feet, but she waited before calling her mother. She wanted to talk to Aidan first and couldn't wait to get his call. She knew he was either working or traveling to Benji's funeral, so she decided to wait him out rather than interrupt him. Waiting on Aidan to call also meant she couldn't call and let Sorcha know either. She knew there would be heck to pay over that little admission. As it was, she had sworn Jesse to secrecy and had managed to extract that promise even as her nephews had filled the living room waiting on Jesse to answer what had caused her to holler out when Anna gave her the good news. Once the boys knew the secret, Eadie would know and then the whole town would as well, including Aidan. She wanted to be the one to tell him and gauge his reaction.

She went about her preparations, notifying her landlord of her plans the very next day and contacting local stores to ask if they would save boxes for her to use for packing. Anna wasn't as type A as Jesse, but she was still a planner in her own right. She tried not to count the hours waiting for Aidan to call, but he was always a shadow in the back of her mind. She couldn't wait to give him the news so that she could get on with it and tell Eadie and Sorcha. By the end of that week, her nerves were on edge, anxious to hear from

Aidan and how he had managed through Benji's service and his travels to Texas. To fill her evenings, she started the task of sorting through closets and gathering stuff to donate so there would be less to move. Anna was a fairly sentimental person, but the huge shock of changes in her life over the past several months gave her enough of a detached, irritated, and excited mindset that helped her power through the task of ridding herself of unnecessary junk. Into the donation bags went clothes she hadn't worn in a while, CDs she no longer listened to, and just about everything that Travis had ever purchased that had been left to lurk about the home they had shared. Saturday morning had been fruitful with her decluttering, and by the afternoon she had just finished filling yet another bag and hauling it to the garage when the phone rang.

"Hello?" she said with a smile; it was Aidan.

"Hey, Anna, I'm so sorry it's taken me this long to call you!" he said, his voice filling her stomach with butterflies. How long had it been since she had been enamored with the very sound of a man's voice on the other end of the phone?

"Aidan, it's fine. How are you? How was the service?" she asked, wincing and wondering if there was another way she should've asked.

He sighed and answered, "It was very well done. They did Benji proud, I think," his voice tapered off a bit. She paused, waiting for him to speak when he was ready.

"I got there on Monday evening and met up with some of the guys from our squad. We haven't been together in years, but it was just like it was when we were together. Isn't that crazy when you can pick right up with people, just like it was when you left off, no matter how much time or crazy life has happened?"

"Yes, I love friendships like that," she said, Sorcha and Jesse popping instantly into her mind.

"We had a few drinks which turned into more drinks, which turned into a little bit of a hangover for a very tough morning on Tuesday. The service was packed and there were several present from the military. I haven't seen that many uniforms since I separated. The hardest thing though was seeing Benji's wife and their little one. My God, to leave behind a child you never even had the chance to meet," he said, twisting Anna's heart.

"How sad, I'm so sorry," she said, tears welling up in her eyes.

"Yeah. The guys and I talked, and we each threw in a thousand dollars to help with immediate expenses. Sarah hasn't been working since the baby came, and his benefits will kick in, but it'll be tight in the meantime. We didn't want her to be more afraid than she has to be right now, you know?"

She already knew she loved him, despite the ridiculously short amount of time they had been involved, but at that, her heart nearly jumped out of her chest with pride. "Aidan, that is so kind and generous of you all. She's lucky that Benji had such amazing brothers."

"Well, we loved him. That means we love her too. I flew

back on Wednesday and had to go back on thirds that night, and since then I've just been bushed trying to get back into the routine. I couldn't wait to hear your voice. What's new with you?" he asked.

Finally, she had the chance to let him know she was moving home, but she felt oddly nervous all of a sudden. She asked herself how embarrassed she would be if he wasn't into her as deeply as she was into him. Either way, her plans were set and she was excited to be moving home, Aidan or no Aidan.

"Here goes. I have some big news," she said, taking a breath to steady herself. "I found out Monday night that my position is being eliminated due to lack of funding in our district's budget. Ten of us at the primary school where I teach are being let go." Anna paused, the words still feeling like a kick to the stomach. She absolutely loved her job and was heartbroken that her length of service would be used against her. She had been at the school several years and had done well on each evaluation, however there were other teachers who were excellent as well, and they had been with the school longer.

"Anna, I'm so sorry!" he said. "What are you going to do?"

"I'm going to finish out the school year, seven weeks and counting," she said, the butterflies in her stomach at a full-out swarm, "and then I'm packing up my stuff and moving home. I'm leaving Denver," she said.

Her announcement was met with silence, and in the

space of a few seconds she imagined every conceivable scenario. Was he excited? Was he nervous? For the first time, Anna wondered if he was panicked, thinking what they had was a fling and now he'd have to fight her off?

"I am so relieved to hear those words come out of your mouth," he said. Her heart stopped. "I have been wracking my brain wondering how in the hell we were going to pull this off with miles between us and I couldn't find one solution that made any sense. When can I come get you?" he said, her heart now pumping furiously. Her cheeks blushed, and her smile felt like it was going to break, it was so big.

"You're going to have to arm wrestle my sister for the honors, I'm afraid," she said, picturing Jesse's face if she even thought Aidan was going to get in her way. "Jesse's already taken off work and bought her plane tickets. She'll be here June 1st to help me haul my stuff home."

"Ah," he said, "I'm not taking Jesse on. She's as scary as Sorcha," he said. "Dang it! Sorcha is in big trouble! She didn't breathe a word to me about this," he said, his irritation easy to read in his voice.

"Well, about that…" she said when he interrupted.

"No way. She doesn't know?" he asked, his smile easy to hear in his voice.

"No, I wanted to be the one to tell you," Anna said.

"Oh! You're gonna be in trouble!" he sang in a teasing voice.

"I know, she's going to be the second phone call on my list," she said.

"The second? Who's the first?" he asked, thoroughly confused.

"My mother," she said quietly.

"Oh! You're in for it!" he said, practically giddy.

At that, Anna knew she had gotten this milestone out of the way, she really did need to tell Eadie and Sorcha. Plus, her nerves were shot after letting the cat out of the bag, and now all she wanted was to have the rest of her loved ones aware of her plans so she could get back to the business of packing.

"You're right. I am about to bust. I'm going to let you go and dive in. Can I call you tomorrow?"

"Definitely. I'll be switching to first shift, so after 6:00 okay?" he asked.

"What, no hot date planned for Saturday night?" she said half teasing, half curious.

"No, my girl is out of town for uh," she heard him rumple some papers, "seven weeks and three days," he said with a chuckle.

"After 6:00 tomorrow night it is," she said, and then said her goodbyes.

With a smile in her heart, she got up to walk Harry and deliver the exciting news to her ecstatic mother and equal parts furious-and-thrilled best friend.

# Ten

THE LAST SEVERAL WEEKS of the school year passed in a blur of preparation and goodbyes. Anna lavished every last bit of her energy on her students, knowing she would remember their little faces forever. She spent time with her close girlfriends when she wasn't busy packing and sorting, and took many solitary hikes along trails she'd dearly miss. She had loved living in Colorado with all the surrounding natural beauty within a short distance from her home.

She found her energy draining earlier in the day and had chalked it up to exhaustion. With one week left to go in the year, she was eating lunch in her classroom, her melancholy over saying goodbye to her classroom had been wreaking havoc with her emotions within the last few days. Anna looked around at the brightly colored decorations that she had so lovingly put up around the room, the cheery little curtains, the reading rug with all the colorful squares where her students sat during the morning leader board, story time, and again during the last story she managed to sneak in at the end of each day. Her heart ached thinking about the students she loved who weren't read to at home in the evenings and before she knew it, she was in full-blown tears.

Her friend Angel sat down at her table and pulled out the contents of her lunchbag.

"Good Lord, Anna, what's wrong?" she asked, her brow wrinkling with concern for her friend.

"I don't know, Ang. I'm just an emotional mess this week. Too much change at once, or something," she said, her voice trailing off as she put her head in her hands. Her friend reached across and put a hand on her shoulder and gave it a quick squeeze.

"It is a lot, I know. Any luck finding a new job in Illinois," she asked, digging into her tuna salad sandwich. Something washed over Anna, and her color changed. She put her hand over her mouth, breathed in deep and tried to ignore the clanging alarm bells that she was about to be sick. She was a Kindergarten teacher for heaven's sake – part of her world was inhaling smells and hearing sounds she'd rather not process. Quickly, her gag reflex won out and she raced to the bathroom just in time. When she walked back into her classroom Angel was white as a ghost.

"Anna?" she asked, standing up as Anna walked back to her table.

"What?" Anna said, a little shook up over getting sick.

"You couldn't be pregnant, could you?" Angel asked with eyes as big as saucers.

Suddenly Anna sat down. She thought back to her last period, and her memory was fuzzy. She quickly got her little planner out of her purse and searched for the little circle she had used for what seemed like an eternity to mark her cycle. She skimmed April, May nothing. Closing her eyes tight she flipped back to mid-March and sat down heavily in her chair.

"Oh my God," she said quietly, putting her head down on her folded arms.

"Oh my God!" shouted Angel. Before she could slap her friend's hands away she was pulled into a huge hug.

"Shhh!" Anna said, trying to quiet Angel. "I don't want anyone to hear you!" she said to her friend who had a smile like the Cheshire Cat.

"Anna, this is crazy!" she said. "Who? Who in the world did you have sex with and why did you not tell me all about it!" she said in a near sulk.

All she could do for a second was think back to the image of Aidan holding Clara closely, the little girl so small in his strong arms. Her next flashback was of her last night with him, when he received the horrible news about Benji. They had been so careful every time, but had they used protection that night? Had there even been time, she wondered, remembering with a deep blush as memories of that night played in her mind.

She heard a snicker come from Angel who was watching this unfold like someone at the movies. All she needed was a bag of popcorn and a comfy seat to make this even one bit better than it was. Anna was floored. How had she been so busy that she didn't notice missing her periods? She hadn't been on the pill, and her periods had always been pretty hit and miss. She had been so busy focusing on the move and job hunting from a distance that she hadn't thought twice about it.

With a big rush of breath, she exhaled and spilled the beans to Angel. She knew she could trust her and that it wouldn't go further than the room – as long as her big scene hadn't been overheard. If she was pregnant, she'd be a little over two months already. She looked at the clock and counted down the hours until she could get to the drugstore for a pregnancy test or two. At the bell, Angel went back to her classroom after giving Anna a huge hug.

"Maybe it's nothing, girl, but maybe it's something. Maybe it's the best thing you'll ever know this side of Heaven. Things don't always go according to plan, but this may be the biggest blessing in your life," she said, leaving Anna wiping tears from her eyes.

Throughout the rest of the day Anna kept stealing glances at the clock and more than once she found herself staring off in a daze with her hand on her middle. What if she was pregnant? She had always hoped to be a mother and obviously loved children. She had thought by now she and Travis would have been married with kids. It had been his decision to prolong their marriage and what a gift that had ended up being. She tried hard not to compare her time with him to her very limited time with Aidan, but as far as she was concerned they were two very different animals.

After what seemed like ages, the school day was over. The stories were read, the desks wiped down, the little chairs straightened and her materials set out for the next day. It was a strange kind of autopilot frame of mind she was in as she drove to the drugstore and picked up a pregnancy test with two in the pack. She went through the motions of driving home, carrying in her things and working against her nerves, she took the tests. Watching a pot boil was nothing compared to watching that little strip change color. Positive. Positive! She was going to have Aidan's baby!

It felt like a thousand different thoughts and emotions washed over her as she soaked in her new truth. She was going to be a mother! She had made a baby with a man she had been on a couple of dates with. Fine, she told herself. He was more than that. He was her best friend's brother; someone she had known for literal decades. Oh my word. What were his very, very religious parents going to say? She didn't have to think twice about it, she knew Eadie would be thrilled, but Ira and Cathleen? Yikes. They were strict in the upbringing of their children and were very traditional people.

Anna was thankful to be thirty years old and able to provide for herself. She knew whether she was judged or not, she didn't have to give two hoots because she could and would take care of this baby by herself or with Aidan. Plus, she'd have access to Jesse, and Jesse was practically a Baby

Whisperer. After raising three sons there wasn't much she couldn't handle.

What in the world would he think about this? Anna was plagued with anxiousness at the thought of telling him, that anxiousness soon turned to nausea, and in seconds Anna found herself getting sick again. When she next lifted her head up, she made a note to call her OB and schedule an appointment, then the realization hit that she wouldn't be in Colorado for the duration of the pregnancy and that it made more sense to wait until she got settled.

She had enough energy left over to drag herself to her bed for a nap and decided how and when to share her news with Aidan, Sorcha, and her family could wait a while longer. For now, she would rest. Anna curled up on her bed with her hand resting on her belly, a quiet, private joy growing in her heart as she drifted off.

THROUGH THE INSANITY of the last few weeks, Anna managed to pack up the rest of her classroom and say goodbye to her students. She exchanged hugs with her teacher friends who were either going on to new jobs at different schools or pursuing other interests. She even managed several conversations with Aidan, Jesse, Sorcha and Eadie where she managed to keep her secret to herself. She just wasn't ready to share and knew she owed it to Aidan to tell him first anyway.

Not surprisingly, the hardest person to resist telling was

Jesse. They had been on the phone and texting incessantly as Jesse planned her and Levi's wedding. They had decided to take the family to Mexico and get married on the beach. It would be a fairly small affair, Jesse, Levi, their children, Eadie, and of course, Anna. Jesse had told her she was more than welcome to bring Aidan, but she wasn't sure of that yet. After all, they had a fling while she was home on Spring Break for Heaven's sake. What was she? Twenty years old? No. She was thirty. And pregnant. With his child. Her feelings seemed to shift with the wind, alternating between excitement and fear, joy and anxiety.

For all she knew, she'd break the news when she got home and he'd be furious and not want to be involved at all. Okay, that didn't seem like Aidan at all, but it was a possibility. After all, she didn't know him that well. It deserved as much to be entertained as a possibility as him sweeping her into his arms and proposing.

As far as that goes, she may be having a baby with him, but she didn't know him well enough to be sure she wanted to marry him. They already would have a permanent tie between them, she wasn't going to add another binding predicament to the mix before she knew him better. She knew where he seemed to stand on family and friends, but what about the rest of his personality? What was he like when he was tired? How was he when he was angry? He knocked Travis to the ground in an instant, but then again, Travis had deserved that punch in the face. A renewed surge of relief hit her then that she wasn't having a baby with Travis.

Anna had made her decision. She needed to get to know Aidan better before she told him about the baby. That way she could make her decision based on her experience with him rather than leaning into his reaction - probable acceptance and excitement over the pregnancy. This approach felt right and made sense to her. She didn't want to end up married solely based on their baby. Jesse would be arriving tomorrow to help her pack up the remainder of her house and the day after they'd start their drive to Illinois. She couldn't wait to start over at home.

EARLY THE NEXT morning Anna was lying in bed rereading her text exchange with Aidan and checking her email on her phone to see if there had been any replies to any of the jobs she had applied to when her doorbell rang. Shocked, she double checked the clock, 8:00 AM. She wrapped up in her robe and checked the peephole. Jesse was standing on her doorstep holding two grande cups of something delicious.

"Jesse! What are you doing here?" she said as she threw the door open with Harry barking wildly and circling them both.

"Surprise!  I got an earlier flight and grabbed a taxi. I couldn't wait to get here to you!" she said, setting her coffees down and wrapping Anna in a hug.

"Well, welcome to my place – for 24 more hours, anyway," she said, rolling her eyes. Jesse hadn't been able to visit her there, with constant turmoil in her marriage, the end of her marriage, her newfound freedom and then of course, the inevitable courtship of Levi.

"Sis, this place is gorgeous. Boy, are you going to miss it," Jesse said, walking into the living room.

"What, the townhouse? It's ok – I mean, it's been home, but…" she answered.

"No, honey. This place is nice," she said, sitting down on the couch with an overly excited Harry doing his impression of a lapdog. "I mean Colorado. Wow. You realize Southern Illinois has fine hills and well, it's home, but look around," she said, pointing out the window. "It's June and it's in the 70s. At home, you step outside and your makeup melts right off your face," she said shrugging her shoulders.

"I know, Jess. I love it here, and it's been so much fun to live in such a beautiful surrounding, but I miss home. I've got nothing holding me here, and, I don't know. I'm just ready," she said.

Jesse looked her square in the eye. "I understand that completely. If I understand anything, it's that sometimes life throws us a curveball. All we can do is swing our hardest and hope for the best, right?"

Without any warning, Anna dissolved into tears. Jesse gathered her up with the protectiveness of a sister and the compassion of a mother. She practically pulled Anna into her lap and murmured gently to her with the comforting noises of someone who loves someone else completely.

"Aww, honey, what's the matter?" she said, holding Anna close.

"Jesse, I wasn't going to tell you, but I can't keep the secret. I'm pregnant," she said, looking into her sister's face. Anna loved her sister and considered her very pretty, but the way her eyes were suddenly too big for her face made her look nearly cartoonish.

"Pregnant?" Jesse said, transfixed on Anna's face.

"Yes, Aidan," Anna answered, a cloud enveloping her. "He doesn't know," she said, transferring her gaze anywhere but Jesse's hazel eyes.

"What? You were home a few months ago, you're what, two months?" Jesse said, her big sister face cementing itself in a near--but not quite--judgmental expression and her hand going to Anna's still-flat belly.

"Aidan," she said again, not annoyed, just relieved that she had someone to tell.

"Anna! Oh, Anna. How perfect!" she said. "You two had such a connection, and that's so what you needed after that spindly little twerp, Travis!" she said, suddenly shifting her gaze as if Travis's ghost would reprimand her for speaking ill of him.

"Jesse! I know. He's perfect, but I haven't told him yet."

"Why?" she asked, her voice suddenly quiet, a strange occurrence for Jesse, post-divorce. Once her sister had escaped the marriage that made her miserable, she sort of blossomed into what Anna could guess was her best sense of self. Ferocious mother bear, confident woman coupled with intelligence and wit, there she could withstand pretty much anything. Anna admired her sister, greatly.

"I'm not sure if it's all going to make sense, or if I even need anyone else to truly understand," she said, looking Jesse straight in the eye and issuing a not-so-subtle warning, "but I want to get to know him more before I throw this in his lap," she said, looking down at the floor.

"He's a good man, a family man," she continued, "but I want to know him more before I make any lifelong commitments," she said, wincing after she realized her blunder.

"Lifelong, I get it," Jesse said. "Initially, I thought I'd be married to Drake till we were old folks," she said, shrugging her shoulders. "Things don't always work out like we think it will, and sometimes that's for the better," she said.

"I didn't mean anything by that," she said, quickly interrupted by Jesse.

"I know, Anna," she said. "It's just sometimes life throws us a curveball," Jesse said, lovingly putting her hand to Anna's still-flat belly. "I can't regret my time with him because of my sons, but I do regret the way I allowed myself to be treated." She walked through the living room toward the stairs where she'd be sleeping. "The best thing I can do now is make sure I'm modeling for the boys how a woman deserves to be treated, and how a man should behave. I think I'm finally getting it right," she said, flashing her bright smile.

Anna was close behind, nodding her agreement. She hadn't planned on telling Jesse a thing, but it felt so much better not to bear the burden alone. The women set to work packing up the remainder of Anna's townhouse while sidestepping the deliriously happy circles of Harry. They managed to both pack the rest of the house and clean and prepare it properly for the landlord's inspection. Before they knew it, a day and night had passed and they were sitting on the deck steps as the movers loaded the moving van.

"Well, kid, I didn't think we'd ever get you home," Jesse said, giving Anna a jab in the ribs with her elbow.

"I know, Sis. I hadn't planned on it, but I think I'm going to love it," she said, patting her hand on her belly.

Jesse shook her head, a smile spreading across her face. She sighed dreamily. "A baby."

"A baby," Anna answered, still mildly disbelieving her situation. She pictured Aidan in her mind, all muscles and gentle smiles. She felt an odd mix of excited and nervous at the prospect of sharing her news with him. One thing was for sure, he was going to be an excellent father. He had all the makings of one. He loved his niece, he came from a big family, and if Anna was looking at it from a brass tacks perspective, he had a good job and would be able to provide for a baby. Now, she just needed to determine if he had the love for her to back up her vision of a family. Otherwise, she was sure she could set up a fair arrangement that would allow him to be present in the baby's life. As it went, she knew a large percentage of marriages ended in divorce, but she wasn't in the habit of lying to herself. There was a tiny spark inside her that hoped they would get a little chance at being together as a family in the traditional sense of the word.

The movers let her know the townhouse contents had

been placed in the moving truck. Jesse and Anna had loaded the special items she hadn't trusted to put in the care of the movers in Anna's Jeep, as well as Harry and an overnight bag for each. Time to head home to Southern Illinois.

## Eleven

Jesse, Anna, and Harry had driven halfway, stayed in a hotel in Kansas City, and continued along their route. Fifteen hours of driving later, they pulled into their mother's driveway. She and Jesse had decided that while it was going to be an exercise in maintaining boundaries, Eadie could use the company and Anna needed a place to stay while she found a job. Jesse's house was already packed to the brim, and she was in the process of deciding where she and Levi, and the five kids between them, would be living.

As Anna turned off the engine, Eadie and Aunt Ruthie flew from the door on their run for the car. Harry went into a barking, circling frenzy and nearly knocked Jesse to the ground in his excitement to greet his favorite older ladies.

"My girls are home!" Eadie cried, thankfulness and joy emanating from her like a force field.

Ruthie leapt for Harry, gathering him into as much as a hug as he'd allow, still frantic with happiness, no doubt anticipating all the extra treats he'd be given.

Anna looked over her mother's shoulder into Jesse's knowing eyes. Anna knew Jesse would never tell her secret, but she also knew the sooner the truth was out, the more content Jesse would feel. It was incredible how much could be communicated with just a glance between siblings.

"Well, I'm beat and ready to get home. Aunt Ruthie, care to run me home in a few minutes?" Jesse asked.

"You got it, kid, let me get my keys," Ruthie answered, Harry hot on her heels as she walked to the house to get her purse.

Jesse walked to the back of Anna's Jeep to unload the few items Anna hadn't wanted to transport on the moving truck. Anna circled around back to help.

"This is going to be a hard secret to keep, Anna," Jesse said in a whisper.

"We've been over this no less than fifty times," Anna said, not wanting to be gruff with Jesse, but so ready to be done with the conversation.

"I know, Sis," she said, carrying the box to the living room, Eadie and Ruthie walking ahead to hold the doors. "I just want you to be all settled and happy. Like me," she said, a wicked smile spreading over her face.

"Understood, Jess. For now, let's focus on you and getting us all to Mexico for your wedding." She smiled back. "I hope my stuff gets here so I can unpack – and then pack again!"

"That's right. Two weeks from now, we'll be in Cozumel, soaking up the sun and sweating our makeup off our faces," she said. "I can't wait."

"Me either. I'm going to have the movers unload the clothes, the rest I'm going to take to the storage unit Mom lined out for me. I'll be over tomorrow to see your dress and have you help me figure out what to wear. Shopping trip in our future?" she said, feeling more and more ready for her bed. The hotel had been fine, but she was bone tired.

"Sounds good, we may not have to go far. There's a new boutique in town that opened and I think I saw a dress in their window downtown that might do just the trick."

Anna hugged Jesse's neck. "Thank you so much for all that you've done," she said, so relieved to not have had to drive all that way alone.

"Wouldn't have missed it, Sis. I'm so glad you're home."

Anna threw her arm around Eadie's shoulder as they watched Aunt Ruthie and Jesse pull out of the driveway, Harry riding in the backseat with his head sticking up just like a person.

"Lord, she's missed that dog," Eadie said, pulling Anna into the house. "Let's get you inside and settled, kid. You look worn out."

*If you only knew*, thought Anna. Her next order of business was to place a call to the moving truck to find out when they were arriving. After that, to call Aidan. A quick look at her watch reminded her that he was underground, so for now a text would have to do. She sent one quickly to let him know she was finally home, and headed to bed for a quick nap. Anna knew her energy was hopefully supposed to pick back up any day now. She was getting closer to her second trimester, and while her stomach was still relatively flat, she could feel the beginning of a bump. She was going to have to be careful not to walk around with her hand on her stomach like she'd been doing for the last month. Thankfully most of her tops and dresses were flowy and not fitted. She'd have to be careful about what she wore or she'd give herself away before she was ready to share the news.

She managed to play it cool through the messages and phone call with Aidan, but by the time he had shut his car door in her driveway, Anna found herself running out the door to meet him. When they met up in the driveway, he wrapped her in his arms and kissed her deeply right there in the open.

Anna felt so relieved to be held against him. She'd spent so much time trying to mentally prepare for the future, to distance herself emotionally in case he bolted – but there was just something about that man.

"God, it's good to see your face," he said, smudges of coal dust lining his eyes. Smiling back up at him, she reached up and wiped at a little black streak on his jaw. "I was in such a hurry to get here that I rushed through my shower at the end of the shift," he explained as he pulled the hem of his shirt up to wipe at the spot she'd just touched, revealing the tight muscles of his stomach. Anna's mouth went dry, in contrast to the rest of her body.

She leaned in, her head pressed against his shoulder, her nose at his neck. She inhaled his scent, and at her exhale he tensed, every inch of his body reading exactly what it was that she wanted. He pulled her back, lowering his gaze as he tilted her face up to his. At that moment, Eadie and Ruthie jostled through the door as Harry bounded across the yard. Anna closed her eyes at the ruckus, begging her flushed cheeks to cool before she turned around to face her family. Aidan recovered more gracefully, smiling over at the ladies who launched into conversation with him. She was going to have to get that man alone as soon as possible.

After the ladies had thoroughly ruined the moment and satisfied their curiosity of how nearly every member of Aidan's family was doing, they bustled back into the house with as much efficiency as they had arrived. As they walked from the porch back to his car, Aidan had his arm wrapped around her shoulders. "Good thing they arrived, I thought you were going to strip me naked right here in the driveway," he said, faking a flinch when she slapped him on the arm.

"I knew I missed you while I was away," Anna said, her hands braced on each of his shoulders, "but I didn't realize how much I missed your abs." He laughed and with a quick look to see if the neighbors were staring, he backed her against his truck and grabbed her butt tightly.

"Well, if we're being truthful, I missed your butt as much as I missed your face," he said, wrinkling his nose at her laugh. "When can I get you to myself?"

Anna looked at her watch, stalling while she argued with herself about whether she should follow her gut. Okay fine, her gut wasn't exactly what was leading her, but she was on the fence about whether she should go for what she wanted, or weigh the concerns of appearing overly eager or overly easy. Anna laughed out loud to herself, much to Aidan's confusion. She realized the concerns over appearing overly easy were a little outdated – she'd jumped into bed with him the first night they ran into each other. Fast forward a week and she was getting pregnant in his house. How in the world was she going to keep this to herself? In the end she shrugged at his stare and asked if she could come over in a few hours. His wide smile spoke volumes, and he hauled her to him in one more kiss before hopping in his truck and promising to shower. Anna grinned her way through dinner with her mother and aunt, and after making certain Harry was settled and happy in his seat between the ladies on the couch, she didn't waste much time getting to his house.

HER KNOCK BARELY sounded on the door before Aidan answered, a wolfish smile on his face. The screen door whipped open and she was inside, divested of her little overnight bag and purse in an instant. A kiss was deposited on her lips as he reached over and peeled off his own shirt. She responded in kind. "Ah," he sighed, "I was hoping you'd play along," he said, fingers tickling the inside of her forearms before they danced down to her jeans. One quick flick of his thumb and finger and they were eased down her hips.

"It's been a long few months," Anna said, returning the favor, dropping his jeans to the floor. They cleared the hallway, a kiss placed right below her ear, his lips against her soft skin.

A groan escaped her lips when he turned her suddenly, his hands moving her hair over one silky shoulder. "I can't even count the ways I've pictured this going down," Aidan said, stifling a laugh at her quick over the shoulder glance at his wording.

"Clever," she said, abruptly shut up by his lips on hers. From behind, he rid her of her pretty bra, leaving her in her panties.

"These, I think I'll keep for a while," Aidan said. His hands traced her shoulders, the strong column of her spine, spanning her waist before wrapping around. As he touched her, hearing her breathing quicken and her back arch in the way it did when she was ready, his game ended and impatience won out. In seconds, Anna found herself on his bed with a very happy Aidan front and center. In true former Marine fashion, he took stock of the situation, figured out his plan of action and didn't relent until the job was well done.

Anna woke to the sun streaming in, curled around a snoring hunk of muscle. A deep feeling of contentment filled her as she lay in his bed. Aidan woke and rolled to face her. He flashed a sleepy-faced grin at her.

"I like finding you here in the morning," he said.

"I kind of like waking up here myself," Anna said, pulling

the covers up over his shoulder like a mother hen. "Aidan?"

"Yeah?" he asked, trying and failing to stifle a yawn.

"This might be a little early, but would you want to come with me to Cozumel for Jesse and Levi's wedding?" she asked, questioning her own sanity. Her initial plan was to distance herself from Aidan a little and here she was waking up in his bed, inviting him on a whirlwind trip to Mexico.

"If I can get off from work, I'd love to go.

"Really?" she asked, her surprise evident. "Do you have a passport?"

He quirked his eyebrows at her. "Yeah, I keep a current one. Once you get used to seeing the world, it's easy to feel hemmed in when you stay put in one place. I don't get too extravagant, but I travel as much as I can," he explained.

A flurry of excitement rushed through her. She had always wanted to travel but Travis had never wanted to use up his vacation days. A little spark lit in her heart, wondering if she'd found someone to really enjoy life with.

# Twelve

L EVI AND JESSE WERE PLANNING their wedding in
Cozumel, Mexico at a fancy resort. It would be a
weekend getaway-destination wedding. Jesse had laughed at
Anna when she asked if was ok if Aidan joined them.

"Sis, we've been expecting that all along," she said,
bugging her eyes out at Anna. "Especially now," she said,
circling her arm around Anna and patting her belly. Anna
nearly jumped out of her skin. She hadn't said word one to
Aidan, or even Eadie for that matter, and was keeping the
subject under wraps.

"Shhh! Jesse!" she whispered, jerking away from her
sister and walking over to the rack of dresses in the boutique
Jesse had insisted they visit.

"Sorry, I forgot," she said, looking around to see if

anyone was close enough to have seen what she did. "I'm just so excited," she whispered.

"I know, Jess. I'm just not ready to tell yet," Anna said. Just then, her hands fluttered over a gorgeous light turquoise dress. Strapless, sweetheart neckline, soft, flowy material with an a-line design. "Jesse, look at this," she said, holding it up for her sister to see.

"Oh, that's gorgeous!" Jesse hooted, taking the dress to the window to see it in natural light. The design was simple, but something about the material screamed for the sea. "This is the one!" Jesse said, heading back to the rack to sift through the sizes. "Here, you've got to try it on," she said, pushing Anna toward the dressing room in the back.

The dress floated romantically at Anna's knees, her skin tone healthy and glowing against the flattering soft color of the material.

"Hey, it even goes with that hair," Jesse said, dodging Anna's elbow. Jesse had never made it a secret that she longed for Anna's strawberry blond hair, though her own dark hair was lovely. Anna twirled around, feeling relieved that the dress had plenty of room in the skirt, camouflaging her precious little secret.

"I think it's perfect, what do you think?" she asked, leaving the final call to the bride.

"It looks amazing on you and the price is perfect," Jesse answered, dropping the dainty little tag. "I love checking things off this list!" she said, pulling out a little notebook and marking off the task at hand. "Not much left to do now," she said.

As Anna changed back into her clothes, Jesse purchased the dress and had it wrapped. The shop owner, Carrie, had been a classmate of Jesse's and was happy to have had just the right dress.

"This will look so pretty on Anna, especially with her complexion," she said. "She's practically glowing," Carrie said, not making eye contact with Jesse. For a second Jesse's heart stopped, wondering if Carrie had seen her pat Anna's belly. She wasn't going to make it worse by responding – Jesse was the world's worst liar. When she did make eye contact, Carrie's bright green eyes were sparkling. She shrugged her shoulders and zipped her fingers across her lips, signing that she wouldn't say a word. Jesse smiled on the outside while her insides turned to jelly. She hoped Anna let the cat out of the bag soon. She didn't want to be the one to leak the news. She was pretty sure Carrie would keep her mouth shut; she was an angel. A very well dressed, very tall, sassy angel.

"We love the dress, thank you. You have so many pretty clothes here! It looks like your shop is doing really well," she said, safely changing the direction of the conversation.

Carrie wasn't one to be put off that easily, though. "Yes, I'm thrilled! We've been open a year now and I hope it only grows from here." She smiled, adjusting jewelry displayed on the shelf. "Jesse, I try not to be nosey," she said, laughing when Jesse did at her emphasis on the word try. "That being said, I just have to say that I'm so glad you and Levi reconnected. I always thought you were a cute couple back in school," she said. "Now tell me all about your dress!" As Anna walked up to the counter, Jesse was happily chattering away about the location of the resort, her dress and flowers.

Anna was excited to see Jesse so happy. Levi had been only too happy to take the kids, his parents, Eadie, and Ruthie somewhere fun for their wedding. Anna had overheard him telling someone at church the past Sunday that it felt like a miracle to have a second chance not only with Jesse, but with marriage in general. Anna knew that Levi had loved his late wife, and that the feelings of his children as well as Jesse's were a primary concern for both of them. While she loved and adored both Jesse and Levi, she was thankful that she didn't have other children to consider when thinking about marriage. She couldn't even dream of how hard it must be to make certain everyone was comfortable and ready for such a big change. If anyone was up for a hard task though, it was Jesse and Levi. Both were such good people, and both had been through their own personal kinds of hell.

Levi's wife had passed a few years earlier and with the help of his parents, raised his precious twins while running his own business. Anna hadn't known his late wife, but Jesse had, and Jesse had liked her immensely. Jesse had survived a long, unhappy marriage at the hands of her narcissistic, antagonistic ex-husband. Drake had been hateful and antagonistic during their marriage and kept it up shortly after their split, but he seemed to be making a little progress. At the very least he had stopped being cantankerous to Jesse on the phone.

As they added the bag to the pile of shopping bags in the back of her Jeep, Jesse caught Anna smiling.

"What are you smiling at? Spill," she said, playfully glaring her eyes at Anna.

"Just thinking about last night," she said, looking anywhere but at Jesse.

"Hot sex, huh? Lord, does it make you wonder how we ever lived without it?" she said, Anna not being able to do anything but agree.

"Yes! I'm almost getting obsessed. I'm trying to be biased about him, examine things from all angles," at this Jesse laughed rather rudely, and Anna gave her the stink eye and kept talking, "but man, I just love it when my bones melt."

"Ah, yes. That's good stuff," Jesse agreed. "Levi and I have been struggling to find alone time. I hope that gets a little easier once we're finally under one roof."

"What did you decide to do about that?" Anna asked, driving toward Jesse's house.

"Well, as much as I hate to move again, neither of our homes are big enough. We've found one a little ways out on Poet's Pass, but it -"

Anna interrupted, "Wait! Poet's Pass Road? Where we all used to go parking?"

"Yes!" Jesse laughed. "You used to go out there, too?"

"All the time!" Anna said, not even bothering to blush. "I didn't see a whole lot of action back then, but my God I nearly kissed my lips off back on that road!"

Jesse threw her hand over her mouth, pretending to be scandalized. As far as she knew, Anna had been Miss-Goody-Two-Shoes in high school.

"One time I pulled back behind the old silos, do you know the ones?" she asked, laughing before she could stop herself at the memory. "I was sort of dating Max back then, and we pulled back behind the silos, flicked off the headlights and cranked up some Prince." She laughed.

"Prince?" Jesse asked, laughing hard now.

"Yeah, I bought his Greatest Hits CD twice in high school."

"Why twice?" Jesse asked, wrinkling her brow.

"Well, I bought it before church camp, pitched it after I was there, then bought it again once the guilt subsided," Anna explained.

At this point, Jesse was cackling. "Go on, back to the silos..."

"Yeah, we had just started kissing, and just then a cop pulled behind us and turned on his lights," she said, wincing even then.

"Oh my God. What happened?"

"Well, I had just enough time to get my shirt over my head –"

"Wait, I thought you said you had just started kissing?" Jesse asked, eyes wide.

"Hey, Max was efficient if he was anything," Anna said, waggling her eyebrows. "At any rate, I couldn't even bring myself to make eye contact with the officer, I was so humiliated. I turned off the CD, rolled down the window and tried not to die. He said, "You can't do that here, get on home," and I answered, "Yes, sir." We drove home and Max just had to deal with blue balls. He survived, but he dumped me on the following Monday.

Jesse was reeling and saw Levi come out onto the porch. He saw them laughing and smiled, leaning back against the railing, arms crossed in front of him. Anna had to give it to Jesse, Levi was still hot. Her sister had done well for the second round.

"Okay, back to your house! Give me the scoop, please."

"It's a huge old farmhouse, and needs quite a bit of work. Gutted, really," she said wincing.

"He looks pretty capable," Anna said, nodding her head at Levi.

"Yeah, he'll do nicely. Even better, he's tight with a plumber and an electrician, so between those guys and their friends, they'll probably be able to handle it. It's a big mama with six bedrooms and sits on a few acres. Nothing too outlandish, but it'll at least fit all of us comfortably."

"You nearly need a hotel with all those kids," Anna teased, already dreaming of Thanksgiving and Christmas dinners at Jesse and Levi's new home. Jesse was a pretty good cook, and she loved nothing more than hosting big dinners. She did chaos well.

Jesse laughed. "You're right, we nearly do. Who knows, you might catch up with us in a few years!" She reached over and gave Anna's stomach a little pat and said to her belly, "Aunt Jesse loves you, Little Britches."

Anna fought the lump in her throat and smiled at her sister. Today was just what she had needed. With a glance up at the porch Anna said, "Looks like he's ready for you to come in, I think."

"Yeah, I think he misses me," Jesse said, love shining in her eyes. "I'll tell you more about the house later. I'd better get going."  As she climbed out of the Jeep, Anna circled around back to pull out Jesse's bags. Before she even lifted them out, Levi was there to help.

"Hey, kid, glad you're home," he said, pulling Anna into a hug with his free arm.

"Me too!" she said. "What a whirlwind, huh?" she shrugged.

"Yeah, life's never predictable, but some of the best things happen when you least expect it," he said, nodding his head at Jesse. "So what's the story with Aidan? Do I need to give him the talk?" he asked, his face going serious.

In a panic, Anna looked at Jesse who shook her head "no" in reply.

"What talk, Levi?" she asked, trying to keep her face from being weird.

"Well, you like him, right?" he asked, looking at her like she was dense.

"Yeah."

"Well, he's a former Marine so I'm pretty sure he could take me, maybe even kill me, but I can at least offer to kick his butt if he breaks your heart, right?"

Unable to stop herself, she laughed. "Yes. You can definitely give him the talk," she said. "Better do it fast though, you'll want to scare him before he comes with us to

Mexico," Anna said.

"That's my girl, she finally asked him, huh?" he said, spinning back to look at Jesse.

"Finally!" she answered.

Anna threw her hands in the air in mock annoyance and got back in the car. Backing out she hollered out the window, "I'm heading to Sorcha's now, talk to you later, bye," she said to the pair of them, waving her off.

BEFORE ANNA CUT the engine, Sorcha was running to her Jeep with Clara smiling on her hip.

"Is it really happening?" she said, grinning as she threw her arm around her best friend. "Do I finally have you back for good?" she asked, squeezing Anna for all she was worth. Clara wrapped her arms around Anna's neck and transferred to her arms like a little monkey.

"It's true!  Officially unemployed, but still happy to be here," she said, walking up the steps and into Sorcha's home.

"Well, something will turn up, I'm sure of it," she said, walking into the kitchen to get Anna some tea.

"I've applied to a few schools in the area, but I've got my heart set on our grade school," she said, cupping little Clara's face in her hands. "This little stinker will be there before I know it; wouldn't it be something if I could be her teacher?" Anna said, smiling as Clara scampered off her lap and off to her bedroom to start dragging in her favorite toys.

"I know you're obviously hoping for a teaching position,"

Sorcha said, settling onto the couch, "but I think they're looking for a secretary out at the mines if you want something in the interim."

Anna shrugged her shoulders. "I may as well look into it. There sure don't seem to be many prospects right now with the schools. Thanks."

"Sure, I'll send you the number to the office," Sorcha said, fiddling with her phone. The resulting 'ding' on Anna's phone gave her a little feeling of excitement.

"I'll be glad to get a paycheck! I love my mama, but I'm thinking Harry and I would be happier in our own place for the long haul," she said, instantly thinking maybe she was wrong. She might appreciate a second set of hands (and third set if she counted Aunt Ruthie) once the baby came. Anna had to practically sit on her hands not to let them drift to her belly. Sorcha wouldn't miss a trick; she had to be careful.

"Maybe Aidan will swoop in and marry you. Then we'll officially be family," Sorcha said, grinning wildly.

"Slow down, slow down…" Anna said, but she couldn't help but smile back at Sorcha. "I am excited to see him though," she said, looking at her watch. "He gets off in a few hours and I'd like to cook him supper tonight."

"Nice, whatcha cooking?" Sorcha asked, arranging all the baby dolls that Clara was piling on top of her.

"Meatloaf, mashed potatoes, green beans, maybe rolls," Anna answered, her stomach and growing appetite fully excited about the meal.

"Oh yeah, baby. Going in for the kill," Sorcha said, laughing at her friend.

"Hush!" she said laughing. "I need to get to the store. I'll come back by in a few days. Maybe we can get out for a little while and go walk at the track or something, or take hot stuff here to the p-a-r-k."

"Sounds good! We're always up for an adventure," Sorcha answered, getting up to walk her friend to the door. "Good luck with the grand seduction tonight," she said, wiggling her eyebrows at Anna.

"See ya later, Sorch. Love you. Bye, Clara," Anna said, squatting down to give the pretty little girl a hug.

# Thirteen

AIDAN'S MOUTH WAS WATERING before he even finished unlocking his door. Wafting out into the driveway were the smells of home cooking. Anna was moving around his kitchen in an apron no-less, cooking up a storm. An Alabama Shakes song blared in the background and she jumped when Harry bounded through the kitchen to greet him.

She yelled before she could stop herself, clamping a hand over her mouth.

Laughing, Aidan appeased Harry with a rub of his ears and then pulled Anna into a big hug. "I kind of like the sight of this, you all barefoot in my kitchen," he said, smiling down and giving her lips a kiss.

"It's pretty nice to be cooking in your kitchen," she said, pulling him down for one more kiss.

Putting his bucket in the sink and his bundled clothes in the mudroom, he poked around the pots on the stove, giving the air an appreciative sniff. "What can I do to help?" he asked, pulling a beer from the fridge. "Want one?"

"No," she answered, suddenly anxious she'd have to explain why she didn't want a beer. "I've got dinner covered, but if you're really wanting to help, would you run Harry out to take care of business before dinner?" she asked, wrinkling her nose. She'd planned on taking care of that herself, but she didn't want to leave supper unattended.

"Sure," he said, grabbing the leash from where she'd hung it over his doorknob. "How did we get this big guy tonight? Ruthie didn't fight you for him?" he asked, trying to clip the leash on the ecstatic dog.

"She and mom have gone out for the evening. They're having dinner up town and then are actually going to a movie," she said, eyes wide in happiness. "So Big Handsome here needed a little company."

"Fine by me. Come on, Harry," he said, slipping on his shoes and heading out the door. The instant it closed, Anna leaned against the sink, her hand resting on her belly.

"What are we going to do, Little Bean?" she asked, closing her eyes against the rising hope in her heart and the ever present anxiety. She'd have to figure out soon how to tell Aidan she was pregnant. She wasn't ready to do it yet, maybe after Jesse's wedding. She didn't want to shift any attention to herself while she was taking time to see Aidan from different angles.

Her hands traveled up to her chest, which was getting noticeably bigger. She'd been sticking to sports bras over the past few days in hopes that nobody would notice the changes. Thankfully she hadn't struggled hardly at all with morning sickness. Despite her rather thin frame, Anna was a good eater and had no issue keeping carbs on her stomach. She kept a stash of crackers in her purse anytime she started feeling puny, and so far it had seemed to do the trick.

The rolls and meatloaf were ready to come out of the oven and she finished setting the food out on the table as Aidan walked in with Harry. As he washed up, she put the remainder of the dishes in the sink to soak so they could sit down and enjoy dinner.

Aidan made a huge deal over how delicious the food looked, smelled, and tasted, and Anna wondered how someone hadn't snagged him. She was starting to go down the rabbit hole of what might be wrong with him when he interrupted her train of thought.

"Good news," he said, a crooked smile showing on his handsome face.

"What's up?"

"I'm cleared for time off; I can go to Cozumel. Think it'll be hard for me to get a ticket this late?" he asked, making a note to check after dinner.

"Now I've got good news," she said, her eyes wide. His eyebrows raised as he filled his mouth with another delicious bite of green beans. "Levi and Jesse already picked up your ticket; they thought you'd be going all along," she said, smiling at him.

"No way! That's awesome! Find out how much for me and I'll pay them back," he said, his hand on hers.

"I already double checked, and it's on them. Part of the 'destination celebration' they said. They've been working out all the details. We just have to have our passports and show up," Anna answered.

"Man, that's cool. I haven't been to Mexico in years," Aidan said, gathering their plates to rinse and load in the dishwasher. Anna followed behind, carrying dishes to the counter.

"You've been? When did you go?"

"When I was stationed in San Diego. We got to go a few times. Crazy stuff," he said, leaving it at that. Anna wasn't sure she wanted to hear details; a surge of jealously had sprung up in an instant. She wanted to beat back that feeling, but he had been young, single, super sexy. Did he go with guy friends? A girlfriend? Butterflies filled her stomach and she felt embarrassed of her reaction.

"I've never been, but can't wait to see it. I'd like to go snorkeling if we end up having some free time over the weekend."

"I would love to take you! Snorkeling is amazing," Aidan said, taking the last dish from her, standing behind her as she washed her hands in the sink. "It's kind of sexy," he said, a soft laugh escaping as she looked unconvinced at his description. "No, no, hear me out," he said, leading her to the couch.

"It's hot outside, and you're not wearing much," Aidan said, pulling Anna down, straddling his legs.

"The water is so warm that it almost feels like bath water, but it's salty." He punctuated this with a touch of his tongue to her throat. He held her close and inhaled gently, his breath by her ear giving her goosebumps. "Your hair gets all messed up," he said, his lips brushing against hers, her teasing smile urging him on.

His hands lightly traced the skin around her neck, tickling and warm as his tongue tasted her softly. "You feel anxious because it's a new sensation, maybe even a little scared," he continued, his fingers tracing her shoulders, the other roaming around her body. She reacted as much to his description as she did to his touch. "You go deep into the water, and suddenly you focus less on the jolt of the waves and the fear, and instead you feel and see things you never imagined," he said, her mouth capturing his in a kiss.

Her hands moved over his shoulders as he pinned her body against his. Despite the layers of clothes between them, she could feel his desire, pressing as hard as a rock against her. Frantic with need, Anna raised herself up and removed the barriers between them. Aidan started to hesitate, a brief second in which Anna assumed he was going to reach for a condom, but as she lowered her body onto his, ready and warm for him, he moaned against her and all thought was lost.

The moon shone in through the curtains, finding them intertwined in his bed, his chin resting on her shoulder and his arms and legs tangled together with hers. Anna slept deeply, at ease against Aidan. Sometime during the night she awoke, thinking she had heard a loud sound. The room was still, but her dog Harry had nosed his way into the room and was sitting at the door. She turned to Aidan's side of the bed and saw him sitting on the edge, still as a statue.

"Hey, are you okay?" she asked, placing her hand on his back. Aidan jerked as Anna realized his back was covered in sweat.

He was quiet for a minute and she waited, silent and still. He took a deep breath and finally answered, "Yeah, I'm fine. I'm going to grab some water. Be right back."

Anna gave Harry a pat and told him to lie down beside the bed. Aidan came back and curled against her side. "He doing alright over there?" he asked as he leaned up on his elbow to check out how the large dog had made himself at home on a pillow that had fallen off the bed.

"He's fine," Anna answered. "Happy as can be. How about you? Bad dream?"

"Yes," he said, hesitating. "I get them sometimes, but not so much anymore."

His words trailed off like he wasn't sure if there was more to say about the dreams. Not usually one to let a point drop, Anna took a quick look at the clock. Aidan had to be up again at five o'clock in order to be at the mines at six. Anna snuggled against him, silently praying that God would grant him rest and safety. She let a hand press against her stomach as she prayed for their little one and drifted off to sleep.

ANNA WOKE UP to a quiet house and a note next to the coffee maker. The smell of coffee was heavenly, and she remembered as she instinctively reached for a mug in the cabinet that her coffee drinking days were on hold.

"You're going to get me busted before I'm ready to talk about you," she said to her belly. Harry happily walked over to her, his nose cold against her hand. Anna picked up the note and couldn't help but laugh to herself that while he was one of the best men she had ever encountered, Aidan had, by far, the worst penmanship of anyone she'd ever seen. Spelling, A+, penmanship, not so much.

In a mix of cursive and print, he wished her a good morning, let her know that he had walked Harry and hoped he could see her again that night. His message warmed her heart immensely, but she needed to log some time with her mother. She'd figure that out later, she said to herself, walking back in the bedroom to make the bed and tidy up a little before leaving. Plus, she thought, she needed to get some time to talk with Sorcha to find out what she knew about Aidan's nightmares. She felt a sense of unease in her stomach that was attributed to more than the sweet baby growing there.

# Fourteen

STEALING A PAGE FROM AIDAN'S book, Anna showed up at Sorcha's with toasted bagels, cream cheese, and strawberries. Clara squealed approval as Sorcha raised her hands in the air in mock praise. "Thank you, Jesus," she sang. "Breakfast fairies two days in a row." She got down to business making plates for the three of them while pouring orange juice into their cups.

"What's up?" she asked, an auburn brow arched over her cup.

Anna looked to see that Clara was engrossed in smashing a bite of bagel into her baby doll's mouth and unlikely to repeat anything she was about to say.

"I stayed over last night," she said quickly, "and Aidan woke up with a nightmare," she said, trying not to be obvious about her unspoken question.

Sorcha nodded. "Yeah, I think he still has those from time to time," she said. She shrugged her shoulders a little. "It's bound to be better than it was when he first got back, Anna. He saw some pretty awful things when he was deployed." I think he went months without sleeping a full night back then.

Anna's heart sank. She couldn't bear the thought of him having witnessed horrors she couldn't help with. She wanted to ask a million questions but didn't want to press Sorcha to share more than she wanted. They might've always been best friends, but Sorcha had made it clear from the start that she wasn't going to play middle man to their relationship, whatever it turned out to be. Instead, she sipped her juice and picked at her breakfast.

"I don't really know what to share about it," Sorcha said, "and I can't honestly say that I even understand where's he's at completely. He didn't share much when he got home after separating from the Marines, but I do know that he was in a therapy program for a few years."

Anna's eyes betrayed her by filling up with tears. Sorcha put her hand on her arm. "Hey, it's going to be okay. He made it home safe and sound. Aidan was able to get the help he needed when he needed it, and from what little I understand about PTSD, that is a crucial step to healing."

Anna could do no more than nod. Sorcha continued, "So many don't get help when they come home because they fear looking weak or being misjudged as unreliable. He threw that out the window and was able to learn to cope with his experiences. It's a good thing, Anna," she said, simultaneously comforting her friend and wrangling Clara, who at that point had smeared strawberries in her hair.

"I'm glad you shared," she said. "Benji's death hasn't been easy on him. I love hearing him tell stories about those guys. He's been talking about funny stories quite a bit over the last few weeks."

It was Sorcha's turn to nod. "Those guys were like brothers. They traveled the world together, had adventures together when they were able. And they saw the ugliest part of humanity together. I can't imagine the bond they all have that we'll never even understand."

"I'm glad Aidan was able to take that step. What I hate is knowing he saw awful things to begin with. Sorcha, I love him," she said, eyes wide. She hadn't planned to confess it, but she'd never been much for hiding her big feelings, especially not from Sorcha.

Sorcha pulled her friend into a hug. "I'm glad to hear that," she said. "I don't think he's too far behind." Sorcha's eyes glittered as she ushered Clara toward the bathroom, pulling her jammies off as they went. "And you, little miss, are going into the tub," she said, while Clara pranced naked through the hallway.

Anna picked up the few dishes they had dirtied and threw in a load of laundry while she waited for bath time to be over. She was in awe that Sorcha managed to keep her place so neat with that little hurricane of a child bouncing from room to room all day. She realized she'd better figure it out, and hoped she'd have the even-keeled approach to parenting that Sorcha had.  Anna knew nothing about PTSD, but apparently she needed to do a little research. She was just about to start folding towels when Clara streaked out of the bathroom, ready to be dried off.

Sorcha plopped down on the couch, snapping up a warm towel out of Anna's laundry basket. "Hey, thanks for grabbing those. I'm totally behind on laundry right now." As she dried Clara, she tapped her knee against Anna's.

"Aidan's been doing really well for a long time. He gets a little moody sometimes, and when he pulls away we've all learned to give him his space. I think he stills talks to a therapist once every few months at the VA, just to stay on track and vent if needed. He and Evan talk sometimes, but they don't really share that with me much. I can't help but think there are some things you just have to experience to understand, and thanks be to God, I haven't seen what they've seen."

"Sorcha, thank you so much for letting me know. I don't know a thing about this, but I'm going to learn. I want to be ready or at least know what to say or do – if I can," Anna said, hands busily folding.

"That's good to make yourself aware, but remember, there's not much more you need to do than just love him, if you love him," she answered.

"I think that's going to be the easy part," said Anna, grinning over at Sorcha.

"On a lighter note, he's going to be able to come to

Cozumel for Jesse's wedding!" Anna shared, smiling ear to ear. I've got my stuff all organized and really it's such a short trip, there's not time for much."

Sorcha narrowed her eyes. "I'm so envious!  Sunshine, sand, margaritas," she mused dramatically. "Maybe even the possibility of a nap!  I kind of hate you, but I'm glad you get to go."

At the mention of Mexico, Anna decided she'd better skip out on the visit. She didn't want to chance Sorcha ferreting out any information before she had a chance to talk with Aidan. She knew she'd have to spill the beans soon. Maybe on their trip if things went well. Her stomach churned at the idea.

Anna pulled Sorcha into a hug and planted a smooch on top of Clara's little head. "I'm going to go hang out with Mom and spend a little time this afternoon refreshing my resumé and references. I nabbed an interview tomorrow about the mine secretary position."

"Yahoo! That job might be a great temporary gig, or maybe you'll hate it. Who knows?" she said, laughing.

Anna walked to her Jeep with a smile on her face, ready to spend some time with her mama. She was so close to being able to take a deep breath and get past having a secret. She was nearly exhausted from turning down coffee and the foods she suddenly couldn't eat. *Who knew that pregnancy could be so restrictive on a diet?* she thought to herself. She was only a trimester in and she was already craving sushi. Thankfully the obstetrician she had visited right when she arrived home had given her the rundown on what she could and couldn't do.

Anna had been with her OBGYN in Denver for years and had forgotten how utterly awkward it was to meet a new doctor. To make it worse she couldn't exactly work it into conversation with Jesse or Sorcha about who they went to for their checkups. As involved as they were in each other's business, they both knew she had her yearly appointment around Christmas and it would be a little suspicious if she were anxious about finding a new doc locally as soon as she relocated.

Right before she moved Anna had called ahead to the hospital where she knew most people delivered their babies in her area. It happened to be about an hour away in the most decent sized city in the area. It was large and a little impersonal, but it had a nice labor and delivery unit and even a NICU, she had learned on the tour. Anna was fine with the anonymity, and didn't mind the drive time. She remembered hearing Eadie say that first babies usually came in their own sweet time, so she wasn't overly concerned with the distance.

Anna had chosen a female OB and had instantly liked Dr. Han. She was tall and willowy with red-brown hair. She couldn't help it, she always appreciated fellow gingers. Dr. Han was patient and actually listened when Anna talked. What she liked best though, was that when she asked if the father was involved, she didn't outwardly judge Anna when she said he would be involved, but Anna wasn't ready. She'd never forget what Dr. Han had said.

"Anna," she said, putting down her tablet where she had been taking notes. "It's good for pregnancies to be low-stress, but just hear me out. From what little you've shared, do I understand the scenario? It's a healthy, compassionate relationship, correct?" she asked, red-brown eyebrows raised, expression serious.

"Yes," Anna answered. "He's a wonderful man. I know he'd be a wonderful father, too. Or will be, I mean. I just need a little more time to be sure he'll be in the relationship for me and not just our baby."

Dr. Han nodded. "Okay. Follow your gut, but keep in mind two things for me please. First, it might be nice to have someone to share in this with you, even as a good, supportive friend. Second, if he really is a good, supportive, and wonderful man, I believe that's the description you used, right?"

Again, Anna nodded, a lump in her throat keeping her from speaking.

"Don't forget he might be bitter if you wait too long. He might feel cheated out of this experience, especially if it's going somewhere," she finished.

Anna had said that she would keep it in mind. As she dressed after the exam, she felt like her heart had been bared, and it had been hurting in a way she hadn't been willing to truly face. She realized that she could take Dr. Han's advice in two ways. First, she could be highly offended that someone who hadn't even met Aidan would offer up their two cents on whether she should tell him, and when. Second, she could take the advice for what it was, an opinion. She was going to do what she thought best anyway, but had it really wounded her to hear out the doctor's opinion? Of course not.

That appointment had been two weeks ago, and while Anna's anxiousness about her pregnancy had diminished, baby seemed to be doing fine, and she was ready to include Aidan in the pregnancy. Now to find the right time to tell him.

# Fifteen

ANNA ROLLED INTO THE MINE parking lot deciding not to let herself cringe over the gravel dust coating her freshly washed Jeep. Dressed in a cream colored suit, emerald silk top and heels, she worried that she had overdone it a little. She hadn't interviewed for a job in a long, long time, and her nerves were shot. She stood outside the door and took a deep breath, trying to steady herself. Plastering a smile on her face, she stepped into the office and crashed smack dab into a very dirty, very familiar man. Evan grabbed Anna in an attempt to steady her, leaving a giant black streak of coal dust on her cream colored sleeve.

"Oh crap," he exclaimed, looking wildly around at the secretary's empty desk and grabbing a box of tissues. He waved it in front of Anna who looked at him like he was absurd. Evan's panicked reaction to her expression caught her by surprise and she lost it. Anna laughed hard and it was like all the tension she'd been holding in burst right out. She plucked a few tissues out of the box he was still holding and dabbed at her eyes.

"Good Lord, Evan, way to make an entrance, huh?" she said, putting her purse and portfolio down in the lobby area chair.

He was muttering his apologies for getting her dirty and she shook her head at him.

"Seriously, I don't know what I was thinking wearing a cream suit to coal mine." She shrugged, noticing for the first time that there was someone behind Evan. Mr. Darby, the HR Manager stepped up and offered a hand.

"Mine's clean," he said, with an elbow to Evan. "I leave the hard work to the young pups. I stick to pushing paper," he said with a self-amused laugh.

Evan mouthed a silent "Sorry" and slid out the door. Anna smiled at him. What else could she do?

The interview went well, and Anna was relieved that the manager wasn't concerned with her previous experience having been within the walls of a Kindergarten classroom.

"Hell, that'll make you fit right in here." Mr. Darby laughed. "Our biggest issue is keeping people on task and listening to them tattle on each other in this office."

Anna understood that her duties would be pretty varied. The office was small and people wore multiple hats trying to pitch in and keep the mine running smoothly. If she were to be offered the position, she would be responsible for keeping time sheets organized and submitted on time, running payroll reports, collecting requests for time off, answering phones, sorting mail, receiving visitors and scheduling appointments. It sounded like a lot, but when she factored in the tasks she used to accomplish daily with 20+ tiny people, she figured she could pretty much do anything.

"Kid," Mr. Darby said, "I could drag this out or just be quick about it. We've had six people apply for this position already, but you're the most qualified."

Anna beamed, thinking of the relief it would be to land this job and stop worrying about the impact her move was having on her savings account.

"I know you're good people; I knew your father," he said, giving her a solemn nod. "My condolences for your loss."

Somehow Anna was able to keep the tears that welled up in place. She was quickly learning that the grief was impossible to predict. Coupled with pregnancy, she felt like she was always one breath away from a sob fest.

"I'd like to go ahead and offer you this position, but I have one concern," Mr. Darby said, pausing heavily. "I think you'd do a fine job at this and we'd be happy to have you, but you have to make me a promise."

"What's that?" she asked, brows furrowed.

"No more white outfits. This is a coal mine, and it's dirty," he said, barely holding in his mirth.

Anna threw her hands up in the air. "Deal," she said.

"Okay, down to brass tacks. Let's talk about salary, benefits and a start date," he said, shifting into HR manager mode, shuffling papers like a professional.

In the end, Anna accepted the position, surprised that the pay was significantly more than she had expected. It wasn't quite what she had made as a teacher in Denver, but it would help her sock away some savings and be more than enough to get by on for now. She was pleased with benefits and more than ever, was thankful to have them knowing the Little Bean was on his or her way. It had been agreed that she could start in a little over a week, which would allow for a few days of training with the person vacating the position.

When the air in Cozumel hit Anna's face, she felt like she had been slapped with a hot, wet washcloth. The Colorado girl in her was still adjusting to humidity in Southern Illinois, so the situation in Cozumel was nearly an affront to her senses. The saving grace was the breeze wafting across the island. As she looked around at her family descending the steps of the plane, she realized she didn't care if she was on a trip to the surface of the sun; she was happy. Aidan took her hand at the bottom of the stairs and hauled her bag as well as his on his strong shoulders. Jesse, Levi and their five kids between them scattered out like ducks. Levi's sister, husband, and their son added to the number; his parents, Stanley and Myrtle, walked with Eadie and Ruthie and brought up the rear. Anna couldn't help but feel so thankful for the size of their family. Walt's absence threatened to choke her at times, and she caught herself looking around for him frequently. If someone told her even one more time that she'd be "adjusting to her new normal" in regards to grieving and missing her father, she wasn't sure she could be held responsible for her actions. Of course people instinctively know these things. They know life will go on, and that it's a blessing that it does. What people need, Anna thought, is time to grieve in their own way without being scrutinized. She made a quick swipe of her eyes with her hands and Aidan jerked his head her way. Without a word he pulled her close, his arm around her shoulder. God, she loved this man. She only prayed he didn't hate her when he learned she'd been keeping the baby a secret for nearly three months.

Jesse, in her typical state of project manager proficiency, had instructed each of them on what papers to have ready so that getting through security and customs would be as quick and efficient as possible. As they walked through the glass doors of the airport, Jesse stood smiling at the door as she held it open for her family. Anna beamed seeing the absolute joy in her sister's face. She had earned it, by God. In and out of the airport within an hour, a feat for such a sizable group, Anna sat beside Jesse on the bus that would take their crew to their resort. She couldn't help but exchange a grin with her sister as both stared a few seats up at Levi and Aidan.

Levi had started up a "brotherly conversation" with Aidan a few days before they were set to travel to Mexico. He had imparted that in no uncertain terms, no matter what this thing between them was and despite the fact that Aidan could kick his butt, Levi wouldn't stand for it if Aidan broke Anna's heart. The posturing seemed a bit ridiculous, but

Anna appreciated it nonetheless. It was a nice feeling to have a protector in the family, even it if was a bit redundant.

Aidan had of course not mentioned the conversation; however, Levi had told Jesse all about it when they were alone right before they left for the trip.

"Jesus, Jesse, have you ever really looked at the size of his arms?" he had said, eyes wide. "I mean, I'm sizable, my job requires a lot of lifting so I stay in good shape, but man."

Not knowing exactly what was safe to say, and not really wanting to admit that she had in fact noticed the size of Aidan's arms, she took the safer route. "I don't know, baby, you guys look pretty much the same to me," she said, taking any chance she could get to put her hands on his own arms. She made an effort to stroke his ego as much as she could; he was a pretty incredible specimen himself.

"Well, he could've bitten my head off, but he took it like a man," Levi said, smiling down at Jesse and pulling her into his arms. "I think he's a really good guy, Jess. I think they'll be happy," he said, placing a quick kiss on her lips.

"I think so, too," she admitted. Keeping the secret about Anna and Aidan's baby was proving sheer torture for Jesse. There was nothing like a baby as far as Jesse was concerned. She was a pro. She had raised three of them, for Pete's sake. Jesse couldn't wait to get her hands on Anna and Aidan's. She was going to be such a good aunt. There wasn't much that could throw her, which would make her the cool aunt. Jesse couldn't help but curl her lip in a sneer. She had forgotten to take into account the Sorcha Factor. Sorcha was going to absolutely be the cool aunt. Jesse would have to come up with something else. At any rate, she knew she was going to love the socks right off that baby, and she for one would be happy when everything was out in the open. More than anything, she knew their mother would love to have something joyful to celebrate.

Jesse didn't like keeping anything from Levi. She had spent an entire marriage having to keep her thoughts and feelings hidden behind a brick wall. Having something that brought her joy that she couldn't share with her favorite person was tough. She could only say her prayers that Anna would let Aidan know what was going on already. What Jesse did like was to be able to look over at Anna and see her smiling up into the face of what seemed to be a gentle giant. Aidan dwarfed her in size, but seemed to draw her up. Anna looked stronger at his side; at least compared to when she was with Travis. *Stop it, not again!* she said to herself, trying to break the habit of comparing men. It had taken her every bit of the last six months to stop comparing Levi with her ex-husband in regards to their approach toward relationships and life in general. There was nothing to be gained from it except, she guessed, to feel better about her own growth as a person and tolerance for what type of people she was willing to allow into her life.

As for Anna, Jesse assumed she'd have to break the news in her own darned time, but she was ready for the cat to be out of the bag already. She was getting married to one of her best friends. Her mother seemed to be easing her way out of the fog of depression that goes hand in hand with grieving. Her children and Levi's children were doing well so far with the adjustment of merging families.   Anna's uncertainty hovered a bit like a lone puzzle piece not in place. Being the big sister was hard sometimes. She wanted to rush in and fix everything, or at least sway it one way or another. Stepping back and watching was new to Jesse, and she wasn't a fan. The fact that the wedding and combination of two families occupied most of her capacity was probably a very good thing.

EVERYONE SURVIVED THE bus ride to the resort, and they decided to get settled into their suites before reconvening for dinner or ordering room service. Eadie, Ruthie, and Stan and Myrtle had each voiced no less than 80 times over the past eight hours of travelling that they couldn't wait to put their feet up. Jesse was anxious to stow away their belongings and set up an appointment with their wedding planner to triple check that all the I's were dotted and T's crossed for their ceremony the next morning. Levi was ready to do anything in order to get Jesse to relax, including shepherding the five children in order for her to take care of the minutia of the event. Anna and Aidan's top priority was booking a snorkeling excursion for early the next morning.

Anna took the cart of luggage to their suite while Aidan made arrangements with the person in charge of arranging the snorkeling tours. She had already gotten the all-clear from Jesse to be absent for a few hours in the morning. Their ceremony wasn't until early afternoon, so there was plenty of time to have their little adventure.

"Are you sure you don't mind if we go?" Anna had asked Jesse once they had arrived at the resort.

"Don't be silly, you know me. I've got this thing planned down to the gnat's ass. We're going to have a big breakfast with the group and basically watch the clock. Everything's all set. The only thing the hotel has left to do in the morning is place the flowers at the veranda where we'll be," Jesse said.

At that, Anna put her hand on Jesse's arm. "You're getting married tomorrow," she said with a huge, cheesy grin.

"I know. Man, can you imagine what life might've been like had we just done this right the first time?" Jesse answered, a sort of wild look in her eyes.

Anna shook her head. "Jess, you can't go there," she said, hoping Jesse wasn't about to crack.

"I know, but sometimes it's overwhelming to think of what we've all lived through," she said, tears welling up in her eyes.

Without even asking, Anna knew Jesse was thinking not of her own sacrifice and hardship that she endured during her marriage to Drake, or even that of her sons. Her heart was filled with grief for Levi and his kids, Hannah and James, and for their loss of Emma.

"You've all been through so much," she said, taking Jesse's face in her hands. "We *all* have," she said, her voice nearly choking on the words. "That's what makes this moment so much sweeter. You've got a gift and you're grabbing it with both hands. That's the way it should be," Anna said, pulling Jesse into a hug.

"Same goes for you, kiddo," she answered. "Grab this chance with both hands, Anna."

Anna nodded, intent on doing just that. She was in love. She was growing a baby. She was in a virtual paradise with nearly all the people in her life that she loved, except for Sorcha. It was a good, good feeling.

ANNA HAD JUST enough time to hang their dress clothes and order room service by the time Aidan arrived in the hotel room. He smiled like a madman, which instantly put her on guard. Something was hidden behind his back and he wouldn't let her see until she sat quietly on the bed.

"So," he said, "the snorkeling is arranged for early tomorrow morning," he said.

"How early?" she asked, wincing as she looked at the late hour on the clock. Just then, there was a knock at the door. A muted "room service" was called out, and Aidan gave her a quick nod before obtusely working to keep whatever it was that he had hidden as he made his way to the door. Minutes later, their food was arranged on the small table in their suite and Anna was about to jump out of her skin with curiosity.

"As I was saying, the trip is early. We have to be downstairs at 8 AM," he said, wrinkling his nose.

"Ugh, that's brutal, but it will give us plenty of time," she said. "What are you hiding? You're killing me here."

Aidan laughed as he tossed a little bag to her on the bed. Anna opened it to find the tiniest dark blue triangle top bikini that she had ever seen. She closed her eyes for a second as she tried to decide if she was flattered or heartily annoyed. His answering guffaw tipped her over the edge to flattered – and amused.

She picked the tiny thing up with a finger and said, "I think it'll be a little snug for you, don't you think?"

"Yeah, baby, but my ass will look fantastic," he said, jumping on her on the bed. "It's not for me, goose. It's for you. I saw it and it took me right back to that little bitty pair of dark blue panties you had on that night in that treehouse we – ahem – explored – back in the day," he said as he buried his nose into her neck, making her squirm and laugh at the feel of his hot breath.

"You remember the color of underwear I had on?" she asked, quirking her head to look at his green-brown eyes.

"Oh yeah, those undies and what was underneath them got me through many lonely nights in the Marines," he said, waggling his eyebrows at her.

"You're hopeless," she said. "But that's kind of hot," she said, pushing him off of her. "Now, let's dig in and see if I can still squeeze into this thing in the morning." She hadn't planned on wearing anything so revealing around him, and had prayed for a lack of light anytime they were getting naked. Anna wasn't showing much in this early stage of pregnancy, but there was a beginning of a definite baby bump. Jesse had even teased her asking if she was really pregnant or had just eaten a few burritos. The clock was ticking though. She planned to tell him about the baby after Jesse and Levi's wedding.

Aidan wasn't one to give up so easily. He coaxed her back into the moment when he took her into his arms. His teasing kiss melted away her anxiety and most of her coherent thoughts as his hands traced up her arms and shoulders, caressing her neck as his fingers worked at the knot securing her halter sundress.

Anna heard a moan escape her lips as Aidan traced a path from her mouth to her shoulders. Inch by inch he burned off her hesitation and built her desire. Strong hands roved her body, gently kneading her shoulders, back, and lower still. His hips pressed against her as his strong leg parted her own. None too gracefully, they transitioned to the bed, half-smiles flashed and faded as their breathing quickened. Whispered words, telling groans and the eventual and inevitable sounds of passion filled the room against the backdrop of the setting sun through the balcony view.

# Sixteen

THE ALARM BUZZED EARLY THE next day. They were running late so she missed the debate about whether or not she'd be having coffee, but they did manage to snag some fruit on the way out the door. The resort was situated directly on the beach, so they were able to take a boat out a bit further into the water.

Anna listened attentively to the instructions and descriptions given by their instructor. Aidan had of course been several times, so he was as relaxed as he could be. All Anna could think about was the time Eadie had shared her near-hyperventilation story during the time she and Walt had tried snorkeling on their 40th anniversary. Anna made a mental note to not try and breathe through her nose, the last thing she wanted was to dork out and ruin the experience for herself.

She put the mask and snorkel on her face, added sinker weights to her belt and checked her flippers for the tenth time. She easily entered the water from the boat and took her place next to Aidan. Her body was electric with both nervousness and anticipation. There were two other couples out in the boat with them, talking to their partners in rushed and excited conversation.

As long as she lived, Anna hoped that she never forgot the look on Aidan's face before they put their faces into the water. His eyes were bright and clear, his happiness showed on his face despite the mask and the snorkel. She put her face into the water, so he did the same. Though the water was clear on the surface, Anna was not prepared for the clarity under the surface. It was like she'd been looking through her regular world with a blurry filter, and suddenly everything was much more clear and crisp than she'd ever seen before.

Aidan looked over at her and she nodded her head to show that she was okay. The brightest school of little yellow fish swam right beside her and she was in awe. They weren't in a very deep area, being that it was her first taste of snorkeling, however she was amazed at the color of the coral. She couldn't believe that this whole other world existed just a few precious feet under the water's surface.

She felt Aidan's gaze before she turned to see it; he was pointing off to his left. Anna saw a big, beautiful stingray swimming along, like it was completely normal for the pair of them to be hanging out in his home. Her joy at seeing this underwater world overcame her fear, and she gained a little more confidence with every second.

Anna moved through the water free of worry over what Aidan would think about her keeping a secret from him. The weight of worrying if she would be a good mother, maybe even a single mother eased its way from her shoulders. The leaden feeling of gut-wrenching grief that still threatened to choke her over the loss of her father, as well as the worry for Jesse and the boys as they transitioned into a new life with Levi and his sweet twins drifted away like a pile of glitter in a strong breeze. It all scattered as she absorbed the colorful fish and never-ending display of plants and coral that she had never dreamed of seeing in her life.

She couldn't help but be sad when their two-hour excursion was over. Before she was ready for it to end, it was time to go back up the ladder to the boat, shuck off her snorkel, mask, fins, and belt, and saddle back up with her anxious burdens. As the speedboat whooshed back to the resort, Anna looked back over her shoulder at the spot where they had been. She'd been weightless and out of her own head for those precious few hours. She already missed it. As if he could feel her reluctance, Aidan pulled her close.

"We'll come back sometime soon, Anna. I promise," he said, pressing a kiss to her salty cheek.

She could only nod in reply, turning her face away as a tear slipped down her face.

JESSE HAD CHOSEN the perfect location for her wedding to Levi. The veranda where they would marry looked out onto the ocean. Chairs were arranged in two small rows, and sprinkled here and there were the prettiest arrangements of fuchsia lilies mixed together with calla lilies tipped in turquoise. The effect was breathtaking against the blue of the water in the background.

Levi stood at the linen and bougainvillea-draped arbor, dressed in a white button down shirt, vest and khakis. James, Luke, and Ryan were talking with him dressed in similar fashion sans the vest. Their sleeves were rolled up, and they looked the very picture of relaxed and content. The boys had turquoise ties while Levi had a fuchsia one. Anna and Hannah were preceding Jesse down the aisle in turquoise dresses. Hannah was every inch the doll, her curls framing her sweet little face, two strands at her temples in braids.

Levi was thankful that Jesse had styled her hair that way. He didn't want a breeze to rob him of the happy expression on her little face. He had taken plenty of time talking with Hannah and James about his marriage to Jesse, making sure they were on board and comfortable all along the way. The children missed their mama dearly, and Levi had every intention of keeping pictures of them with Emma up and around their house wherever they would be living. The children were happy reminiscing and retracing every single story that Levi could remember of Emma and he was happy to do it. He had even gone so far as to write them all down in a journal so that the kids could have it one day.

Jesse wasn't replacing Emma for them, she was supplementing their lives. He was so thankful to finally have her back in his life that he still caught himself not quite believing how things had fallen into place. To think he was getting to marry his high school sweetheart after all they had been through in their lives along the way. It was a gift he was going to cherish for the rest of his life.

He looked from Hannah and saw Anna beautifully dressed behind her. His heart warmed at the way that Anna looked at Aidan as she took her place at what would be Jesse's side. As the music started to play, his eyes jerked to the doors of the veranda. Michael emerged first, holding his hand out to his mother. Levi saw Jesse's smile before he registered anything else.

She was breathtaking. Her dress draped from shoulder to floor, sleeveless and with a v-neckline. A slender, fuchsia colored belt banded her waist, and the long skirt parted on a lace slip covered slit. Modest, yet sexy, a lot like Jesse herself, Levi thought. Her brown hair curled around her shoulders, and her eyes sparkled with joy. Levi had known Jesse since they were kids and he had seen her at all stages. Never did he think she had looked more beautiful than she did at that very moment.

Michael walked her to her place beside Levi and gave her a kiss on the cheek. He extended his hand to Levi, who used it to pull him in for a hug. He loved her boys and was so very thankful that they had been welcoming in this process. He knew it was impossible to think there wouldn't be challenges down the road with blending families, but he also knew he had been gifted by God with a tremendous family to join.

Levi turned and took Jesse's hands and they exchanged a look that they had shared a hundred times over the course of their friendship, courtship and lifelong love for one another. They had this unspoken way of communicating with one another. He couldn't help it, he reached up and touched her cheek before putting her hand back in his, much to the delight of the family watching in the seats.

As the reverend walked them through the ceremony, Anna had to work to peel her eyes from Aidan. He watched her closely, a half-smile lazily taking in the proceedings. He always seemed so at ease, Anna had to work hard to remember there were still demons that he faced. She knew that she loved him enough to jump into that dark ocean and be there for him when he needed her. Anna had never been an impulsive person, yet here she was in love with someone she'd not been with for long, pregnant with his child, and wishing it was them getting married at that moment.

The ceremony seemed to be over quickly, as weddings always do. Months and months of planning goes by in the blink of an eye, and soon it's time to move along to the next event. A short reception had been planned indoors at the resort, as the sun was high and hot outside despite the breeze. The toasts were made and eyes were blotted as they are at all good weddings. Music filled the room and after Levi and Jesse had their dance, Aidan happily pulled Anna into his arms.

"May I have this dance?" he asked, his handsome lips curved into a smile.

"Of course," she said, slipping onto the dance floor, relaxing against him, thankful for the nearness.

"This is pretty romantic, isn't it?" he asked, turning her in a slow circle before pulling her gently back against his chest.

"Yes, I think it's been just beautiful," she said, smiling up at him. She was beginning to feel exhausted and was looking forward to kicking off her heels.

"What would you say if I asked you to marry me?" he said causally, his cheek pressed to her hair, moving gently to the music.

She jerked her head back and met his eyes, her expression shocked.

"Easy there, Anna," he said, his hands down to her waist as if he had all the time in the world and hadn't completely taken her by surprise. "What would you say?" he asked again, grinning down at her.

"We… we can't right now… it's Jesse's day and…" she stuttered, as he touched his thumb to her jaw, his hand lacing at the base of her hair.

"I know it's their day, but what if we could slip back to the veranda?" he asked, calm as could be, swaying with her to the music. "What if I had asked for the reverend to stay for a few more hours so that we could do this the minute we could get away unnoticed?" he asked, his voice low and deep.

Anna couldn't help herself, her eyes welled up with tears. Her emotions seemed to be completely at the surface these days. "So you're really proposing?" she said softly, feeling as if she were in a dream.

He turned her then, taking her chin in his palm, as he kissed her. He looked at her so intently she felt the burn of his brown eyes right into her soul. "Anna, will you marry me?" he asked quietly, his gaze unwavering from hers.

"Yes," she breathed, pulling his head down to hers for a kiss.

"Okay then," he said, relaxing his arms to a light hold as they finished their dance. "We can slip out in about ten more minutes."

As THE RECEPTION wound down, the older folks gathered together to drink coffee down at one of the resort restaurants while Sarah, Levi's sister, and her husband corralled the kids. Jesse and Levi had the housekeeping items to tend to in regards to paperwork that would need to be filed with the Office of Authentication at the State Department in order for their license to be official once they returned to the United States. Without it, their ceremony would be deemed nothing more than symbolic, and they'd have to redo things stateside. Neither were interested in doing the ceremony again; the one they had enjoyed with their family had been just perfect. Happy to be married to his best friend, Levi trailed alongside Jesse as she chattered, remembering things to do as she went.

While the others dispersed, Anna and Aidan slipped back to the veranda where, as promised, the reverend was patiently waiting. While Aidan made the introductions, he produced copies of their birth certificates and their passports from his jacket pocket. The reverend had Anna and Aidan sign the marriage license. He himself witnessed the signatures as well as an assistant and two others who flitted to his side when it was time to sign their names as well.

Within minutes, Anna found herself taking vows to bind her life to Aidan's, her hands held in his. She had always considered herself risk averse and had pretty much colored inside the lines for her entire life. Once her relationship with Travis had ended, she had found herself taking one risk after another. She had discovered fairly easily that life held so much more for her than she had let herself feel. Without fear and anxiousness hemming her in, she lived more fully and second guessed herself less. Anna enjoyed the power that stemmed from that kind of life. Because of that, she cast out the shadows of fear and worry that marrying Aidan was rash and crazy.

Anna loved him. He loved her. They had made a new life together. She knew his family was incredible and that they already loved her, and she knew her own family loved him, if anything, by sheer association with Sorcha. So she allowed herself the freedom to banish her fears, revel in the moment and repeat after the reverend as she sealed her life with Aidan's.

As with Jesse's wedding, within minutes it seemed the ceremony was over. The reverend gave them instructions on filing paperwork when they got back to the U.S. Aidan was clear on what had to happen, so they said their goodbyes to the reverend and his assistant and wound their way back to the suite.

Giving a quick look each way in the hallway to be sure they wouldn't be seen by anyone from their own party, Aidan whisked her up into his arms and cradled her against him after she unlocked the door. She threw her head back and laughed as he closed it behind them with his foot.

Aidan deposited her on the bed and dropped to one knee in order to remove her shoes. She moaned as he took her feet into his hands, rubbing the soreness from them as she threw herself back on the bed in ecstasy.

"Keep moaning like that and you're going to give me a complex," he said to her, a devilish smile on his face. "I've made you make a lot of noises," he said, eyes going wide in mock surprise at her expression of complete exasperation.

"What? It's true, I've made you make a lot of noises," he said again, cocky and plenty pleased with himself. "But, I don't think I've made you make noises like that!"

"Ugh, it just felt so good," she said. "You've made me feel good in a lot of ways, but that might be the best," she said, squealing when he flipped her over and gave her a swat on the rear.

"Hold still, I've got to get you out of this dress," he said as his fingers found the zipper. He pulled it slowly down, the mood changing from teasing to electric with every snag of the descending zipper. He traced the path with a finger, starting at the base of her neck and not stopping till the base of her spine. He parted both sides of the dress and his lips followed the same path.

Anna had been nearly overtaken with tiredness when they entered the room, but now every nerve was at attention and she needed him badly.

She rolled over and her dress slipped, exposing her breasts to him as she did. He stood and gently pulled the dress down and off of her.

"You're so beautiful," he said, his eyes covering every inch of her.

She typically wasn't one for praise or flattery, but his expression and tone registered something deep within her. He loved her as strongly as she loved him, she was sure of it. The understanding of it gave to her a power she relished.

Her fingers traced his shirt front, each button a small obstacle as she nimbly worked them free. She removed his shirt and felt his heart pounding as she noticed his breath becoming shallow. Anna slowly undid his belt and pants and failed at hiding a smile at how he quickly bobbed to attention. He didn't bother trying to hide his pleasure at being alone with her with nothing but a small bit of lace between them. He eased back onto the bed and with her hand, pulled her down with him.

Anna heard a groan escape her own lips and electricity shot through her as she realized this was the signal he had been waiting on. His hand dipped down between them, fingertips dancing along the edge of her panties. He looked into her eyes and she nodded, and in a quick jerk of his hands, the little garment was ruined and tossed to the side of the bed.

"Caveman," she said, her hand wrapping around his neck as the other braced against his shoulder.

Aidan grunted in reply as her hands tangled in his hair as she moved against him. Her legs circled his hips as he bucked against her, his hand under her body, cradling her as they moved together. His tongue tasted her lips, her neck, and back to her lips. When she came, Anna arched her back and he smiled against her neck. He loved that he could completely undo her.

Though she felt boneless, she held him as tightly as she could while he moved against her, his breath labored, his body hot and hard. When his body went rigid, she held him close, not moving an inch. She was still until he slowly relaxed and rolled them down to their side.

"I guess we don't have to worry about condoms anymore," he teased, his lips against her collarbone.

Anna froze against him. He felt her odd reaction and looked up at her face. "We're married now, I guess we don't have to worry about condoms anymore, right?" he asked, his brow wrinkled in confusion.

This was it. There wasn't any way to avoid what she needed to say. Anna looked at him and nervously smiled. "Well, there's something I've been wanting to tell you but I couldn't really figure out how to say it, or when," she stammered.

Aidan propped his head up on his arm, elbow balanced

on the bed. "What are you talking about, Anna? You can tell me anything," he said, his other hand tracing a path from her shoulder down her arm.

"Aidan," she started and then stopped. "Aidan, I'm pregnant. We're having a baby," she said, forcing a smile to her lips.

Agony filled her at the thought of ever having to witness his face undergo the change it did ever again in her life. Aidan changed from gentle confusion to hardened warrior in mere seconds. He didn't look furious, but he looked as hard as stone.

"You're pregnant?" he asked, light brown eyes locking on green. She nodded. "How far along?" Aidan asked, expression unchanged.

"Aidan, I wasn't sure exactly what I…" she started when he jerked his head once, from right to left, choking the words from her throat.

"How far along?" he asked again.

"Three months," Anna said quickly. "It happened when I was home in March, the night you found out about Benji."

He allowed his pain to wash over his face for a split second, and if she hadn't been watching so closely she would've missed it. His expressionless mask was fixed back in place quickly. He mechanically got up from the bed and stood for a second, a perfect statue of tensed muscle. Once he saw where she had placed their clothes, he dug around for a t-shirt and boxers and crossed to the bathroom.

While he dressed, she ran to the suitcase and threw on

pajamas. She felt awful and pathetic and bare and wanted to be hidden from him, but she wasn't going to let herself shrink back from him. She had her reasons for withholding the news. Anna was perched on the bed when he came out of the bathroom.

He yanked a blanket from the closet on his walk to the bed and looked at her for a split second before pulling two pillows from the bed.

"Aidan, I wasn't sure what to do, or when to tell you," she started, tears welling up in her eyes.

"How about the first minute you knew?" he said, his pain clear in his eyes. "Anna, how could you keep this from me?"

The tears crashed from her then, all the insecurity and anxiousness she had been holding in for the last three months just poured from her body.

"I didn't know what was going to happen with us," she sobbed, trying and failing to regain composure. Anna hated not being in control of her emotions, but there was no keeping the tears at bay.

"Would what happened with us make a difference in whether you kept the baby?" he asked, an incredulous expression filled his eyes.

"No, of course not," she said. "I was afraid to tell you because I knew you'd be all in, right from the start," she said, flinching as he threw his arms up in the air in disbelief.

"All in? Jesus, Anna, is that a bad thing to have the father of your child be?" he asked, shaking his head in confusion. "I can't believe you kept this from me!" he roared, catching himself and checking his volume before the whole resort came into their room to check on them.

His temper flipped a switch in her, and she felt an unholy white hot flame well up in her soul. "I wanted to know you wanted me for *me*," she hissed, "not just because we would be a ready-made family!"

Aidan's eyes flared at that, his pride stung in more ways that he could even pinpoint at that moment. He had just found out that she was pregnant, that he was going to be a father. This was supposed to be one of the happiest moments of his entire life. Instead, he roared and she spat fire at him. He felt a level of betrayal that he had never felt before in his life.

He had seen some terrible, terrible things in his past during his time of service. Aidan had seen pure evil and lack of respect for human life. One of the things he most treasured during those dark times was the idea that someday he'd be in love and start a family. He loved kids and he loved loud, crowded families. Finally, he had a taste of what he had always wanted, and it had been tainted and transformed to vinegar on his tongue.

"I'm disgusted that you would keep this from me, take even these three months from me," he said, his voice catching. "Have you been to the doctor yet? Do you know if *we're* having a boy or a girl?"

"No," Anna answered, shaking her head slowly. "I have an appointment next week for that and was going to ask you to come," she said.

"Were you?" he asked, a mix of doubt and sarcasm so thick that she couldn't determine which he intended.

"Yes. I was planning to wait until tomorrow to tell you the news, this day was supposed to be about Jesse and Levi," she said.

"Oh," he said, eyebrows raised to the sky. "Now you're sorry we even got married?" he asked. "Wait a minute," she said, her finger pointing right at him.

"Don't point your teacher-finger at me," he said angrily. "I'm not one of your students."

She took a deep breath and put her hand down. "Please don't put words in my mouth here," she said. "I thought I was doing the right thing by waiting to see if you loved me rather than taking me part and parcel in the deal," Anna said.

Aidan stood for a second looking hard at her, trying to decide if there was anything left to say. He turned, flicked off the light and laid down on the floor where he didn't sleep at all that night.

Anna went to the bathroom and washed her face, pressing a cold wash rag to her eyes. "How has such an amazing day gone so terribly wrong?" she asked herself, knowing full well the answer. She truly had thought she was doing the right thing. She'd never pretended to be perfect. This was a new experience for her as well.

She went to lie back down in the bed, waiting for Aidan to say something. He didn't. They spent their first night as husband and wife lying awake and broken hearted, together but apart.

# Seventeen

DAYLIGHT FORCED EVERYONE FROM their rooms, including Aidan and Anna. Around the breakfast table, everyone chirped pleasant conversation while Anna felt a tremendous hole in her heart.

"Are you feeling alright, dear?" Eadie asked her, head cocked to one side.

"You look like hell, honey," Aunt Ruthie said, catching an elbow from Eadie. The older ladies looked between Anna and Aidan, noting the puffy eyes and irritable moods.

Anna shrugged and muttered, "I'm fine, just tired," she lied, risking a quick glance at Aidan, who stared a hole through her head. Anna looked back down at her plate where she forced bites of pancake down her throat. She was repulsed by her own appetite, but my God she was hungry. She felt weak from skipping supper the night before and though the food tasted like clumps of wet paper, she had to eat.

Aunt Ruthie started to say something to Aidan but was stopped by Eadie.

"How do you think your sister is getting along with dog sitting Harry and Oscar, Aidan?" Eadie asked, receiving a dirty look from Ruthie that clearly begged the question why it was okay for Eadie to talk to him but not her.

"I'm sure she's doing fine," he said forcing a smile at Eadie. "We've got a big family, so we're used to chaos and kids," he said, piercing Anna with a glance.

"Well, everyone, if we're all done here," Levi said, reading the weird vibe at the other end of the table and anxious to be rid of it, "we'd better get back and get our stuff loaded up. The bus will be here in an hour to take us to the airport," he said as he raised up to his feet.

Everyone stood and made their way to their room.

"What the hell was that about?" Levi asked Jesse.

"Better sit back down, I've got something to tell you," she said, launching into Anna and Aidan's news.


ANNA COULDN'T STAND the silence any longer as they packed up their belongings in their room.

"This is ridiculous," she said. "Are you going to talk to me at all?" Anna asked, stopping to look at Aidan.

"I do have a question," he said. "When is the next appointment? I'd like to be there."

"Of course! It's Friday at 10 AM," she answered. "I want you to be there," she added quietly. Her heart sank and her spirit deflated when he didn't respond or even look at her. Was he who she even thought he was? It was a little late now, she thought. She was married to him now!

Suddenly she looked at the clock. "Aidan, we need to hurry and file those papers! If we don't the marriage won't be official when we get home," she said, eyes huge.

He looked at her like she was crazy and slowly shook his head. "No way. I can't do that now," he said. "Anna, I can't trust you."

"Come on, Aidan, it's not like I lied," she started, but then realized the weakness of her own argument. Instead of trying to fight a battle she wouldn't win, she just nodded her head and did her best to stifle the sob that nearly erupted from her body.

THE NEXT EIGHT hours of travel were sheer torture for nearly everyone. The older folks were tired from the trip, the young folks were squirmy and ready to be home. Jesse and Levi felt tense on behalf of Anna and Aidan, and Anna and Aidan were so upset they wouldn't even look at one another.

All cars had been parked at Jesse's. Aidan thanked Levi and Jesse for the trip and congratulated them once again. He said his goodbyes to the children and the parents and tossed his bag in his truck and drove off. Anna stood on the porch feeling like her heart was going to explode. After everyone else had left, Anna and Jesse had to go and pick up Oscar and Harry from Sorcha's. As soon as the vehicle door clicked closed, Anna threw herself into Jesse's arms. She didn't know how she had more tears to cry after the awful night she had just had, but they streamed hot and wet against her face. She told Jesse everything, and Jesse cried with her.

Though her attempts were feeble, Jesse tried to reassure Anna that everything would work out. When Sorcha threw the door open and saw Anna and Jesse's faces red and puffy, she pulled them inside amongst the prancing, barking dogs. Evan took one look at the ladies and ushered both Clara and the dogs outside for just one more walk.

"What the heck is going on, Anna?" Sorcha asked, pulling her friend close in a hug.

Anna winced, for the first time wondering how Sorcha was going to handle the news. "I did something that I thought was right, but it happens what I did was awful," she said, her voice catching on her words.

Sorcha led Anna and Jesse to the couch, taking a seat in the chair next to them, nearly dying from curiosity. "Enough already, spit it out!" she said, waiting impatiently, as she bounced her foot nervously in her chair.

Anna dried her eyes on the tissues she offered and stared hard at her best friend. "Sorcha, I'm pregnant," she said, and threw her spread hand up at Sorcha's delighted screech of joy.

"Wait, you're going to be pissed," she said, looking down at the floor while she sorted out her words. This was the part she dreaded. Sorcha said from the get-go that she wouldn't be taking sides, but Anna wasn't so sure she'd hold to her position.

"Aidan and I were *together* when I was home in March, and I got pregnant," Anna said, looking into her friend's eyes. Sorcha beamed and nearly bounced on the couch with joy. "I wanted to wait to tell him until I was sure we were going to work out so that he didn't just take me on because of the baby," she said.

Sorcha stilled and tilted her head to the side, trying to decide how she felt about the matter.

"So wait," she said, sorting it all out as quickly as she could. "You're pregnant, you and Aidan love each other, what's the big deal?" she said. "Oh," she exclaimed, sucking the air in as it hit her.

"Yeah, he's furious that I kept it from him," Anna answered, wringing her hands self consciously. The thing is, I didn't mean to do it *to* him, I was doing it *for* me. I didn't want someone to love me or try to love me – or pretend to love me because of the baby. I know it sounds screwed up, but I'd rather co-parent with him separately than live together when we aren't in love," she said, exasperated.

"But you are in love," Sorcha half asked, half answered.

"Yes," said Jesse, nodding emphatically.

"Yes," said Anna, "but I think I broke it."  Her voice cracked and Sorcha dove at her best friend, pulling her into her arms. Holding her friend as she sobbed, Sorcha patted Anna until she finally pulled back.

Anna took the tissue Jesse was offering her and looked at both women. "There's something else," Anna said looking at both women.

"Oh God, what, Anna? Twins?" Sorcha said, ducking Anna's swat.

"No. I mean I don't think," she said, her hand firmly planted on her belly. "I have that appointment on Friday. Surely I'd know by now, right?" Anna asked, eyes bugged out.

Sorcha shook her head. "I don't know. I've got twin brothers, it's in the blood. And I had a cousin not find out till the sex reveal at 20 weeks."

Anna shuddered. She loved kids and would love twins, but the idea of two babies at once while she was by herself was a little unnerving.

"Back to it, Anna. If it's not twins, then what?" Jesse asked, impatient to hear what else she had to share.

"Jesse, after your reception, we went back to the veranda," she paused, trying to decide just how she would word it.

"Spit it out, Sis. I'm dying here," Jesse said, as she gestured with her hands for Anna to get on with it.

Anna took a deep breath, "We went back to the veranda and got married," she said, closing her eyes as a fresh wave of pain washed over her.

"Oh my God," Sorcha said quietly, laying back against the side of the couch. "Oh my God, this is the best thing ever," she said, eyes closed like she just couldn't believe her good fortunate.

Anna stared at her and was about to ask how it was the

best thing ever that she and Aidan kind of got married but kind of weren't talking.

"You what?" Jesse screeched. "You got married without me?" she said, hurt filling her eyes.

Anna suddenly felt like a little kid again, reporting to her big sister. "It was the most romantic thing I could have ever imagined," she explained. "Jesse, we were dancing at your reception and he proposed right there on the floor. He had the reverend hanging back in case I said yes," Anna said, as she patted her hand on Jesse's knee.

"All my life I've been careful and reserved and I've over thought every decision that I make to death. This time he asked, and I went for it," Anna said, as she placed her hand on her heart.

Jesse threw her arm around her little sister. "I'm glad you went for it, Anna, I just would've liked to have seen it," she said.

"I know, Sis," she said, then turned to Sorcha. "You too, Sis," she said, then laughed despite herself.

Sorcha leaned up from her spot on the couch. "Sis," she said, and rolled her eyes. "Just what I need, more siblings," she joked, then put her arms around Anna and Jesse.

Anna pulled away and grabbed another tissue. "The thing is, we were supposed to file the papers before we left or the marriage doesn't count in the U.S."

Sorcha bugged out her eyes and Jesse moaned.

"Jesus, Anna. Everything is complicated with you guys. It'll work out," Sorcha said, dismissing it like it was just a small hitch before moving on.

The room was quiet for a moment as the ladies soaked in all the news.

Sorcha's eyes rested on a pile of Clara's toys in the floor and her heart welled with happiness for her brother and her best friend. "Oh, Anna, you're going to be a mama," she said happily, her own eyes filling with tears.

"I am," Anna said, a half-laugh bubbling from her throat.

"I'm going to be an aunt!" Jesse said smiling wildly.

"Me too!" hooted Sorcha.

The women huddled and laughed and cried together while Evan and Clara, Oscar and Harry walked circles around the block until the sounds of chaos subsided from the living room.

Once Jesse and Oscar had been safely deposited at their home, Anna drove home with Harry. Despite her heartbreak, she was looking forward to giving her mother some good news. She was tired of holding in secrets and when it came down to it, Aidan was either onboard or not onboard.

Anna entered the house to find Ruthie already gone for the night and Eadie waiting up in the living room.

"Hey, Mom, are you worn out?" she asked, sitting beside her mother on the couch as Harry tried and failed to insert himself between them. Anna moved the big fellow to a better spot and saw Eadie studying her.

"Whatever it is, kiddo, let's talk about it," Eadie said, her worry showed clearly on her face. Anna smiled at her mother and used a line she had heard Jesse's kids say a hundred times. "Okay, but don't be mad…"

EADIE CRIED FIRST with joy that Anna was having a baby, then cried with shared heartache that she and Aidan had gotten married in secret then fought. She hated to see her own baby struggling so hard with someone she was clearly meant to be with.

Anna accepted her mother's arms greedily. No matter her age, there was no comfort like a mother.

"It'll work out, Sweet Pea," Eadie said, smoothing Anna's hair away from her face like she had done a hundred times before.

"I hope so, Mom," Anna said. "I love him."

"He's a good man, honey. He might be a stubborn mule, but he's a good man. You've got to let him have time to deal with his hurt," Eadie added.

"You're probably right," she said, not missing the arched eyebrow as Eadie heard the word probably.

"Give me a break, I'm the mom. I'm always right," Eadie replied. "You'd better get used to that, you'll be saying it before you know." At Anna's expression she said, "No, don't give me that look. Over the years I've said a hundred things my mother used to say to me that I swore I'd never say. You become a mom and it all just bubbles up from somewhere."

"I might be a little old to say this, but this didn't happen in the order I always thought it would happen in," Anna said. "I hope you're not embarrassed."

"Oh, kid. Come here," Eadie said, putting an arm around Anna's shoulders and her hand on her knee. "Listen, first off, you're 30 years old. I'm way past being anything but proud over anything you kids have done or will do," she said, giving Anna a squeeze. "Second, I've never told either you or Jesse this because I didn't think it would set a terrific example, but," she paused, choosing her words carefully, "I was expecting a baby when your father and I were married."

Anna could've been knocked over with a feather. She was stunned, then confounded as she calculated Jesse's birthday. Before she could ask, Eadie jumped in.

"Not Jesse, hon. A little boy baby," she said, her face soft with remembrance. A tear slid down her cheek and she reached to the side table for a tissue. "My, my," Eadie said, shaking her head slowly. "I haven't cried over that sweet thing in years," she said.

"Oh, Mom, I'm so sorry," she said lamely, unsure of what to say.

"It's an awfully sad thing to lose a baby," Eadie said, "even when it's really, really early." Eadie dabbed again at her eyes, tucking the tissue into the sleeve of her shirt the way Anna had seen her do a million times before.

"We didn't talk about loss back then of course, the way ladies do now." She slapped her hand on her knee, punctuating her feelings. "I'm so thankful to see that some of the stigma is being taken away from such a hurtful subject. Why should people be forced to be quiet about miscarrying, like it's something shameful?" she asked Anna.

"I don't know, Mom," she said, her hand going to her own stomach. Even putting a voice to something that terrified Anna had her a little uneasy.

"Well, sweetie, I'm exhausted and ready for my own bed. I'm glad we got this out of the way. I've been worried sick since breakfast today," Eadie said, wincing as she stood up from her seat. "And stiff. My word, I can't wait to lie down," she said, giving Anna a smile.

Anna smiled and stood to hug her mother one last time. "I'm beat, too. I'll take Harry out once more and lock the doors.

"Sounds good, night night," Eadie said, her house shoes making a shuffling sound as she walked down the hallway.

ANNA LATCHED HARRY's leash and opened the door. Harry let loose a bark that made the hair on Anna's neck stand up straight. Aidan was sitting on the porch swing in the dark. He greeted Harry with his hand out, and the ferocity vanished and was replaced with joy.

"Easy, big boy," he said to the frantic poodle. Anna's heart was about to leap out of her chest. She didn't know what to say or do, she just froze where she stood.

Aidan stood, reaching out for Harry's leash as he gave the command to heel. Anna woodenly handed him the leash and followed him to the driveway. They walked in silence a little way and finally he held his hand out to her. He gave hers a squeeze and they continued walking.

After a few blocks, Aidan finally seemed to decide what he wanted to say.

"Anna, I'm sorry," he said, looking from the ground to her face and back to the ground. "I can't say I wish I had the moment to do over again, but I wish it had gone differently."

She stopped walking and turned him to her, her head resting against his chest. He wrapped an arm around her but didn't hold her as close as she craved.

"I'm so sorry that I hurt you. I had to see that you loved me for me, not just for our baby," she said quietly. She held stock still as she heard his breath catch, and couldn't bear to look in his eyes, so she stayed as she was. After a minute she felt him slightly nod his head, then he stepped back.

They started walking back toward her house in silence. Once they got to the door, the awkwardness of the moment was nearly paralyzing.

"Where's your appointment on Friday?" he asked, his hand at her waist.

"Robertsville, at the Women's Hospital," Anna said.

He nodded. "I'll see if I can get off. Would you like to drive together?"

"Sure, that would be nice" she said, feeling weirdly shy.

"Okay then, I'll pick you up at 8:45 if I can get off," he said, sending up a prayer that he could get off on such short notice. "And we get to find out if it's a boy or a girl?" he asked, a half-grin appearing on his face.

"Yes," Anna answered, eyes glimmering with tears. She couldn't wait for the appointment. She'd only known she was pregnant for a little over a month, but nearly every minute since that positive test had been filled with a mix of worry and wonder over this Little Bean.

He nodded his head and reached out to hold the door for Anna and Harry to go into the house. She looked at him hurt and confused, expecting a goodbye kiss or hug. She reached a hand out to him and Aidan shook his head at her in a small jerk.

"Anna, things aren't fixed between us," he said, surprise registering on his face. "I'm more thoroughly pissed than I've ever been in my life, but I don't want it to be mean between us."

Anna didn't even have the words to match her thoughts or feelings, so she did the only thing she could. She slowly turned and walked into the house, shutting the door closed behind her.

As she got into bed that night she lay there exhausted but wide-eyed, looking up at her ceiling. Anna tried to ignore the ache in her chest and the thoughts that raced through her mind. Her hands rested on her belly and she whispered a promise to the baby that it would be loved and all would be well. She didn't know what that would mean in the end, but she was going to make sure everything would be okay.

# Eighteen

THE FIRST FEW DAYS OF July arrived with searing temperatures and humidity that made clothes cling and hair frizz. Anna spent the few days between arriving home and the Friday doctor appointment indulging in a little online shopping. While there was a terrific little boutique in town, and a Wal-Mart, of course, there wasn't much else in the way of maternity clothes or baby nursery items to be found nearby.

She wasn't certain what kinds of decorations she wanted to choose because she was still on the fence about so many other things. Anna wasn't sure she really wanted to find out the sex of the baby. There was a lot to be said for finding out, but then again, what kind of surprise would ever rival finding out if she was having a son or a daughter? She didn't know if she was going to stay at her mother's house until the baby was born. She clearly couldn't bank on everything turning out all sunshine and roses with Aidan; he wouldn't even give her kiss, for heaven's sake. Anna slammed her laptop shut at the thought of that moment, the rejection still stinging. She had completely misinterpreted his presence at her house the night they got home from Mexico.

Deciding she had had quite enough stewing, she threw on her workout clothes and laced her running shoes. Harry bounded for the door, eager to go on a jog. Anna took it easy, the heat absolutely draining. She alternated running and walking each block and allowed her mind to float away from her worries and focused instead on her breathing.

Without intending to, she found herself in front of Sorcha's house. Clara saw her first and hooted and banged on the glass front door hard enough to bring Sorcha there at a run.

"Anna, good God, are you trying to kill yourself out there?" Sorcha said, unlocking and throwing the door open.

"Sorcha, I run all the time, what are you talking about?" Anna said, annoyed at her friend.

"I don't know how. I've never once ran unless chased, and I sure as heck never ran in the middle of the afternoon in July," she said, pausing, emphasizing Anna's idiocy by looking over glasses at her, "with a bun in the oven."

Sorcha sat a tall glass of ice water down in front of Anna and put a cold water soaked dishrag on the back of Anna's neck. "You're as red as a beet, lady," Sorcha said, plopping down in the kitchen chair beside her.

"I'll be fine, just a little hot," Anna said, smiling as she watched Clara. She had squatted down in front of Harry and was talking to him full throttle in her really loud, really high, little girl voice. Harry responded by plopping down on the air vent and turning his head to the side like he was trying to puzzle out whatever Clara was blabbering about.

"So, have you talked to Aidan?" Sorcha asked, eyebrow raised in suspicion.

"Not since the night we got home," Anna said, "but he did send a text that said he was able to get off for our doctor appointment tomorrow." Anna didn't say anything else after that. She wasn't particularly interested in giving away any details of their conversation at her house the night they got home. Her level of rejection was absolutely off the charts and it pained her greatly.

"Well, I imagine he'll have an interesting story to share with you when you do talk," Sorcha answered.

"Oh, Lord, I'm afraid to ask," Anna said with her eyes closed.

Sorcha nodded. "Oh yeah, it's big. He told our parents you two were having a baby." At that, Sorcha pursed her lips and waited for Anna to say something. Anything.

Anna opened her eyes. Sorcha's demeanor spelled doom. The two of them had done a lot of stupid things over the years as best friends, but it was easy to read that Sorcha was happy to have not been the one who had screwed up this time.

"How did they take it?" she asked, wincing already.

"Well, let me put it this way," Sorcha said, "it turns out Dad can still yell, really, really loud, and Finn is no longer the family screw up."

Anna sighed and put her head down on her arms at Sorcha's table. Finn had stolen a car when he was 15 and had been arrested. He claimed it had been a joke, however the officer took more of an issue with the open bottle of Jack Daniels in the console than the unlawful possession of Finn's grandma's car.

"I'm sure Aidan will fill you in tomorrow," she said, shrugging a shoulder when Anna looked up and glared. "Come on, Preggo, I'll drive you home." Sorcha got up and grabbed her keys, scooping up Clara who was trying to put a baby bonnet on Harry. She held her up, sniffed her pants and smiled. "No messy pants for you!" she said to a giggling Clara.

"Gross," Anna said, disgusted.

"Just wait," Sorcha laughed, secretly thrilled at all the many unsavory things Anna had yet to learn about the inner workings of motherhood. "While we drive I'll tell you all about the enormous blood clots and mesh underwear that go with labor and delivery."

AIDAN PULLED UP at Anna's house at precisely 8:45 AM on Friday morning. She took a breath to steady herself and waited until he rang the doorbell before jerking the door open. Anna wanted so badly to be impartial to him after he humiliated her just a few short days earlier. She wanted not to see his broad shoulders and sexy arms and flash back to the sight of him poised above her, merging their bodies as one. She didn't want to see in her mind the way his eyes crinkled at the corners when he laughed. Anna especially didn't want to remember the tender moment he let her cradle his head to her body as he cried for his friend, the very night they made their baby.

She plastered a fake smile on her face and grabbed her purse as he held the door.

"Good morning," she said, "perfect timing."

"Thanks, and thanks," he said as she handed him a big cup of coffee in a travel mug.

"I can't drink it, but man, I love the smell," she said, shrugging as she walked to the passenger side of the truck. Aidan closed the door behind her and walk around the truck.

He took a drink of the coffee and buckled up. "So, no coffee," he said pausing. "What else can't you have?"

"Well, it's a pretty good laundry list. Let's see, first, the worst...no sushi," she said, grimacing. "At least not the kind I like that has raw fish." She sighed so heavily that he laughed.

"No more medium rare steak, no lunch meat unless it's piping hot – and who eats it that way?" She cringed.

"No bologna? Dang, that must be hard for you!" he said with a grin.

"Ick, bologna? You're not even allowed to live in Denver if you eat that crap," she said, sticking her tongue out in an awful face.

"What? There's nothing better than fried bologna, hot sauce and white bread. Even better if you throw on some American cheese, processed plastic wrapped goodness," he joked, enjoying making her cringe.

"I can't even think about it," Anna said. "You're lucky I'm past the puking stage or you'd need to wash out your truck."

"Easy. I'm not a fan of other people's puke."

"Definitely avoid talking to your sister then, she gave me the rundown on motherhood, from labor through potty training." Anna paused, the seriousness of her feelings stealing into the truck and taking up all the air. The light hearted teasing was gone right out the window.

"I hope I'll be a good mom," she said quietly.

He looked at her quickly, waiting for her to continue.

"I gross out so easily. I'm impatient. I'm 30 years old, dang it. I'm used to everything being pretty much my own way. Neat and tidy, naps, vacations..." She shrugged a shoulder.

"I know it'll be fine," she said, shaking her head. "I'm just a little freaked out."

"Yeah, I get it," he said. "I mean, I've only had four days to soak this in," he said, throwing a hand up in the air to call off her attack in case she was ready to have a fit. "I'm used to things a certain way too. It's a little scary. It's not just me anymore," he said, a weak smile flashed her way. "I've got everything I need right now, my little house, my truck, I've got a life insurance policy and all that crap," he said, but I've got to get a will made out, a trust set up for the little guy, a..."

"Or girl," she said.

"What?" Aidan said, puzzled.

"You said little guy, it might be a little girl," she said.

"Okay, got me there, or girl," he said. "Either way, only a few days in and I've already lost sleep each night worrying over what I need to get set up to provide for the baby.

The way he chose his words made Anna's stomach turn. It sounded like he had zero expectations of them getting together and raising their baby as a family. She knew she had needed to prepare for that as a possible outcome, but he sounded like he'd already made up his mind.

Anna's disappointment was palpable. Aidan sensed her mood had changed, but he didn't realize what he had said to put her in a bad mood. He thought things were going well enough on the drive, all things considered.

They made the rest of the drive in silence. Anna stared out the window and Aidan kept his eyes ahead. The feeling was tense for the rest of the time they were in the truck and as they checked in at the doctor's office. Anna was sullen and Aidan was annoyed. He didn't even know what it was that he did, but he wasn't going to beg her for an explanation. She could either be an adult about it or she could try to deal. He didn't want to be a jerk to her. He had enough women in his family to know that pregnant women didn't need to be stressed out. He even did a little research online about pregnancy and what stage she was, how big the baby would be and what she should be experiencing as far as the textbook experiences.

Anna's name was called and they made their way back

to the ultrasound room. He sat down in the chair as she laid back on the table. The tech greeted them, introduced herself and made chit chat as she lifted Anna's shirt and spread goo on her belly.

The room was still as the technician did the ultrasound. Aidan watched Anna, her face tense and her hand clasped in a tight fist at her side. Even anxious she was beautiful. He hated that she had even thought to keep their baby a secret. He wondered when she would've told him if they hadn't been together in Mexico. Or, what if they had been together but hadn't gotten married? Would she have mentioned it before the baby was born? He felt enraged that she would keep such an important secret from him. It tugged at him no matter what it was he was busy doing, alone, whatever and whenever he was awake. He had always been so careful when he was with a woman. Making a baby outside of marriage was not tolerated in his family or his church, neither, he knew, was sex outside of marriage. He fought back the reaction of his parents. He didn't want to play that back through his mind, at least not right now.

Aidan had already missed so much, he didn't want to miss this moment, too. He took a big breath to calm his anger and regain his focus. He checked his pride and scooted his chair close to Anna on the table.

Anna nearly jumped when she felt Aidan reach over and take her hand. She tore her eyes away from the monitor to look into his eyes. Girl or boy, this would be one beautiful baby, she thought, looking at his handsome face. He gave her a slight smile and she watched his eyes drift back to the monitor. She let her eyes follow, amazed that the technician could make heads or tails out of what she was looking at.

"Well, the doctor will go over this with you in greater detail, but so far everything looks fine with baby," she said, smiling at the couple. "Are we finding out the sex of the baby today?" she asked, her preliminary report instantly calming to Anna.

She turned to Aidan and raised her eyebrows at him, disbelieving that they hadn't covered that singular topic on the drive over.

"I'm going to leave that up to you," he said, his eyes on Anna's.

"Come on now, tell me," she said to him. "Which do you prefer?" Anna asked.

"Honestly, this is the best gift I've ever had in my life, and I'd be fine with it being a surprise," he answered almost reverently.

"Me too," she said, inwardly groaning at the trouble she was going to catch from Jesse and Sorcha, her two detail-obsessed loved ones.

"Okay," the technician said, "I'll make a note that we're waiting." Anna and Aidan watched her cursor move along the screen as she tilted it a bit more to face them better. "Here's the baby's head, arms, that's the heart, spine, tummy, legs," she said. "I'm going to skim past the private bits. I don't want to give anything away. I will have you know that I checked everything already, and things look just fine."

The sight of their baby's profile caught Anna and Aidan by the heart. Each fuzzy detail of the precious little head, tiny nose, the jaw seemed to act like an eraser for the hurt that had ricocheted between them over the past week. Contempt was overcome with joy; anger overcome with hope. Aidan crowded in over Anna to see the monitor more clearly. Anna was in awe of the baby, moving its little hand around, as relaxed as a baby could be. Anna made herself a promise at that moment to reign in the stress that had been flooding her body since their wedding. Aidan could be her son or daughter's father or he could be her husband and part of the very fabric of her life, but either way, she would give this baby love and stability.

Aidan wiped the tears from his eyes, embarrassed at his emotion. He was a battle hardened warrior. He'd seen more of this world than he'd ever imagined he'd see, but nothing had prepared him for the torrent of emotions coursing through him. He looked down at Anna and decided right then that he would try and find a way to forgive her for her lack of trust and mutual love. His pride had been ripped in half as well as his heart when he learned she had kept such an utterly dear secret from him.

He may be flawed, and may wrestle certain demons, but he was a family man through and through. That little boy or girl on that monitor and in her belly would be his whole world.

Once the ultrasound was over, the technician printed off pictures, carefully avoiding those that might spill the beans on the sex of the baby, wished them a good day, and stepped out of the office.

"That was incredible," Aidan said, the first to find his words.

"We made a beautiful baby," she said, pulling him into a hug.

For half of a second she was worried he wasn't going to hold her back, but slowly he wrapped his arms around her, his posture transitioning from rigid to warm. He felt like her Aidan. She sighed and relaxed in his arms. She enjoyed the feel of him against her body for a minute, then gradually built back up her fortress. She wanted to be ready in case he turned standoffish again. Anna wasn't going to allow herself to be hurt and then upset; she had just had the gift of seeing the baby she had to protect.

Eventually they separated, drawing up their respective walls, but maybe this time not quite as high. After a brief waiting period in the lobby, they were called back to see Dr. Han.

"Do I get to come?" he asked her as she rose from her seat.

"Sure, absolutely," Anna said, reaching out her hand to him. They walked back to Dr. Han's exam room tentatively holding hands. Aidan glanced at the six-month-old magazines while she undressed and dressed again in the flimsy gown for her exam. She took her seat and he took his in the little chair that was typically hidden behind the curtain where patients dressed. Anna was happy that he would be up so high near her head during the exam. They had made a baby, they had been together even five short days before, they had even promised to love and cherish one another, but then the bottom had dropped out. Suddenly there was such an awkward gulf between them.

With a light tap at the door, the nurse came and checked Anna's blood pressure, weighed her and asked her questions about her general health and how things were moving along. The nurse was in and out in two minutes flat, and then they sat again in silence.

Aidan looked at his watch and gave her a weak smile. "Hospitals make me nervous," he admitted, looking a little embarrassed.

"You?" she grinned. "I didn't think anything would make you nervous."

"Oh yeah, lots of stuff does, I just try to keep it all shoved way down deep inside. You know, real healthy," he said, nodding in an exaggerated fashion.

"Ah, good to know," she said, loving the sound of his laugh.

A quick knock on the door announced the arrival of the doctor. Dr. Han walked in and smiled at the couple, then looked directly at Anna, reading her face. Anna had only met with the doctor one other time but had immediately liked her. She almost wished she could speak to Dr. Han privately and unburden herself to this relative stranger. Anna fought the feelings back and decided she needed to log some time with Jesse soon. Jesse was the closest thing Anna had to a therapist, which might be just what she needed at this time. She felt like a ping pong ball bouncing from one emotional extreme to the next. She wanted to be calm and composed during this pregnancy, knowing the stress could have an impact on the hormones rushing around in her body.

"I'm Dr. Han," she said, extending her hand to Aidan. "Nice to meet you."

"Yes, ma'am, I'm Aidan Doherty," he replied, shaking her hand and sitting down after the doctor was seated.

Dr. Han gave Anna the side-eye, seeming to approve so far of Aidan. "Well, it's good to see you again," she said, "and even better because I get to tell you that your baby looks healthy. The baby is a perfect size and length for the gestation."

At this, Anna felt the breath she hadn't realized she'd been holding escape her lips. Aidan reached over and took her hand.

"So, now your turn, how are you feeling?" Dr. Han asked, looking directly at Anna.

"I'm feeling good," Anna answered, nodding. "I seem to be getting tired a little easier than normal, but maybe it's the scorching heat."

Dr. Han nodded, "Yes, the heat is pretty intense. Are you staying cool when you can?  Drinking lots of water?" Anna continued answering questions about her water intake, her sleep habits, her diet, and her exercise.

"How about stress? Are you controlling the stress in your life?" she asked, looking to both Aidan and Anna for a response.

"Trying to," Anna answered. She wasn't prepared to jump into all the gruesome details in front of Aidan. She didn't want to seem like she was vilifying him or excusing herself from the blame of their situation. Avoiding the mess, Anna quickly changed subjects. "I do start a new job next week, so that should be a positive change," she said.

Dr. Han nodded. "Great. Tell me about what you'll be doing." Anna rattled on until the doctor was satisfied that she was taking actions that would be good for her and the baby.

"Anna," the doctor said poking around on her tablet as she spoke. "Your blood pressure is a little high," she said. "Not much," she said, patting Anna on the hand, "but a little." I want you to make sure and follow my instructions so that this small issue doesn't turn into a problem, okay?"

Anna instinctively put her hand to her stomach and Aidan was on alert.

"Keep eating healthy, and you can go ahead and continue exercising at this stage. What are you doing now for activity?"

"Jogging, walking, a little cardio here and there using some DVDs on the really hot days when I don't want to get out," Anna answered.

"Great, keep it up for now. We may taper it off a bit or knock down to just walking," said Dr. Han.

Anna nodded her assent and the doctor went down her list as she washed up for the exam. "That's really all there is to do at this point. Eat well, be active, reduce stress in your life as much as possible, and get plenty of rest."

"Okay, that I can do," she said, looking back at Aidan.

Dr. Han made conversation as she went through the exam, putting Anna at ease. Aidan still looked a little green about the gills for being present during a pelvic exam, but he stayed on his little seat right near her head where Anna preferred him to be.

"Well, Anna, things seem to be perfect. Aidan, it was nice to meet you. Take care of your girl, here, and I'll see you at your next appointment," she said as she washed and dried her hands. With a smile and a nod, Dr. Han left the room.

Aidan drew his first easy breath once the doctor had left the room.

"You're a new patient of hers, right? You just started coming here?" he asked, stepping to the far side of the tiny room so that Anna could dress.

"Yes, I've only seen her once before, but I like her," she answered.

"Me too," he said, then added under his breath as they walked down the hall, "I'm just not sure it's reciprocated."

THEY HIT A greasy little diner on the way out of town for a burger and shake. The popular place hadn't filled up yet with the lunch rush and they were actually able to hear each other speak.

"Since we're not finding out what we're having, what are we going to tell people?" Aidan asked. "Is this a common thing to do?"

"Most of my friends have always found out, but those who didn't usually griped about people giving them a lot of flak," she said between bites.

"It's weird the stuff people find to get worked up about," he said, finishing off his food.

"Yeah, I think most of the complaining is about how to shop." She shrugged. "The way I see it, you need about the same stuff no matter if it's a boy or girl: a crib, a swing, a bouncy seat, blankets, burp rags and a boatload of diapers. That stuff comes in yellow and green as easily as it does pink and blue."

Aidan nodded his head, but something had changed in his eyes. Anna felt her stomach turn a little, almost wishing she had a rewind button and could do it all differently. If she had, they might be snuggled up close together instead of sitting awkwardly at the booth.

"Speaking of cribs and stuff," he said, looking down at his food, "what's the plan, just buy two of everything?"

Anna looked into his eyes, his lips pulled into a harsh line. She shrugged her shoulders a little. "I hadn't really thought that far yet," she said, quickly looking away. "Ah, guess I kind of ruined the plans a little when it bothered me not to know I was going to be a father for three months more than I could've," he said, a sharp edge filling his voice.

"Aidan, let's not do this here," she said, looking over her shoulder at the line of people starting to trickle in.

He just sat there staring at her until she finally became uncomfortable enough to look back up to his face. Aidan leaned in toward her and said quietly, "You're going to have to give me a little more than a week to get over this. You realize this, right?"

The combination of the sarcastic tone he was taking along with his body language made her blood boil.

Calmly, through nearly gritted teeth she said, "We've been over this. I've explained my reasons for doing what I did," she said, breaking off when he leaned back and looked away. "I'm not going to keep rehashing the same exact argument, Aidan. I did what I thought was right."

At that, Anna loaded up her purse and tray, pitched the trash and walked out the door to stand beside his truck. He was behind her in seconds. Surprising her, he reached to her side, pulled the door open and held it while she climbed into the truck.

Anna's heart was pumping and she quickly argued with herself over his right to be furious and her surprise that this level of fury was maintainable. She didn't look through his window to see him standing there, eyes closed and taking several deep breaths before getting into the truck.

Aidan stood there, collecting his anger and trying to release it. Dr. Han's words about limiting stress rang in his ears and he did not want to make things worse for her or the baby. Once he was in control of his temper, he got in the truck.

Before starting the ignition, he exhaled. "Anna," he started.

"Listen," she said, green eyes flashing.

He shook his head. "No, I need you to listen. Please."

She held still, hoping this would end quickly.

"Anna, you're not understanding me. I'm not upset because I wasn't there to get you crackers or hold your hair while you puked," he said, exasperated, "although I would've liked to have been there for that, too." As he spoke he was irritated with himself that his words weren't coming out right.

"What I can't wrap my head around is how you didn't know from the start that I already loved you."

All the air seemed to suck out of the car as the words Aidan said landed home. Her heart leapt to her throat and her eyes filled with tears.

"But it was so fast!" she said loudly, unable to stand the shrill sound of her own voice.

"Screw fast! Who cares that it was fast? Anna, this isn't high school. It's not college. There's not a time limit on something like this," he said, knuckles white on the steering wheel.

"We've known each other all our lives. Our families already love each other. We somehow ended up back in our hole-in-the-wall town," Aidan said, his voice getting calmer. "Anna, all the hard stuff is already sorted out."

Anna let his words reverberate around the cab of his truck while she tried to get a handle on her feelings. She dug around in her purse for a tissue as quiet sobs escaped her against her own will.

Anna quickly wiped her tears and held up a hand. "I

don't want to argue right now. We just got really, really good news," she said, turning toward him. "We got to see our baby. He or she is healthy. Can't we just soak that in for a few hours?"

"That's all you have to say?" he asked, the hurt palpable.

"I need to think," Anna answered.

"Okay," he said in utter disbelief. He had just said that he loved her, and that he loved her from the start and she needed time to think.

She stared out the passenger side window, wiping tears from her eyes. She was so tired of tears. Anna didn't know whether to chalk them up to heartache or hormones, but she was drained from crying.

They drove in silence for an hour, and Aidan parked in her mother's driveway. He turned off the ignition and she threw open her door. He walked behind her, and placed his hand on her shoulder as she dug in her purse for her keys.

"Hey," he said softly, so relieved when she turned and leaned against his chest as he folded her into his arms.

"I don't want it to be like this," she said quietly. "It's not supposed to go like this."

He cradled her head in his hands and said against her ear, "I know, honey, me neither." He stood holding her there until the dog made so much noise that they could hear either Eadie or Aunt Ruthie walking toward the door.

Former Marine or not, Aidan didn't want to look into either elderly lady's face when they saw Anna had been crying. He quickly touched his lips to hers and walked back to his truck. Anna wiped her face one last time and put a fake half smile on her face in time for her aunt to open the door.

"Well?" she exclaimed loudly, "Are you having a girl or a boy?"

In answer, Anna raised her hands and shrugged. "We're waiting to find out."

"Well, I'll be," Aunt Ruthie said as her face fell. "Eadie, get a load of this…" she said, closing the door as Anna stepped inside, muttering under her breath about her niece moving to Colorado and coming back a hippy.

As the bathtub filled, Anna dumped extra squirts of bubble bath in, figuring if she couldn't make the water as hot as she normally liked it, she'd at least have it smell and feel amazing. Her phone chirped beside her, jolting her from her daydream state at the sight of Aidan's name.

"Hello?" she asked, her stomach suddenly in knots.

"Hey, Anna, I'm sorry things got so heated today," Aidan said.

She wasn't sure how to feel about how badly she needed to hear those words. Anna was almost tearfully exhausted after the emotional roller coaster of the day. She paused before answering and tried to decide what she even wanted to say.

"Anna, are you there?"

She sighed. "Yes, sorry. I'm so danged tired tonight." She

stifled a groan as she slid into the water. She propped her feet up on the edge of the tub, and she leaned her head back. "I'm sorry, too. The last thing I want to do is fight anymore. Can we put this day behind us?" she asked, closing her eyes and letting her hand rest on her belly.

"I think we should," he answered, then added, "all but the part about that baby. I can't believe something so small could make me feel something so huge," he said, laughing at his own comment. "I mean, I know that sounds so stupid, but my God, there it was, little heart pounding, little arms and legs moving. It was incredible."

Anna loved hearing the excitement in his voice. It was the first time she felt like he was really on board with this baby.

"I know, and that sweet little head. It almost makes me sad that we have to wait so long to meet him or her."

"Yeah, I get it, but there's so much to do still, right?" he said. "Good grief, where are we going to find that many yellow and green outfits?" he asked, genuinely puzzled.

"Easy, tiger," she said laughing at his eagerness. "We can pick out the basics, the rest can be purchased in December when he or she is born."

"Oh," he said, and almost sounded a little deflated.

"My family's going to go nuts probably, especially if the baby is a girl. With Jesse's three boys, we've had blue out the wazoo for years. My mom would probably swoon if she got to buy something pink," said Anna.

"Mine's had their fair share of both, I guess," Aidan said

thinking back to his bevy of cousins. "I just can't believe it's me that's finally getting to have a child."

"I didn't know that was even on your radar for now," Anna replied, wondering what other secrets he had.

"Well, it wasn't really on my radar, but I was starting to think it might not happen. I'm getting a little long in the tooth to have not settled down just yet," he said, then tacked on, "in case you haven't noticed."

"Oh I've noticed." She laughed.

"Well, back to why I called," he said, clearing his throat. "Would you want to go on a hike or something with me tomorrow? You could even bring Harry," he said.

"Sure, the weather's supposed to be nice," Anna said. "That's one thing about living with two older women. You always, always know what the weather's supposed to be."

"Yeah, I can see that," he said with a chuckle in his voice. "How about this, I pick you up around eight o'clock before it gets too hot. You can pick where we go. Sound good?"

"Sounds good. I'll be up and at 'em."

"Okay, see you then," Aidan said, disconnecting the call.

Anna laid her phone down on the sink and sank back down into her bubbles, content as she could be. Harry wagged his tail as he sat on the mat waiting for Anna to get out of the tub.

"Harry, you're too much for words sometimes, buddy," she said as he wagged his tail harder. "Were you listening in on my phone call?" Sometimes she thought he smiled.

# Nineteen

DRESSED IN A TANK TOP and shorts, hiking boots and her favorite button down shirt to deflect the sun and hopefully ticks in the deep woods, Anna waited on the porch steps with a very excited dog. If a person so much as put their hand near the leash while wearing shoes, Harry was on cloud nine and wasn't afraid to show it. Eadie and Ruthie sat on the porch swing enjoying their coffee.

"Did you put on your sunscreen?" Eadie asked, mentally running through the list of things to do/pack/be afraid of while exploring the great outdoors.

"Yes, ma'am, I even brought some with me in my bag," Anna answered, wondering which supply she'd ask about next.

"How about water?" Eadie said, earning a sideways look from Ruthie.

"Yes, Mom. I have a few extra bottles, as well as tissues, Tylenol, and hand sanitizer," said Anna, smiling over at her mom while tossing a tennis ball to Harry.

"Well, what about –" Eadie started, only to be interrupted by Ruthie.

"Well, what about a condom?" Ruthie yelled, cackling at her own joke.

Anna put her head in her hands. "That ship has sailed, Aunt Ruthie," she said laughing.

Eadie glared at her sister. "I was going to ask about first aid supplies," she said, looking annoyed instead of amused.

"Oh, come on now, Eadie," Ruthie said, giving her sister's knee a light slap. Ruthie looked over at Anna and bugged her eyes out. Eadie's sense of humor still wasn't back up to snuff, but she was certainly making progress.

Just then a truck engine announced Aidan's arrival. He parked in their driveway and intercepted Harry with a few good rubs behind the ears.

"Morning, ladies," he said, holding out his hand to help Anna up from her seat.

"Morning, Aidan," Eadie said, pulling him into a big hug. "I can't believe we're going to have a baby!" she said, smiling for the first time that morning.

"Yes, ma'am," he said, his eyes crinkling at the edges in the way that made Anna's heart flutter a little faster.

He certainly was a handsome thing, Anna thought, letting her eyes drift down from his light brown eyes to his wide shoulders and strong legs. Anna felt a little shiver as he reached back for her hand after telling Eadie and Ruthie to have a nice day.

Anna turned back to the ladies and waggled her eyebrows at them a bit, not missing the smiles on their faces. She could see the wheels turning as Eadie and Ruthie simultaneously mentally planned their "real" wedding. Tulle, as far as the eye could see.

She snorted a little as he started to shut her door.

"What are you laughing about?"

"I get a kick out of those two," she said, not quite ready to make light about their failure of a first wedding ceremony.

"They're a pair," he said.

When he climbed into his side of the truck, Anna told him what Ruthie had said about the condom and he actually laughed. She could hear that sound every day of her life and not get tired of it.

"Where to?" he asked as he pulled into the gas station to fill up.

"How about Copper Creek?" she answered, settling Harry back into the second seat in the cab. He kept trying to slowly sneak his way into the front seat like maybe she wouldn't notice a 60+ pound dog sitting in her lap.

"Sounds good to me, I haven't been there in ages," he answered. "Want me to get you anything from inside?"

"Nah, I'm set," she answered, her bottle of water by her side as always.

He fired up the truck and set out toward the southeast end of town.

ANNA LET HER HEAD drift back to the seat as she looked out at the fields as they drove. Green soybean fields and high tasseled corn fields, coupled with the breeze whipping through the cab of the truck, made Anna feel a surge of something in her stomach that felt a lot like nostalgia and happiness at being home. She put her hand to her stomach absentmindedly and enjoyed the view.

"Are you okay?" Aidan asked, putting his hand on hers.

"Yeah, just happy to be home. It's been a long time since I've seen so many corn fields," she answered, smiling.

He nodded, looking relieved.

"They have farms there too, of course, but none that I saw that rivaled this," she said, looking back over the view. "I miss the mountain scenery, but I love this too. Dad used to pull over on this road and let me and Jesse take turns driving. It made mom a nervous wreck, but we loved it."

"That's one thing my parents didn't do," he said, "but then again there were five of us. We'd have never got where we were going if we all had a turn."

Anna laughed thinking of all the Doherty kids piled in their station wagon.

"Man I loved riding in that wagon," she said. Your mom always stuck me and Sorcha in the rear-facing back seat. We always pretended we were riding a train."

"I can't blame mom for that, you two were wild back then. She probably did that so she didn't have to listen to the chattering."

"You're probably right. You know, I think you are because she sure switched us to the bench seat behind her when we were in high school, probably listening extra close then."

"Probably so. I always thought Mom walked the fine line between being in awe of Sorcha's personality and in fear of it."

"Might be onto something there, although I was always pretty sure Cathleen could take Sorcha in a red hot minute."

"Yeah," he said, turning off into the parking lot of the park, "where do you think she got the temper from?"

Anna stepped out of the truck as Aidan rounded it, pulling a backpack out of the bed of his truck.

"What've you got there?"

"Just some supplies if we need them," he answered, shrugging.

"Good, my mom asked me a hundred questions about what I was bringing," she laughed, "maybe you have whatever I forgot."

"I've got it covered," he said, reaching his hand out to Anna.

She slipped her hand into his and they walked together to the mouth of the trail. The sun was shining but it wasn't oppressively hot yet. Anna was thankful for the early start. She loved the outdoors but liked to limit her sweat sessions to her runs.

THEY ENJOYED THE rays of the sun peeking through the

leaves, talking when it suited them and enjoying the sound of the forest around them when they didn't. Anna tried not to compare Aidan with Travis, but she couldn't help noticing she felt comfortable in his silence where she always felt she had to fill the air with conversation with Travis.

The sound of the creek met their ears before they could see it. Anna felt instantly relaxed. The combination of the lightly rushing water and sunshine on her skin took her back to her youth. She looked over to Aidan to see him smiling, watching her.

"You really love this place, don't you?"

"I do, it's one of my happy places," she said, finding a rock to sit on as she removed her boots and dipped her feet in the water.

"Ah, we're going full Monty here, huh?" he asked, removing his shoes as well.

"Not quite, just the shoes. Go big, or go home, right?"

Something changed in his eyes when she said that, but she wasn't sure what. His mask had slipped for just a second and she wasn't sure whether to question it. They were finally having such a nice time; she didn't want to ruin it. Making a mental note to ask later, she reached for his hand as she stepped into the cool water.

Aidan stepped in behind her, broadly smiling as he wiggled his toes in the clear water. "As many times as I've been here, I've never actually gotten in the water."

"When did you come here?" she asked, walking in little circles, enjoying the moment. Harry splashed around them in big circles, submerging himself as much as he could.

"We used to camp out here a lot in high school," he said, following her path. "There would be half a dozen of us all with our beat up trucks and tents. We mainly just made a fire and drank as much cheap beer as we could hold.

"Drinking in high school? Underage? Shame, shame," she fake-scolded.

"I know, I know, so rebellious. Don't try to act like you didn't get your fill of – what was it back then? That cheap strawberry wine?" he asked, eyebrows raised high.

"Ugh, yes!" she said, scrunching up her nose at the thought of the cheap wine and red plastic cups from days gone by. Just the mention of that made her involuntarily put her hand to her stomach, remembering silly times and next-day hangovers.

Aidan caught her action and a half smile lit his face. He stood behind Anna and wrapped his arms around her, placing his hand beside hers on her stomach, the other around her chest. He held her close for a few moments, just drinking it all in.

Anna shut her eyes and leaned her head back against his chest. This was much more like what she had hoped her time with him would be like. Relaxation flooded her senses until she felt him go completely rigid.

"What? What's wrong?" she asked as she turned to look up at him.

Without even an answer, Aidan jerked her up into the air and carried her like a baby as he ran for the creek bank.

Harry barked and chased them out of the water, raising nine kinds of heck.

"Aidan! What the hell is going on?" she asked, alarmed.

"Water Moccasin," he panted, as they both started fumbling with their socks and shoes. "Big son of a bitch! Get your shoes on and let's move!"

"Right behind you!" Anna couldn't help but get tickled once they were away from the snake. "How in the world did you pick me up and run like that?" she said, amazed at his agility for a big dude.

"Grace of God, I guess," he said, ducking her fake slap. "You might be pregnant, but you're still little, for now," he joked, not evading her swat on his arm.

"Yeah, just wait. Who knows what this Little Bean is going to do to me," she said. "It'll be worth it though."

"Absolutely," he answered, holding his hand out to her. They walked up the path with Harry circling around them and entered a clearing. Just off the bank of the creek, a bit down the way from the snake incident, sat a modest little country church. The white paint had faded in places, and a window was broken out, but other than that the old church dripped with charm.

Anna walked to the door and gave it a tug, but it was locked. They circled the building to peek into the broken window and found their view inside. Sunlight streamed through the windows on the far side, and the pews were still intact. Leaves were all over the floor and a variety of critters had no doubt found a home there. Dust motes filled the air, and Anna decided that old church was one of the most romantic places she'd ever seen. She stepped back and looked at the little parking lot and the cemetery off to the side.

"Would it be morbid to walk through the cemetery?"

"I don't think so. These old stones probably don't get many visitors."

They walked holding hands, sharing surprise at the early dates on the tombstones, and commenting sadly on the many stones of children. Life would've been so much harder back when these folks were making their life out in such a rural setting. Anna was very thankful to be living in the time she was born.

"I can't imagine having to rough it like these people did. I don't think I'd be able to live without my creature comforts."

"Yeah, it would've been completely different back then. It's something else when you're out in the middle of nowhere with a pack of gear to live off of.

"Did you have to live like that when you were in the service?"

"Yeah, there were some times when I thought I'd never get the sand out of my... there was lots of sand," he said, smiling at her laughter. Anna looped her arm through his.

"None of that for me, please," she said, "unless it's a vacation. Then, I can deal with the sand in the nooks and crannies."

"Agreed. None of that for me anymore either, I've traded it for coal dust." Anna patted his arm and gave him a little squeeze. "So what was it like in the desert?"

"Well, the closest I can come to explaining it is this. Preheat your oven to 400 degrees. When it gets there, open the door and put your head in it. And imagine walking in sand."

Anna couldn't even respond except to feel immense pride in Aidan and men like him. They shared a smile, hers forced and his obligatory. He didn't talk much about those times for a reason.

"You know that there are people who live out in the boonies though, right? Survivalists?"

Anna stopped in her tracks. "Are you serious? In our area?"

"Absolutely. They live way up in the hills and rarely come out. I've only ever encountered a few of them. When Benji came up to visit once we took a couple of packs, drove up as far as we could go on one of the trails and hiked to see what we could see. They grow their own food, don't get down out of the hills much and, as a rule, are pretty freaking scary.

"Hmm." Anna acted like she was truly pondering the lifestyle. "Nope, couldn't do it," she said, picking her way up the path. "I'm going to admit something to you that probably could've gotten my Denver Resident Passport revoked."

Aidan looked up at her with a smile on his face before she even finished her sentence. He believed he had been justified in his reaction to the news of their baby, but he felt horrible for the way it had unfolded. He was glad to see her joking again, and dang if she didn't look pretty with the sun shining on her red-blond hair.

She stopped walking and put her hand on his arm in mock seriousness. "I like hiking," she said, throwing a look over both shoulders and conspiratorially whispered, "but I hate camping." Anna scrunched up her eyes like she was too afraid to see his reaction. When she opened her eyes, she was taken aback at his expression. Aidan was grinning at her, his light brown eyes warm and soft.

He stepped around to face her, put his hands on the tops of her shoulders, and slowly pulled her close. His hand wrapped around to the base of her neck, the other cradling her face, and he kissed her tenderly. Anna felt momentarily lost with the sensation of his hands and lips on her body, enjoying feeling small against him. The sounds of the birds and bugs doing their thing in the woods only enhanced the moment.

Aidan grew bolder in his kiss, his hand trailing down to the base of her spine, molding her against him. Anna felt herself melting, awakening to him and felt for a minute as if they were the only people in the world, until of course, they weren't. Aidan stepped back from her and pulled her his direction off of the path as an older couple walked by with matching walking sticks. The woman in front had a very dour expression, while the older man turned and flashed Aidan a thumbs up.

He laughed as he leaned his forehead against Anna's, then they started back on the path holding hands. The rest of the afternoon was comfortable, and the drive home casual and quiet. Anna admonished herself for feeling butterflies as they neared her driveway. Their child grew in her stomach, shouldn't she be past the stage?

Aidan walked Anna to the door of her house and felt a little like they were teenagers again.

"I feel like I need to be watching out for your mom to come around the corner or something," he said, looking over her shoulder to see if Eadie was staring out the front door.

"I know," she said, "I look forward to getting my own place, but I need to make sure the new job works out first."

"Makes sense. Tomorrow's the first day, right?"

Anna nodded. "Yes, I'm a little nervous. It's been a long time since I've done anything outside of teaching Kindergarten."

"Just don't try to tie the boss' shoe or correct his spelling and you'll be fine," he said with a smile. He kissed her and she let herself wish for a minute that things had been different. They could've gone back to his house and made love all afternoon if she hadn't insisted on keeping their baby a secret, part of her argued.

# Twenty

THE BUZZING ALARM announced Monday's arrival and jarred Anna out of a deep sleep. Her resulting growl earned a large, dog-sized sigh from Harry, happily cuddled in his dog bed. Anna had hoped to jump back into her 5 AM wake-up schedule so that she would have plenty of time to get ready and settle her nerves a bit before her first day at work.

Taking into consideration the advice from her interview, Anna dressed in dark colors. She packed her lunch, did a weird little 'you can do this' pep talk on the first half of the drive and blared Mumford and Sons for the remainder of the drive. Though it would probably stink in the wintertime, she enjoyed the trip through the country on the hot, summer day. There were soy and corn fields all around her, and the hills looked a rolling, green backdrop against the clear blue sky. The drive only took fifteen minutes and Anna decided she could totally handle working around a bunch of men. *She was used to Kindergarteners, how different could it be?* she asked herself, hoping against hope that the first day went well.

THE FIRST DAY was mainly a tour. The HR Manager, Mr. Darby, had her spend the first few hours going over the benefits package and signing forms. The pay was decent, the hours were good and the benefits were terrific.

She met Mr. Roberts for the first time and decided she'd suspend judgement on him. He had been a coal miner since he was in his twenties. He was charming, but Anna also had the sense he could rip someone a new one in the blink of an eye. She didn't have to interact with him much, and usually Anna wasn't really the type to provoke people anyway. That was more Jesse's forte.

Within a few days, Anna had been introduced to the other admin staff and she was beginning to learn what she'd actually be doing for a living. She familiarized herself with reports and settled into her routine. It wasn't long before Anna realized that she actually really liked her job. It was a world apart from teaching and being responsible for 20+ little people every minute of the workday. She still had responsibilities, but found a certain amount of peace that went with not having to speak aloud every minute of the day. She was isolated in the front office and found she could even play any kind of music that she liked. It was like an oasis covered in coal dust and men.

For the most part the men were friendly. When they came in the office they dealt with her for whatever it was they needed. She booked appointments with Mr. Darby as well as handed out and explained, to the extent she was able, the different types of forms they needed to complete. If there was anything the HR department was not lacking, it was forms. She quickly adapted to the routine of the job and though it wasn't her calling the way teaching was, she liked the work and the time passed quickly.

As THE SEASONS changed and colored their beautiful surroundings with the shades of summer and eventually fall, Anna and Aidan cycled through their own seasons. They dated, dreamed of a future together, fought over idiotic things and moved backward to step one. Jesse had remarked more than once that Anna and Aidan deserved each other. Anna's hormones were all over the board and he seemed to keep a marginal amount of control over his smart mouth. When he pushed, she pushed back and they imploded. Eventually Anna would miss him and he would do something sweet, and the cycle would repeat itself.

One lazy October weekend afternoon Aidan stepped out of the shower and slung a towel around his waist. He tiptoed into the bedroom to find Anna asleep. She dozed on the bed, laying on her side with her hair spread around her head like a coppery-blonde halo. He crawled in beside her and watched her sleep. Aidan hadn't completely forgiven her for keeping their baby a secret, but he wanted to.

He burrowed under the covers, and Anna instinctively moved closer. Her eyes flickered open and a smile crinkled the corners of her eyes. They had been together a few times over the last few months, but every time it got really good, one of them said something to set the other one off. Aidan knew in his heart that he loved Anna, and what he thought was screwing them up was that she had another safe place to land. He knew once she was 100% in the relationship, that they'd find a way to work it out without Anna running back to her own turf each time they disagreed. He just had to get her there.

Aidan touched the hand curled up under her cheek. He lazily stroked her skin, enjoying the way she watched his face while he touched her. Aidan traced her arm up to her shoulder and across her collarbone. He could see her pulse flickering in her neck and wanted to taste that spot.

Anna's eyes closed as his lips found her skin. She reveled in his touch and his warmth, admiring his ability to make her feel so safe and loved. Aidan was real, her protector, her lover and refuge. She moved to her back as his hands roamed and caressed her. He brought his face back to hers, his kiss gentle. Anna smiled in response as she felt his lips shape into a smile and his hands moved over her belly. There was no way to not be somewhat amused when you look like you swallowed a basketball. He quickly switched gears though, moving around to cup her rear. He deepened his kiss as Anna responded in kind. Her breathing quickened and her hands moved across his broad shoulders and strong arms. He moved against her as she explored his back with her hands. Every day they weren't together, she wanted him more.

# Twenty-One

ANNA SAT AT HER DESK, changing her desk calendar to November and counted out the weeks till Christmas. She usually did all her shopping online and early, but this year had been so busy, she thought, absentmindedly rubbing her lower back. She was trying to decide if she wanted to answer emails or voicemails before sorting through invoices when George, one of the surface miners, came flying through the door.

He had his phone up to his ear when the door slammed.

"Yeah, we've got at least one pinned, maybe two, they're trying to get them untangled and onto the stretcher" he said, walking quickly through the office to the superintendent's office.

Anna's heart lurched into her throat and was on George's heels, Mr. Darby, the HR Manager close behind.

"Go ahead, we'll do our best to get him out quickly" he said, hanging up the phone as Mr. Darby started firing questions. Mr. Roberts, the superintendent, interrupted him with his own questions.

"What have we got, George?" Mr. Roberts said, his lips set in a hard line.

"Two guys down, one a roof bolter. Had a big rock fall, so far just two pinned. There's a helicopter on the way from Robertsville and the guys are working to get them out," George said, already shifting on his feet to head back in the direction of the door, "one of them is James."

Mr. Roberts nodded, grabbing his phone and starting behind George, Mr. Darby right behind him. "Aidan," she whispered. "Aidan is underground," she said, fear choking her throat. Anna didn't feel herself hit the floor, and for a second couldn't feel anything. The next thing she was aware of was a huge weight that seemed to press on her chest and her belly. She couldn't breathe and was so afraid that she couldn't get a grip on her thoughts. She took jerky little breaths and knew she needed to calm down. There was nothing she could do for him if she gave in to a full-fledged panic attack. She eased herself into a sitting position but didn't move from the floor.

John, one of the miners, came flying in the office to get a folder from the superintendent's office. He looked to his left and saw her on the floor.

John dropped down to his knee and knelt beside her, "Anna, are you okay?"

She didn't realize she was crying till she heard herself choke out the words, "Okay, I'm okay."

"You don't look okay. Want up?" John asked, as he put an arm around her back to help hoist her up at her nod.

"Who's hurt?" she asked, as soon as she was in her chair, her words barely understandable.

John knew she and Aidan had been involved and that she was very pregnant. He wished he could've eased her mind, but they hadn't said who was pinned. "I'm not sure who is still hung up down there, but they're bringing Evan up on a stretcher now," he said, unprepared for Anna's howl.

She hadn't even thought about Evan. She felt so horribly selfish. *What would Sorcha do if he was hurt or killed?* John's eyes bugged out, he grabbed her in a hug then ran out the door with the folder for the Super. Anna heard him yell, "Someone needs to get in here, Anna's shook up."

She felt a pain shoot through her belly and clenched her muscles against it. A groan escaped her as she clutched her stomach. Right then Mr. Darby stuck his head inside the door.

"Oh, Jesus, Anna," he muttered, crossing the office to her desk. "Are you okay, kid?"

"I don't know," she said, wincing as another pain grabbed at her. "What do we know? Who's hurt?"

"We're still finding out. Evan's got a hurt leg, they've just got him out and are loading him up in the ambulance. We're waiting to see on the others."

The breath she'd managed to catch rushed out of her. *Oh God, please let them be okay*, Anna prayed. What would Sorcha do without Evan? What about little Clara? Anna stood up and knew something was wrong. She felt wet all of a sudden and feared that her water had just broken. She looked down and saw a dark stain spread over her pants. Anna raised her eyes to Mr. Darby's face and felt nothing short of horror at his expression.

In seconds, Darby was out of the office and coming back with one of the EMTs on his heels.

"Okay, ma'am, let's get you laid back down, feet raised, please," the man said, wadding up her coat to put beneath her feet. "What's your name please?"

"Anna Fraser."

"Anna, we're going to need to work together to answer a few questions real quick so we can figure out what's going on and get you out of here, okay?" She nodded mutely in reply as her mind swam with fear for Aidan, Evan, and now her little baby. Hot tears streaked down her face and her hands shook as she tried to stay calm.

"My name is Mike and I'm going to help you, okay?" he asked, putting a blood pressure cuff on her arm. Anna nodded. "Alright, Anna, your blood pressure is good. How old are you?"

"Thirty."

Checking her pulse, he continued with his questions. "Is this your first pregnancy?"

The tears were streaming fast now as her mind raced with fears that the baby wouldn't make it. "First, I'm 32 weeks, 32 and a half today," she said, fighting to keep her voice from quivering.

"Alright, have you been having any problems before now?"

"Not one," she said, doubling over as another cramp seized her body.

"How far apart are your contractions, Anna?" Mike asked as Mr. Darby nervously paced the office.

"I haven't been watching them, I didn't think to look," she answered, eyes wild.

"15 minutes," Mr. Darby answered. "They're 15 minutes apart."

Anna's eyes were huge as she looked into Mr. Darby's face. He smiled a fatherly smile and continued to pace.

"That's good, thank you, sir. Okay, Anna, I need to get you straight to Robertsville. I need to step outside here and get your ride arranged."

He stepped in the next office and shut the door. Anna overheard him say that she was in labor and needed the next ambulance headed to Robertsville. She knew then that the baby must be coming without any hope of stopping labor. Robertsville was the closest hospital with a NICU. Thankfully it's where she had hoped to have the baby in several months with Dr. Han. As quickly as he left, Mike was back.

"Anna, we're going to need to get you on the next ambulance to Robertsville," he said, giving her hand a little reassuring squeeze. "Is there someone we can call to meet you there?"

She nodded. "My mother and my sister. Mr. Darby, take

my phone and call Jesse please. She can get my mom and meet me there."

Mr. Darby was happy to be of use. "I'll call her right now, then I need to get outside to see what's going on with the men. Will that be okay?" he asked both Mike and Anna. In response to their nods, he grabbed Anna's hand, gave it a quick squeeze and stepped into the side office.

Anna listened to his voice, muted by the closed door. Anna's head was spinning. She knew she had to stay calm for the baby, that the more she cried, the less she was able to focus, but she was just so scared. She was scared for the baby, for Aidan, for Evan, for the rest of them. Regret washed over her and she thought about the time she had wasted with Aidan by keeping their baby a secret.

Mr. Darby stepped back out of the office and put Anna's phone back in her purse. "Your sister is on her way to get your mother. They'll be in Robertsville as soon as they can.

"Mr. Darby, you've got to find Aidan and tell him what's going on," she said, her eyes wild. "He's got to know!" she sobbed, not believing this was happening. *This wasn't how it was supposed to be*, she thought, trying to control her tears.

A second EMT came in to help get Anna on a gurney, and Mike started her IV. With a nod he said, "Mr. Darby, we've got Anna from here. Thank you for your help."

Mr. Darby handed Mike Anna's bag and gave her hand a squeeze. "You're going to be okay, kiddo. I'll tell Aidan when I find him and I'll check in with you once I get to the hospital, if I can."

Tears streaked down her face as she nodded, so thankful to work with such a kind man. She stared up at the sky, afraid to look around as her gurney was taken outside. She was afraid to listen to the sirens of the police cars and ambulances as they arrived at the mine. Anna couldn't believe this was happening. It had started off like such a normal day.

# Twenty-Two

WHEN ANNA WAS UNLOADED at the hospital, the first face she saw was a welcoming one. A very petite, very kind looking nurse was there to take care of her.

"Anna, I'm Dawn, I'm the charge nurse," she said, introducing herself as they got Anna settled in a wheelchair. How many weeks along are you? Tell me what happened today please," she asked, peppering Anna with questions as they moved her down the hall and into a room. Dawn peeled back Anna's bloody clothes as she questioned her.

Anna recited the details, "I was at my desk and one of the men ran in and said there had been a rock fall," she paused, her voice sounding foreign to her own ears. "My baby's father, my hu…" she paused, correcting herself. "My boyfriend, is underground today," her voice choking on the words. "I don't know if he's hurt. I don't know if he's alive," she sobbed.

"I'm so sorry, I need you to keep breathing nice and calm, okay?" Dawn continued to examine Anna as she listened. "What's his name please?"

"His name is Aidan Doherty. I felt my knees give out and I landed in the floor. My belly cramped and I started bleeding," she said.

"How far apart are your contractions, Anna?"

"Ten minutes apart," she answered.

Dawn nodded as the doctor entered. As Dawn explained Anna's situation, she looked into the hallway to see Jesse and her mother looking through the glass. Their presence was reassuring. At least she wasn't completely alone. She turned her attention back to the doctor.

"I'm Dr. Pearson, Anna. I see from your chart that your OB is Dr. Han, correct?"

At her nod, he continued. "Dr. Han has been called, however we're going to need to get you moving before she can get here today, alright? The first thing we're going to do is get you going on magnesium sulfate to see if we can slow these contractions down. Next, we need to give you steroid shots to help with the baby's lung development in case he or she..." At that he raised his eyebrows to see if she knew the sex of the baby. At her shrug, he continued, "decides to make an early entrance."

"But I'm only 32.5 weeks!" Anna said, fighting the acceptance that their baby was coming today.

"We'll do what we can to extend your pregnancy, but we need to figure out why you're bleeding. In the meantime, we'll do what we can to give him or her what is needed."

"She's dilated to three centimeters, Dr. Pearson," Dawn said.

"Okay, check her again in ten minutes please. We're going to do what we can to prevent delivery, Anna, but if we must deliver, we'll need to do a c-section. A vaginal delivery would be too hard on the baby right now, alright?" Anna could only nod as hot tears streaked down her face. She hated the feeling of helplessness. She always kept control, that's just who she was. Anna couldn't have been in any less control than she was right now, at the most important moment of her life. She had been so careful through every step of her pregnancy. It wasn't fair that this was happening. It wasn't part of the plan. *Nothing else had gone to plan, wasn't she allowed at least a long, healthy pregnancy?* she asked herself.

As Dawn added the magnesium sulfate to her IV two more nurses came in the room. While one gave her the steroid injections in her thighs, another worked to strap a fetal monitor on her belly. The nurse with the shots left the room, but Dawn stayed while the other nurse continued to move the monitor around. As the reason the nurse kept moving the monitor around her stomach dawned on Anna, she went completely still. Dawn moved to her bedside and held her hand. Anna started to shake from the sheer overload of fear, but she didn't make a sound. The other nurse continued to move the monitor slowly around. Three sets of eyes were glued to the heart monitor. Suddenly, the line jerked and started a rapid pattern. All three women exhaled with relief. Anna couldn't hold her emotions in any longer. The fear and shock from the day erupted from her body at once.

Dawn leaned down right into Anna's face. "Listen honey, I know you're scared right now, but you have got to get ahold of yourself. You can fall apart once this is all over, but your baby needs you to put that on hold right now. I've called down to the ER and a friend of mine is going to call once she finds out the situation with the baby's father."

"Okay," Anna answered. "Okay." Anna risked a look out through the windows at her mother and Jesse. She tried to smile but couldn't.

"We're going to check you again in a few minutes to see if you're dilated any more, Anna. If you'd like, I can let your mother and sister in briefly. Is that alright?"

At Anna's nod, Dawn left the room and spoke quickly to Eadie and Jesse. They entered the room and embraced Anna together.

"Oh, Anna, I am so sorry, sweetie. You have to be so scared," Eadie said, placing a kiss on Anna's forehead.

"Mom, you can't be nice to me right now. I swear to God if someone is nice to me right now I'm going to start crying and won't stop," she said, wincing as another contraction passed over her.

"I know, kid, I'm the same way when I'm upset." Eadie nodded.

Anna could hardly make eye contact with Jesse. They

knew each other too well. Jesse couldn't hide her fear from Anna, and she certainly couldn't lie about the direness of the situation, and Anna didn't want to read it in her face.

"Have either of you heard any updates on the accident? Do we know if Aidan's okay?" Anna asked, not missing Eadie's eyes jerk to Jesse's. "What? Tell me!"

"Aidan's okay, Anna. There was a rock fall where they were working and a few of the men were injured. Aidan has a few pretty deep cuts on his arm and face and is downstairs getting stitches right now. He's going to be sore, but other than that he's fine," she said, patting Anna's arm as she sighed with deep relief. "Evan was hit hard on the leg and is having surgery right now. He's going to be fine, Sis."

"Thank God," Anna cried. "I have been so scared wondering about them."

"They had to bring Evan out on a stretcher, and brought him in an ambulance. Aidan rode along but wasn't happy about it. It turns out he's not a very good patient," Eadie said.

Anna couldn't help but laugh, having no problem imagining Aidan being a jerk, given their recent exchanges. Relieved by the attitude in the room, Dawn smiled as she reentered the room. "It sounds like your sources are faster than mine. All good with Aidan?" she asked. Pleased with the report she said, "Anna, I need to check you again, ladies, you can stay in the room, if it's okay with Anna," she said, waiting for Anna's nod.

"That's fine, thanks."

Anna stared up at the ceiling, relief rushing over her that

Aidan and hopefully Evan would be okay. Now to try and keep the baby from coming.

"Anna, you're dilated to six centimeters right now. The magnesium isn't helping. I've got orders for you to get your epidural if you progressed to a six, so we need to do this now, alright? One of you can stay to hold her hand, but the other needs to leave the room please," Dawn said, removing her gloves and heading back to the station to notify the doctor.

Anna held out her hand to her mother and Jesse gave Anna a quick kiss on the cheek. "You're going to be fine," she whispered to her sister. "Your baby is going to be fine," Jesse said, leaving the room and walking down the hall so that her sister couldn't see her cry.

Eadie held tightly to Anna's hand throughout the waiting period for the anesthesiologist. He introduced himself, quickly explained the process and placed the epidural within minutes. Eadie half-listened to the doctor explain how long it would take for the medicine to work. She simply sat by her daughter, smoothing the hair from her forehead every so often. Sometimes there just weren't any words to say.

Dawn entered the room and checked Anna's response to the epidural. "Alright, it's time. Go ahead and say goodbye for now, we're going to take you down to the OR," Dawn said, nodding her head toward Eadie.

Eadie leaned close to Anna. "I love you, Anna. You're going to be just fine," she said as she patted Anna's belly.

Anna was wheeled out and prayed harder than she ever had in her life for the safety of their baby. She fought back the thoughts of how the day was going nothing like her plan. She had counted on having a full nine months to grow this baby, to have it with Aidan by her side. She stopped herself then, she had to focus on thankfulness that Aidan and Evan were safe. *One thing at a time, Anna,* she told herself.

She was transferred onto the operating table, surprised by the amount of people in the room. Her nurse introduced her to a few of the doctors as a courtesy, but their names went in and out of her mind. A thermometer strip was stuck to her forehead as her nurse reminded her that in recovery she would probably get the shakes, but that it was a side effect of the magnesium. Anna had heard that earlier but didn't think much of it. A curtain was between her and the doctors except for the anesthesiologist who sat near her head.

A tugging sensation could be felt, but no pain. Anna let her head drift to the side where she saw two nurses positioned beside a portable incubator. She didn't dream there were more tears left in her body, but she felt them anyway. How she wished Aidan could be beside her right now. He always made her feel strong, except when he was making her infuriated.

The doctor stepped toward Anna with a tiny, red-skinned little baby, and offered its head to her lips. "Meet your son, Anna," he said, as the smallest little head was pressed to her skin. "We need to get him cleaned up and checked now," the doctor said, just as fast.

She stared as she felt her body being moved around, knowing her placenta was being removed and her body stitched back together. Mutely, she stared at the nurses as they suctioned her son. Her son! She had a son. She hadn't even decided on a name yet, and here he was. *Dear God, let him live. Let him be healthy*, she prayed to herself. The nurses had wiped down his little body and the doctor intubated him right there in the room. Anna could barely breathe as she watched all this happen in a haze. She noticed her arms shaking and felt a nurse put a warm blanket on her arms and chest.

"It's okay, honey. It's just the medicine," she said, trying to comfort Anna when nothing but a healthy baby would make her feel comforted ever again.

"We're going to take your son to the NICU now, you're going to be moved to recovery in a little while, and then we'll take you up to see him after, alright?" the doctor explained.

Waves of sadness washed over Anna as the nurses quickly wheeled her son out of the room. All the terror she had experienced over the last several hours poured from her body. Anna had tried to keep it in as long as she could, and all she could say were the words *I'm sorry*. She was sorry for crying, sorry to the baby for having him early, sorry for the time she wasted with Aidan. Sorry that she didn't even have a name for her son yet.

A nurse patted her shoulder. "Let it out, Anna, it's okay. You've been doing your best to keep it in, just let it out," she said. Anna did. She cried until she thought didn't have any more tears left to shed. Before long, Anna was transferred to recovery and consoled by the nurse again that the shaking in her arms was completely normal. A part of her feared that despite the reassuring words, her shaking was a sign she was going to die and leave that poor little nameless baby without a mother.

Eadie and Jesse were allowed into the room and sat with her as she tried to compose herself. There weren't many words to say as they waited to learn more about the baby. Anna stared at the ceiling, trying to reign in the fearful thoughts that raced through her mind. Would the baby live? Could babies born so early be healthy? She fought hard to not even give voice to the terrors that threatened to tear her to shreds. Anna tried not to compare her reality with what she had pictured the birth of her child would be like. She thought she and Aidan would be together. Her plans included that she would carry to full term and be big as a whale, ready to have the baby and groaning about being miserable like so many of her friends had done. In her mind she had envisioned a birthing experience like some kind of TV movie where the mother strained and struggled, and eventually her reward would be a gunky, gorgeous baby, placed on her chest as it peeked out and wailed a big lusty cry.

Instead, she had an emergency c-section all alone, where she barely saw her nameless child before he was taken away. Deep down she knew she should focus on the blessings. Aidan was alive. She had made it to the hospital. Her son had been delivered in a hospital with neonatologists and a NICU. She didn't mean to be pitiful or obnoxious, but she knew she had a right to be sad, and a reason to be thankful.

The curtain around her bed swished to the side as a nurse held it open for someone to enter. Aidan stepped through the partition and Anna caught his eye as his face transformed. His face at his first step was a forced smile, but when he saw her lying in that bed, pale and worried, something broke inside him. The regret and hurt that he had been carrying around like a sack of bricks on his shoulders dropped and vanished.

He half sat, half fell beside her, jumping as Eadie rushed forward with her hands hovering over Anna's stomach to be certain he didn't come in contact with it. "Sorry," he whispered to Eadie and Anna both.

"I'm so sorry I wasn't here," he said, emotion choking his voice.

"Aidan, your head," she said, placing her hand near his bandage that stretched from his cheek to his jaw. "Your arm," she said tearfully as her hand trailed down to a bandage from his bicep to his forearm.

"It's okay, I was so lucky." He shook his head, wanting to dismiss her worry. "Evan's going to be okay. He broke his femur which is going to be a bitch to heal, but he's going to be fine."

He pushed her hair back from her forehead and kissed her there, then kissed her lips tenderly. Eadie and Jesse stood to leave the area and give them a little privacy.

"Sis, we're going to go get some coffee and see if we can find out if Sorcha's here yet, maybe sit with her for a few minutes," Jesse said, giving Anna's hand a squeeze.

"Okay, I'll text you if anything changes and we get to see him," she said.

"Him," Aidan said, trying to smile and failing. "We have a son."

"We have a son," she said, her voice thick and strangled-sounding.

He held her as best as he was able while they cried, the fear from the day wracking their bodies. After a few minutes, Anna pulled back from him. Aidan handed her a tissue and pulled a chair closer to her bed.

"I haven't heard anything yet other than they'll take me up - take *us* up," she corrected, "as soon as it's okay for me to get out of here. Aidan, he was so red and tiny. I only saw him for a second and they had to whisk him away."

He nodded, not knowing what to say. He had very little in the way of experience with babies, having just one little niece to spoil.

A nurse entered the area to check on Anna. As she went about her tasks she gave Anna the news she so desperately wanted to hear.

"I see you've stopped shaking almost altogether. That's good, I know it's scary," she said, giving Anna's shoulder a little squeeze. "I just got the call from the NICU that your baby is stable and is on a ventilator now to breathe for him. This is not uncommon," she said quickly, seeing the panic in Anna's face.

Anna and Aidan both nodded, neither familiar with anything having to do with premature babies. "Before we go up there, I want to explain a little about what you should expect to see, alright?" she paused, waiting to see that they were soaking in the information. She did this nearly every day and knew that half of what she said was going to go in one ear and out the other. She knew they were distraught, exhausted, and totally unprepared for this.

"Your son, as you saw, is very small. He is the perfect size for his gestation; he weighs four pounds and six ounces and is nineteen inches long," she stopped, trying to read them. Once she saw she could go on, she did.

At 32.5 weeks old, he'll typically be on for a day or so before they try to wean him off to see how he tolerates oxygen. For now, he has a tube in his mouth."

They looked at each other and Aidan squeezed her hand in reassurance. Anna looked positively numb. The nurse continued, "Alright, next step. More tubes. There will be a lot of tubes and wires right now. He has a vent tube in his mouth that is breathing for him. He has an IV. He has leads on his chest to monitor his heart rate and respirations. He has a lead on his foot to monitor the amount of oxygen in his blood so that we can see how well he's oxygenated, understand?"

They nodded. *What else could they do?* The nurse thought to herself. As many years as she had been doing this job, it never got easier to tell terrified new parents what to expect. Just like she knew she'd have to look away the moment they laid eyes on their tiny child for the incubator for the first time, there's not much that can match the level of helplessness and fear than a sight like that.

"For now he's under a bright light to help lower his bilirubin levels; he's just a little jaundiced, which is common. He has what looks like a little blindfold over his eyelids to protect his eyes. This is perfectly comfortable for him. Do you both understand?" she asked, waiting for their reply.

"Yes," Anna answered, her need to see the baby nearly overwhelming her.

Aidan answered, "Yes, may we see him now?"

The nurse nodded. "I'll take you up there. The NICU is a busy place and the quarters are pretty tight. There will be other families visiting their babies, and we need to keep them in mind as well during our visit. It's a fairly intense, loud place with a lot of noises, so brace yourself against the alarms."

"I understand," Anna said, wondering how possible it was it brace yourself against what she was about to see for the first time.

She was silent as the nurse pushed her bed through the halls, Aidan walking beside her when possible and  behind them when it wasn't. Anna overheard him flag down Eadie and Jesse in the hallway.  They added to the train of people headed to the fourth floor to meet their son.

Anna's head was swimming with all the turns they were taking and all the long corridors. She wondered how she would ever make it to the NICU without someone to take her. Her sense of direction was dismal on a good day.

Aidan looked down at Anna when he could, dismayed at the transformation she had underwent. He was used to seeing her full of fire, and now she looked like a shadow of herself. She looked impossibly small and fragile. Though she was trying to be stoic on the outside, her beautiful eyes betrayed her terrible fear, like her soul was on the brink of bailing from its shell. It broke his heart to see her so afraid, and he was going to spend the rest of his life making sure she was never this afraid again.

He replayed the rock fall in his mind, the darkness and then the bright light in the area. The scenes flashed like screenshots or segments rather than the fluid experience that life really is. He heard Evan cry out when the rock hit his leg, heard the screams of the men as they reacted, then stifled, resorting to their drills and training for such an emergency. Coal mining was a dangerous job where every man was as important as any other; every job as important as any other job. It was a dangerous job, but not one to be fearful of. Aidan knew the risks, but he also knew if he had been scared to death every time he went to work, he wouldn't have gone in. After years of being a coal miner, even after the horrors of the day, he knew he'd be back when he was healed up. There was a camaraderie underground that he loved, much like that in the service.

Aidan had faced fear earlier in the day, but the pain and worry of the rock fall were a drop in the bucket compared to the moment John had told him Anna had been taken away in an ambulance, that she was having contractions. *She was only eight months along. If she delivered in the ambulance, would the baby make it? Would Anna? They were supposed to have more time*, he thought, hating himself for the arguments they'd been having over the baby. He had handled a lot in his life, not to mention the things he had witnessed in the Marines. That was a different set of feelings than what he experienced when he learned Anna and their baby were in danger.

He knew he loved her, but at that moment he knew without fail she was the only woman for him. He felt convicted about his treatment of her, his process for filtering his emotions at her idiotic decision to withhold information about the baby. He jerked his head at his own thoughts. He had to remember that she had as much right to her own feelings as he did his own. She had her reasons. He'd work on understanding that some other day. Right now the only thing that mattered was getting her well and begging God to let that baby be healthy.

As they entered the double sliding doors to the NICU, the alarms startled Aidan. The nurse had warned him, but he was still unprepared to see tiny bodies in warm incubators, so vulnerable and dependent on the attention of those around them. They circled around to the back of the room as Aidan marveled at the way the nurse glided the bed through the tight spaces. Finally, they stopped in front of their little incubator with the name Baby Boy Doherty taped to the side. *Doherty*, he thought with relief. He hadn't realized he had been afraid Anna would have not given his son his last name. *We'll straighten it all out later*, he promised himself. *Just be there for her now.*

ANNA HELD HER breath as the nurse used the antibacterial soap foam dispenser on the wall to clean her hands, as well as directed Aidan to bring enough for himself and Anna. Anna inhaled as she used the soft cleaner on her hands, knowing full-well she'd never forget that smell.

The nurse had positioned her bed as close as she could get it against the incubator. "Alright, Anna and Aidan, this is your son," she said, opening the little circle-shaped windows on the side. "Remember, his skin is very sensitive. You can touch him, but gently place your finger and don't move it around just yet," she said, watching the pair gingerly place their hands inside the incubator. The humidity wafted out from the clear plastic box as Aidan and Anna placed a fingertip to their son, tears streaming down both their faces.

"I want you to keep in mind that this is not a permanent situation. As he grows, you will be able to touch him more. This is a precaution for now to guard against over stimulating his very sensitive skin, alright, Anna? Aidan?" The nurse looked away, unable to bear the hurt on the mother's face. Next to them, another mother held her preemie daughter against her skin. Their NICU was an advocate of Kangaroo-Care, placing the baby against the chest of the mother. The skin-to-skin contact benefited the baby by stabilizing the heart rate, potentially improving the breathing pattern, oxygen saturation, and could even help with weight gain. The mother benefited by increased breast milk production and having an opportunity to bond with the baby, a healing experience that goes far in repairing the heartache that happens when things don't go according to plan. The nurse knew she needed to get the mother to her room now and let the baby rest, but this was the part she hated most. She nodded over to another nurse who was watching for her signal. The nurse came over with a digital camera.

"Hi, guys, I'm going to take a quick picture for you to take back to your room with you today, okay?" she said, Aidan and Anna taking the nonverbal cue that their time with their baby was finished for now. Anna wiped tears from her eyes as Aidan placed a kiss on her head. The nurse took the picture and closed the little doors on the incubator side. "I'll have this printed off by the time you maneuver your way back to the front door," she said with a smile and was gone. Aidan stepped to the side, and Eadie and Jesse ducked out of the way so that they could wipe the tears from their faces before seeing Anna.

"You know what this means, right?" Aidan said gently to Anna, bringing his head down level with hers.

She was so far beyond cognitive thought that she just raised her eyebrows in answer.

"We need to choose a name," he said gently.

Anna nodded, staring as hard as she could at the tiny baby boy in the incubator, soaking up every second she had with him.

Their nurse nodded to Aidan, and he, Eadie, and Jesse stepped back in a little nook so that they could follow the nurse as she pushed Anna's bed. Anna closed her eyes against the other little babies and parents, doctors and nurses. The nurse at the door handed four copies of the baby's picture to Aidan as he passed the desk. With no words and a small smile, he handed copies to Eadie and Jesse, each of them hugging him in return.

As they followed behind her, Eadie asked if he would be staying the night, or if there was anything she could get for him.

"I think I'll see that she's settled in and figure it out from there. I ought to be fine. I've got to call Mom and Dad and check in with Sorcha to see how Evan's doing. My God, what a day, huh?" he asked, his chin quivering as he looked at Eadie.

She wrapped him in the kind of hug that only a mother can offer, patting his back. No matter the difference in size between them, at that moment, she was a mother and he was a big, tired, terrified child.

"You take care of her, kid. She's going to need you," she said.

"Yes, ma'am. I'll take care of her for the rest of my life," he answered.

"Good. Good," Eadie said, pulling away and giving him a kiss on his uninjured cheek. "You try and get some rest, son, you've been through the wringer today."

"Yes ma'am," he answered dutifully. He tucked the remaining pictures inside his back pocket and followed the nurse through the door to Anna's hospital room. He looked around and noted the tiny room, the three-feet-long bench seat and the tile floor and shrugged. He'd often slept in worse conditions in the service. He wasn't going to leave her.

THE NURSE THAT had taken care of Anna from delivery to this point introduced Anna to the nurse that would be taking care of her on this floor. Maybe it was her exhaustion, but Anna disliked this woman on sight. She hated to be that way, but there was a hateful glint in this woman's eye that Anna couldn't stand.

Anna was listening to the nurse's quick list of instructions which was mainly just to rest at this point in time. As the nurse removed Anna's catheter, she explained that an aide or nurse would be in every few hours to check her vitals, and a nurse would check her dressing and massage her uterus. She was told to breathe into a contraption that would help her keep from getting pneumonia and her legs had some kind of amazing massage setting on them that would keep her from getting a blood clot.

"When do I try to pump?" Anna asked, eyeing the yellow breast pump warily.

"Right now, you just need to get some sleep," the nurse said a little harshly for Anna's liking.

"Yes, but, the sooner I pump the sooner my milk will come in, right? Can you show me how to use it?" she pleaded, surprised to be getting resistance.

"You attach the bottles to the suction cup attachment. You attach the hosing from the pump to the suction cup. She gestured across the room, it's all there together for you when you're ready. You hit the button, give it five or so minutes the first time and then you're done," she said, frustrating Anna completely.

"Great. It's perfectly clear. Thank you so much for all your helpfulness," Anna said in a tone that even surprised Aidan. The nurse shrugged and Anna said a silent prayer that she wouldn't be the one taking care of her for the uterine massage.

Eadie and Jesse came in from the hall and said their goodbyes. They said they'd be over as soon as they could the following day, and Anna was almost relieved for them to go. All she wanted was to figure out the pump to spite the nurse and dive headlong into sleep. The thought of her baby being a few floors away from her sunk her spirit like a rock to the bottom of the ocean. She may as well be on the other side of the world for all the good she could do for him.

Aidan held her face in his hands. "Anna, it's okay to rest. I'm going across the hall to refill your cup, the nurse mentioned you need to try and drink as much water as you can."

"Yeah? Well, screw her," she muttered, giving Aidan a dirty look when he chuckled. He wisely didn't look back; he flicked off the harsh overhead light and gave her a minute to herself while he refilled her water cup. Anna knew she was being hateful but she couldn't quite get herself to feel sorry about it. She closed her eyes tightly against the barren hospital room and drifted to sleep before Aidan re-entered the room.

He crept silently into the room and wasn't surprised to see Anna sleeping. He mouthed a silent prayer of thanks to God. His girl was worn out. He settled onto his seat and couldn't help but watch her. She was fiercely independent, to the point she was nearly impossible to help. Aidan couldn't imagine how he was going to teach her that he was there and for the long haul, and that he wanted to be her partner in things. He wanted to be strong for her so that sometimes she could be weak and rest in him. Other than showing up every day and chipping away at that chip on her shoulder, he wasn't sure what else to try. Thankfully, he wasn't the type to walk away from a challenge, and he knew one when he saw it.

# Twenty-Three

ANNA WOKE UP AND realized she needed to use the restroom. She hadn't stood on her own yet and was surprised to find her legs so shaky when she placed them on the ground. Anna grabbed the IV pole like the nurse had told her to do and shuffled her way to the bathroom. Her incision and the dressing felt so foreign, but not nearly as strange as her empty belly. She was able to take care of her business and decided to carefully make her way across the hall to get more water.

On her way back to her room, Anna heard the cry of a newborn in the room next to hers. Her heart suddenly filled with rage that the woman next to her was able to have her baby with her. That woman's baby probably came full-term. That baby was probably chubby and healthy and getting ready to nurse. That woman probably got to cradle her baby the minute it was born and look into its little eyes. Anna sat down on her bed and bowed her head. The mourning of her experience left her body in the form of a low moan, a horrible sound that jerked Aidan to his feet.

Anna jumped, grabbing at her incision. "Jesus, Aidan. I didn't know you were in here," she said, wiping the tears she hated to cry from her face.

"Anna, are you hurt?" he asked, frantically turning on the lights.

"Yes, I'm hurt. I hurt so much I feel like my heart is going to explode," she cried. "The woman next to us is holding her baby, probably nursing it, and ours is in a plastic box, hooked up every way he can be just to keep him alive!" Her body shook with fury and helplessness, and there was nothing she could do to hold it in.

Aidan scooted her to the side of her bed, careful not to get in the way of the IV stand. He laid down beside her and cradled her in his arms the best he could. "I'm so sorry, honey. I know this isn't how it was supposed to go. This didn't happen the way we wanted it to," he said, his head resting atop hers.

"I don't even remember what his face looks like, Aidan," she whispered, ashamed. Shouldn't she remember at least that?

Aidan reached around to his back pocket and pulled out the photo he had tucked there earlier. Her face crumpled at the sight of that sweet, pink little body, covered in leads and wires, his little shades protecting his eyes from the light.

Anna stared at the photo until she couldn't keep her eyes open any longer.

They stayed like that until nurse came in, surprised to see them both in the same bed.

"Anna, I'm Sarah, your night nurse. I need to check you out now. You're going to have to get out of here, sir, we've got work to do," she said, a wry smile on her face. "I wouldn't mind finding a man like that in my bed though," she mumbled.

The comment took Anna so much by surprise that she laughed despite herself. She liked this woman already, even though her laugh cost her tremendous pain. Sarah carefully examined Anna, administered her medicine, took her vitals, and checked her incision. Anna soon discovered there were few things in the world as awful as a uterine massage, but she took Sarah's word for it that it was necessary. Sorcha had warned her of the mesh underwear and enormous blood clots, but hadn't said a word about the god-awful massage part.

Aidan's stomach didn't turn easily, but it hurt his heart to see Anna in pain. What was worse was knowing there wasn't a single thing he could do to help her right now or to make their baby grow healthy and strong any quicker than he was able. While the nurse was finishing her exam, he walked out to the nurse's desk and asked if there were any restrictions for parents visiting the NICU. He was thankful to learn they could go whenever they liked. He knew he'd be off of work for a few days while his cuts healed, and he wanted to spend as much of that time as possible with Anna and the baby. He also found out she'd be cleared to eat soon, so he popped his head in to say he was going to search out what drive-thrus were open this time of night.

Anna was relieved that Sarah was more helpful than the other nurse when it came to introducing her to the breast pump. Thankfully Sarah had set her expectations accordingly so that Anna didn't feel totally disappointed by the result. Rest, checkup, pump, repeat were the orders for now. Food would follow soon.

Morning came fitfully, as the night was a cycle of napping and being woken up. She and Aidan feasted on burgers sometime around 4 AM and Anna wasn't sure she'd ever tasted anything as wonderful in her life. Eadie arrived as Aidan and Anna were getting ready to visit the NICU. Thankfully, she came bearing gifts of clean clothes and house shoes.

"Thanks, Mom. I feel so gross," Anna said, thrilled to be changing clothes.

"Good, honey, that's part of the transformation," Eadie said, a smile in her voice.

At Anna's glare, she shrugged. "Face it, kid, social media lies. There's not much about this first part that will be glamorous at all. The first few months you'll be worried out of your mind. Then comes the puke and poop. Then the snot and drool," she said with a shrug. "But then, it gets better."

"I'll feel better when we get to the puke and poop stage. I'd like to bypass the worry stage."

"Oh, sweetie, that's the one part that never ends," Eadie said quietly. They wheeled Anna to the NICU in a nervous little train. They were given the rundown by one of the nurses that included instructions on hand washing and gentle reminders that the baby couldn't be rubbed yet, just a light fingertip placed on his body.

Though it was killing Eadie not to get in and see the baby as much as she liked, she took a quick look and settled into a chair to the side to give the nervous new parents a chance to stare at that precious little son of theirs. She took out her crochet hook and yarn and set about making a little blue and white cap for her new grandson. She made plans to make many more as she looked around at all the other little ones in their incubators and open top cribs. So much fear and sadness in the world, she thought, wiping a quick tear and wishing Walt were here beside her.

Aidan and Anna were on their own planet, leaning down to look in their baby's humidity-rich bed.

"We need to choose a name," Anna said, giving Aidan a small smile. "I thought we had more time, so I hadn't narrowed it down just yet."

"Which ones do you like so far? Maybe we can make a list," he said, looking at his tiny son, with his preemie-sized diaper folded over in order to fit his body.

"I don't really want to get too crazy with it," she said, "something easy to spell correctly would be good, I think."

"Right, and something where he can find stuff with his name on it," Aidan said seriously.

Anna quirked an eyebrow at him, waiting for more information.

"In my family our names are all pretty unusual, or at least they were growing up. I don't think one of us ever got to waltz into one of those souvenir junk shops and find a bicycle license plate with our name on it as kids," he said in a near-biting tone. "There weren't a whole lot of Aidan, Sorcha, Lochlan, Finn and Cora's running around in the 80s, you know?" He laughed.

"Okay, so we've got simple spelling, Irish, but not too Irish," she laughed, "and nothing that rhymes with his last name."

"Or starts with a D either. I don't want him to be called Double D and made fun of because of it," Aidan said, as serious as he could be.

"Got it," Anna said with an eye roll. "Classic spelling, no D's. I like Brian, Braden, and Liam," she said, her voice drifting off as she continued to think.

"No Liam, license plates, remember?"

"Wow. You're serious about the license plates."

"Serious, serious mental anguish over that one," he smiled.

"Okay…" she said. "Seamus," she said, watching his face as he jerked his head up.

"Anna, no!"

"I'm kidding, take it easy,"

"How do you feel about making his middle name Walter?"

"After Dad? I'd love it," she said, squeezing his hand. "Mom, would that be okay with you?"

Eadie looked up from her work with a warm smile. "I'd love it, sweetheart, he would've loved it."

"I like Braden the best from what we've got so far," Aidan said, saying the name a few times, imagining how it would sound yelling out the backdoor, calling his son inside.

She said it aloud, then wrinkled her nose. "But it rhymes with Aidan."

"Darn it."

Suddenly she thought of the perfect name, but felt hesitant to suggest it. He noticed the shadow cross her eyes.

"What are you thinking?" he asked, his hand stroking hers.

"What about Benjamin?" she asked, watching him closely.

Aidan pressed his lips into a straight line as he thought it over. She watched him swallow the lump rising in his throat.

"Benjamin Walter Doherty," he said, turning his head to look at the baby, weighing each syllable of the name. "That's a very strong name," he said, smiling down at their little one. "I think I love it. How about you? Do you feel like a Benjamin?" he asked, marveling at the perfectly formed hands, four little fingers gripping his thumbnail, a tiny thumb halfway encircling his own.

Anna smiled down at the pair of them, her heart in

her throat. "I'd say he likes it. Hello, Benjamin. Ben," Anna whispered softly.

Aidan's hand cupped the baby's small head. "I think he's going to need a strong name to get through this. His skin is almost red, Anna."

"That'll change soon," the NICU nurse said, coming up behind them. "I'm Alex," the young brunette woman said. Anna liked her on sight. She couldn't help but think she looked like a scrapper, little and strong. Anna could use all the scrappers in her life that she could get right now.

"Do I hear we have a name?" Alex asked.

Anna and Aidan smiled at each other.

"I believe we do. Alex, meet Benjamin Walter Doherty," Aidan said proudly.

"That's a good name," she said smiling. "I'll get the paperwork updated and bring you some forms to sign to make it official. We just had our shift change," Alex continued, "and your previous nurse, Yvette, gave me all the details on this little mister. Nice to meet you," she said with a smile as she handed Anna a hospital-issued cup filled with ice water. "Drink up, you'll want to try pumping again soon, I bet."

"Thank you, Alex. You're right. I hate to leave him here," Anna answered.

"Did Yvette get to show you were the pumping area is?"

Anna shook her head. "We haven't been here long, actually I just realized we're probably here pretty early. What time is it, Mom?"

"Six-fifteen," Eadie answered, looking at her watch.

"Good grief, Mom, did you even sleep last night?"

"Not much, dear. Couldn't wait to get back here."

Alex smiled at the three of them. "Anna, I'll give you the tour. We do shift changes at six, so if you call down to check on the baby, try to avoid right at that time. That's when we get briefed on what's going on with our patients," Alex said, wheeling Anna to the pumping area. "Here we are. It's not fancy, not much more than a glorified dressing room, but it gets the job done," she told Anna.

"It'll be fine, thanks," Anna said, looking at the basket of supplies.

"You can use one of these sets," she said, producing a packaged set of tubing and cups, "and the bottles are here." She gestured to a basket full of plastic-wrapped bottles. I'll have the desk print you off a few pages of pre-printed labels, that way you just stick them on when you're done filling them. You just hand it off to one of us and we'll put it in the breast milk fridge in his section.

I'll come check on you in a few minutes. Don't get used to this A-lister treatment, though. You'll be walking tomorrow," Alex said with a wicked smile.

Anna groaned, wondering if she could fast forward to feeling like herself instead of a bloated slug. She wasn't an idiot, but she was surprised to look completely pregnant the day after having a baby. Everything in her middle was so soft. Thankfully, her pain medicine was working so she didn't feel pain at the incision site, however she did feel like her guts were going to fall out. She kept a pillow positioned over her belly while she fiddled with the pump. She didn't want to continue to dwell on the "what should have been" feelings because she knew in her heart it would be easy to get comfortable in that dark spot. She needed to focus on the positive. Anna needed to push on for Ben. Finally, she settled into a comfortable position and closed her eyes for a few minutes. Eadie tapped on the outside of the curtained area softly.

"Are you doing okay, sweetie? she asked, jolting Anna back to reality.

She looked down, surprised to see about an ounce of thin liquid in the bottles. She was filled with immediate relief. "I'm fine, just spaced out for a minute. Give me a minute to get all put back together," she said, her heart filling with joy. With her many fears, she was terrified she wouldn't be able to provide for her baby on top of everything else.

When she pulled back the curtain for Eadie to enter, she held the bottles out as proudly as she had ever displayed anything in her whole life.

"That's great, baby!" Eadie said, hugging Anna. "You're going to do just fine at this, I promise."

Eadie settled Anna back to the area where Alex was showing Aidan how to change Benjamin's tiny diaper.

Anna marveled at the sight of Aidan nervously raising their son's little feet slightly to slide the tiny scrap of diaper beneath him. It was both beautiful and terrible at the same time. Each time she felt a happy feeling well up, it was matched by equal parts of fear. So many wires and tubes attached to their son.

Tears streaked down Anna's face even though she tried to fight them back. She pressed a finger to Benjamin's little outstretched leg, and she whispered a prayer that he would be well.

"I'd like to go back to the room now, please," she said, feelings of guilt nearly swallowing her whole. Aidan looked at her, surprise clear on his face. She shrugged a shoulder at him, unable to put into words what she was feeling.

Eadie gathered up her things. "I'll take her up, honey. You stay," she said to Aidan. He nodded his reply.

Without a word, Eadie wheeled Anna back to her room.

"Mom, can you hand me my phone, please? I need to check in with Sorcha."

"Sure, but after that, I think you should try and get some rest," Eadie said, unable to help herself.

"Me, too. It'll be time for my next nurse to come in in a minute. I'll cash out after that, promise."

"I'm going to go stare at Benjamin a little more then. That's a good, strong name. I love it."

"Me too, thanks, Mom," Anna answered, ready to call Sorcha.

Instead she found a voicemail from Mr. Darby. He was checking on her and the baby, of course, but also wanted to reassure Anna that they had a temporary secretary they could hire to keep the office afloat in her absence during her leave. With that off the list, she decided to go ahead and call Sorcha.

Sorcha answered on the first ring. "I'm so glad to hear from you," Sorcha breathed into the phone. "I've been scared to call and wake you."

"I'm so sorry I couldn't call earlier. How's Evan? How are you?" Anna said, so relieved to finally get to talk to Sorcha.

"He's in a huge amount of pain, and he's guaranteed to be a tremendous pain in my ass, but he's going to be okay," she said. "He has to be. Thank God. Anna, it could've been so much worse," she said, her voice hitching on the words.

Anna sighed, not even able to touch that place of fear she went to yesterday in the office when John ran in and said there had been a rock fall. "I know, Sorch."

"How is the baby? How are you holding up?"

"I'm scared to death. The baby, we named him Benjamin Walter, will be on a ventilator for a few more hours, then they're going to try and wean him off to see what he'll do. He may have to stay on it for a while," Anna said, her voice trailing off, the vision of all those tubes and wires burned into her mind.

"I can't come visit because of my germ-factory-toddler, but I would be there with you if I could, Anna."

"I know, it's fine. There's nothing to do here except for be terrified or depressed. Pick your poison," she said.

Sorcha wrinkled her face at the phone. That didn't sound like Anna. Sorcha decided she'd give Anna a week before she ripped into her. *Of course she was upset*, she reminded herself. *I've never seen Clara that small, hooked up every which way. I'll give her some space.*

They ended the call as Sarah entered the room to give Anna another exam. Anna endured the checkup and eventually submitted to sleep until the next exam woke her.

THE NEXT MORNING Sarah entered the room and pulled back the blinds. She had some news and needed Anna alert and in a different state of mind when she heard it. She made no effort to be quiet as she moved around the room and adjusted the monitor.

Anna woke up, turning her face away from the light.

"Wake up, Anna, time for your exam. You need to order something to eat, too. What sounds good today?"

"I'm not hungry," Anna answered quietly.

Sarah knew it was time for her to be a little tougher on Anna. It's not really for you. It's for the baby. You need to drink some water, eat some food, and try pumping again. Your milk has come in," she said with a nod to Anna's chest.

"Holy boobs," Anna said, the shock registered on her face as she looked down at herself. She'd always been small-chested. That was certainly not the current scenario. "These are amazing," she said with a laugh.

*Finally*, Sarah thought. *She has a sense of humor after all.* "Let's get this part over so I can give you some good news," she said, starting the exam.

"God, I hate that," Anna said, once it was over.

"It would be weird if you liked it," Sarah answered. "Okay, now that that's over, let's get to the good part. I got an update from the NICU a little bit ago. "Benjamin, nice name by the way, did well when they took him off the ventilator. He's off the vent now and is on oxygen," she beamed.

"That's great!" Anna said. "What about all the other things?"

"He'll have the rest of the leads until he's on his way out the door, Anna. But he's able to breathe on his own now with oxygen, which is huge," she said, eying Anna closely.

Anna nodded.

"Anna," Sarah said, placing her hand on Anna's arm, "there's a lot to be thankful for here, you see that, right?"

Anna didn't say anything.

Sarah took a deep breath and said what she knew needed to be said. "Honey, you need to thank your lucky stars you are alive and your son is alive. Last week a lady bled out before she got here. Her sac ruptured, she died and her baby drowned. Your story is one of the lucky ones," she said, giving Anna a squeeze and leaving the room with tears in her eyes.

Anna couldn't do anything but stare at the ceiling, willing herself to stop being so negative. Sarah was right. She needed to focus on the good stuff. She was alive. Benjamin was alive. He was off a ventilator already. These are good things, she told herself.

# Twenty-Four

THE NEXT FEW DAYS WERE a blur of becoming acclimated to the terminology and blaring alarms in the NICU world. Anna learned about oxygen liter flow, apnea and bradycardia episodes, and how to touch Benjamin to wake him up to breathe when he got so comfortable that he just stopped.

She loved that amazing little face. Benjamin still had the cannula and his feeding tube, however if he continued to bottle feed well today they were going to remove the tube from his nose. He had to prove he could handle the suck/swallow/breathe pattern once more before she was allowed to try to nurse him. So much hadn't gone to plan, she was hoping at least that would.

Aidan walked into the NICU to find her with her hands cupping Benjamin's head and little legs, trying to gently hold him in a sort of fetal position like the occupational therapist had taught her to do.

"Hey," he said, wrapping her in his good arm and giving her a kiss.

"Hey, how's the arm?" she asked, happy to have him next to her.

"Hurts like the dickens, but nothing compared to Evan. I just went down to see him. I don't know if it's better to keep him in here or send him home to Sorcha. She's liable to kill him. He's a terrible patient." Anna watched as Aidan went over to the sink and scrubbed up to his elbows as instructed by the nurse.

Anna laughed in spite of herself. Sorcha thought the sun rose and set on Evan, but she had zero tolerance for whining. Aidan had mentioned that one of Evan's nurses said that a broken femur was about the worst kind of pain a person could be in, so she had zero idea how this was going to work out well for anyone involved.

"The nurse said I'll be going home today," Anna said, not looking away from Benjamin.

Aidan nodded. "That's what they told me, too."

They sat in silence for a little while, watching Benjamin breathe in and out, stretching his little legs and feet as Anna gently guided them back into position.

"He'll be okay here, Anna. It's going to hurt though, isn't it?"

"That drive will be the longest of my life," she answered, trying not to think about it. "It'll be two more weeks before

I can drive myself. Mom said she'd bring me every day that you're not able to."

"I'm so glad to hear that. I just got checked out with my doctor. My stitches come out tomorrow, so I'll have to go back to work the day after," he said, rubbing at the bandage on his face. "I can't wait to get this off my face. It itches like crazy."

"Will you go underground right away?" she asked, fear in her face.

"I'll be above ground for a few days; Roberts needs me for something. But the feds finished the investigation and the area has been cleared, so the guys will be going back underground tomorrow to get the roof repined. Then it's back to business as usual, I guess."

Anna nodded, fighting with herself to trust that the men would be safe. She knew that Aidan was a coal miner at the start of their relationship. She had to accept that the job was dangerous, and that was the end of it. The same could be said for police, military, firefighters, and others, but somehow it was more personal when it was the man she loved.

"Mom and Dad would like to visit today," he said. "This morning if possible. Sorcha lined up a babysitter for Clara so that they can finally get up here."

"Of course. I'm glad they'll get to meet Benjamin."

"Mom's been going crazy having to wait this long. They've had Clara every day and Dad's been terrified to come here. The five of us were pretty big babies. I think he's nervous to see our little guy," he said, his finger resting on Benjamin's little arm.

"It's kind of intimidating," Anna said. "I get it. I feel scared every minute that I'm in here." She winced as a blaring alarm announced that Benjamin stopped breathing again. "The noises don't help," she said, quickly moving her finger on his chest as her eyes were glued to the monitor. "Come on, buddy," she said as the nurse stepped between Anna and Aidan to rub Benjamin with more force than Anna had the nerve to do.

"There, there he is," the nurse said. "You can't be lazy, Benjamin, come on, Little One," she said, not seeing the dirty look Anna gave her. The nurse was new to their rotation and Anna took everything everyone said to heart.

"These hormones are a bitch," Anna whispered to Aidan. "I can't decide if I'm hot or I'm cold, but I know I'm tired and scared and totally pissed off every minute."

His safest option, he decided, was to nod in agreement, but not too much agreement. An hour passed while they just sat and watched the baby, and helped where they could with taking his temp with a thermometer in his tiny armpit and changing his diaper when possible.

The nurse produced a bottle and asked which of them wanted to feed him this time. Anna had done the last, so Aidan was up this time around. Anna watched as Aidan carefully followed the instructions, holding Benjamin halfway on his side so that he could be quickly turned from his back at an incline to the side in case he choked. It was surprising how many different tricks there were to the simple care of an early baby. They made it halfway through the bottle when Benjamin started to sleep during his feeding, so the nurse went ahead and called time on the bottle feeding.

"It's ok, Buddy, the next time will go better," Aidan said, his lips pressed to the baby's little head. The nurse held Benjamin as Aidan unbuttoned his shirt. She helped slide Benjamin against Aidan's chest, then produced two warm blankets that were draped over them. Kangaroo-Care was their favorite part of the day.

Anna wasn't sure that Aidan had ever looked more content than he did at that moment. He was reclined back in the chair, with his son nestled against his skin. If she hadn't already been in love, she would've fallen at the sight of that alone.

She took that time to send a quick update to Jesse about how Benjamin was doing, and that she was due to be released later that day. Anna watched closely as their nurse quietly tiptoed in and out of their space, checking and adjusting different things.

Aidan and Benjamin were snoozing and Benjamin's numbers on the monitor looked amazing. Anna thought this was perhaps the longest he had gone without an apnea or bradycardia alarm. She couldn't wait to see longer and longer periods between heart rate drops and she dreamed of the day they vanished completely. She knew that the goal was for Benjamin to be close to five pounds and his due date, as well as free from heart rate drops for 24 hours in order to come home. She imagined they had at least four weeks left in the hospital.

THANKFULLY, JESSE HAD volunteered to handle updating the masses of people who were kind enough to care about what was going on with Benjamin. Anna had zero patience at the moment and wanted to spend her time focusing on Ben. Jesse was all too happy to take the reins and offered to handle updates to friends and family. Anna was thankful. And tired.

Aidan's phone beeped while they were watching Benjamin, his parents sending a message that they were at the NICU and needed to be signed in. He handed Benjamin back to the nurse so he could be placed back into the incubator. Aidan loved his parents dearly, but they weren't quite ready for anyone else to hold their little man yet. The fear of germs was immense at the stage Benjamin was in, and they were completely comfortable postponing germ exposure any way they could.

Anna realized she felt a little nervous as she adjusted her clothes and put a hand up to her hair, wondering what a strange mess she must look like. She had felt like Ira and Cathleen's home was her second home when she was a child, but she had always found them a little intimidating. They were so much stricter than her own parents, and she had loved them, but from a healthy distance.

Cathleen was the first to make it to Benjamin's area. Before she could stand, Cathleen wrapped Anna in a hug and a quiet sob escaped her lips. Cathleen quickly looked away, wiping her tears with a handkerchief. Ira was more reserved with his greeting, nodding hello to Anna with a small smile.

"Hello, Anna. We've come to meet our grandson," he said, leaning down to look into the incubator.

"This is Benjamin," Aidan said. "He's having a fairly good day today. He made it through half his bottle before he wore out. He's still alarming every so often, but he gained back the ounces he lost over the past few days. He's back to birth weight as of today," he said like a proud father, gesturing to the whiteboard above his incubator.

"He's so small," Cathleen said almost reverently.

"I've never seen anything like it," Ira said, his voice filled with awe. "He looks like he'd fit in one of those oatmeal cylinders.

"Ira," Cathleen scolded.

"Well he does," Ira said quietly.

Anna watched them closely with a small smile on her face. She hadn't seen them in several years. It was strange to see the signs of aging in parents, she thought. Little things had changed. Each had additional lines here and there, softening of work-worn bodies and hair lightened to gray with time. Deep down though, you could see that Ira still blustered as much as he ever did, and Cathleen, a task-master with her children, still catered to him. Anna wondered if it was love and devotion or just expected gender-based servitude that caused Cathleen to dote on Ira so much.

Either way, they seemed happy, which made Anna happy. She stood to greet them properly.

"How are you, dear?" Cathleen asked, gratefully accepting Anna's hug.

"I seem to be healing well, and I'll be discharged later on today," Anna answered, her forced smile communicating her heartbreak.

As Anna gave Ira a quick hug, Cathleen peered closely into the incubator. "Look at those little fingers," she said. "So perfect, like a baby doll."

"When he's able to maintain his own body temperature, we'll be able to put clothes on him. It might be as early as next week, the nurse said. They're pretty careful about not getting our hopes up too high, but we're hopeful anyway," Anna said. "I imagine he'll be swimming even in preemie clothes."

"Leaving him here today will be the hardest thing you'll ever have to do, kiddo, but you can do it. He's in good hands here, right?" Cathleen asked with a kind smile.

Anna nodded, appreciating the sentiment but not quite ready to smile about it. As they got back to Benjamin's area, Ira stood beside Aidan.

"Well, Son, now that the baby's here, you two will be properly married soon, right?" Ira asked expectantly.

Aidan shot a look to Anna. "Pop, we've been pretty preoccupied here," he said, gesturing to Benjamin. "We haven't exactly had the chance to talk about it."

Ira wrinkled his brow and looked at Aidan like he had sprouted another head. "What is there to talk about. You've had a son together, you'll want to have him baptized by parents that are married, correct?"

Aidan raised his hand to signal to Ira that he'd said enough, but the older man clearly wasn't finished.

"You don't want your son to leave this place a bastard, now Aidan."

Between Anna and Cathleen, they nearly sucked all the air out of the place. Anna had been standing but sat down gingerly, looking down at the floor to keep herself from letting Ira know exactly what she thought of him and his opinions. She could feel the color rising in her face and she didn't dare make eye contact with Aidan.

Cathleen, however, took no such approach to Ira's comment. Usually she deferred to him. Usually she stayed a little to the side, giving Ira center stage. At this moment, however, there had been a rip in the fabric of the universe.

"Ira Doherty," she said in a low, lethal tone. "How *dare* you say such a thing to these kids," she seethed. "This baby here is hanging on by a thread. Four days ago your son was nearly killed in a mine accident and Anna's just had a major surgery. How dare you!" she hissed, looking around wildly, shocked at the steadily creeping volume of her own voice.

Anna waved away Nurse Alex, who had been giving the family a little privacy. The little fiery nurse looked like she was ready to bust some heads. Her face was red and she was about two seconds away from throwing Ira out on his ear, size and stature be hanged.

"Dad, we're going to talk about this later, but I think you should go now," Aidan said with gritted teeth. "Mom, I'll talk to you later," he said with a quick embrace. Aidan thought his mother looked like she was going to shatter into a million pieces.

Cathleen gave both Aidan and Anna a quick peck on the cheek, peered in at Benjamin one last time, but didn't even look in Ira's general direction.

Red-faced, Ira nodded to each of them. "Aidan, Anna," he said, turning to follow Cathleen out of the NICU.

Aidan sat down in the chair next to Anna and rested his elbows on his knees, head hanging, with one hand resting on the back of his neck.

A moment of silence passed while Benjamin slept peacefully. "I don't know what to make of him sometimes," he said in a low voice, rubbing his neck with one hand and reaching for Anna's hand with the other. "It's like he still thinks it's the 1970s and he's freaking Archie Bunker."

A laugh escaped Anna. She tried to smother it, but the harder she tried, the more she laughed. Aidan looked at her with his eyebrows raised as a smile spread over his face. She grabbed a tissue, tears and snot streaming down her face, the picture of attractiveness, she was certain.

"I love you, you hot mess," he said as he kissed her.

"I love you too, Aidan," Anna answered.

"Maybe we should go ahead and talk about marriage again. What do you think?"

Anna nodded in agreement. "I'd like that."

"I mean, technically, we're kind of married already," he said, a half-smile on his face.

"Technically, you're right," she agreed, "but only in Mexico."

He watched her as Anna nervously alternated looks between their son and his monitor, and Aidan realized how full she made his heart feel. He looked around to see if there were many people around. Thankfully it was pretty quiet. He knew what he wanted to do, and that there would be a better time and place, but right now the three of them were together. Later today, he'd take her home and they'd leave little Benjamin at the hospital, something he knew would break Anna's heart.

Fishing in his pocket, he felt the box he had purchased the day before. Aidan had endured some incredibly stressful situations in his lifetime. In the Marines, he had been shot at, had swam in the ocean with 70 lbs. of gear and lived on basically nothing in the desert during training. Four days ago he was nearly killed in the coal mines. Those were moments he'd never forget, but they didn't touch the fire in his heart right now.

Aidan dropped to his knee in front of Anna and produced the little blue box. She stared at him for a moment, completely perplexed. Once she wrapped her head around what that box meant, she stood up.

"Aidan, let's not do this because of what your dad said…"

He shook his head. "I bought this yesterday. I wanted to surprise you," he said, raising his eyebrows and grinning. "Surprise."

She smiled and looked at Benjamin. "Look at your dad, kiddo. There probably aren't many kids that get to witness this," she said, remembering how she had told her mother how her life was unfolding in a much different manner than she thought it would.

"Anna, will you marry me?" Aidan asked.

Anna looked down at the gorgeous man in front of her. He was made of so much good. Aidan was loving, affectionate, intelligent and funny. He loved his family, good, bad, and otherwise. He had a hell of temper and was as stubborn as a mule. She had adored him as a teenager and loved him as a man. He could make her blood boil with both lust and anger. He was a handful. And with all of that, he was everything she could ever want.

"Yes," she said, leaning forward as much as she comfortably could.

"Mommy said yes," Aidan said, whispering to Benjamin.

He stood and pulled her into his arms.

"Kiss me," Aidan said, nuzzling Anna.

She did. They hadn't truly kissed in a while and it felt so good to be that close to him for a second. At least it felt good up until the flash went off. They looked over to see Alex with a camera and two nurses smiling like maniacs.

"That is a first," Alex said. "I mean, an absolute first. We have seen some crazy things in here. This place is like a Pollack painting of humanity. Emotions are splashed everywhere. Nothing like this though. Man, what an awesome day," she said, shaking her head.

The nurses dispersed and Anna opened the ring box. Aidan had picked out a white gold wedding band with delicate knot work and emeralds. She had never seen anything like it.

Anna slid it on her finger, and it fit beautifully. She quirked a brow at him in question.

"Jesse helped with the ring size," he said. "Your Aunt Jesse is like a secret weapon, kid," he said to Benjamin. "She knows your mother better than anyone."

# Twenty-Five

ANNA FELT A LUMP IN HER throat as she was wheeled out of the hospital. Aidan carried her bag and a nurse pushed her chair. She felt so empty without Benjamin in her arms. Despite the surprise of the day, she felt like she was carrying a wet bag of sand on her shoulders. She tried not to think of how unfair it was that some women went home with their babies. She refused to think how heartbroken other women were, leaving with the knowledge they would never again hold their babies. Anna focused instead on just trying not to think at all. She took it step by step. *Just make it to the door. Just make it in the car. Just make it to my house. Just get inside the house to my bed*, she thought.

AIDAN SNUCK LOOKS at Anna throughout the drive. Her

hands were clenched so hard that her knuckles were white. He didn't *do* powerless very well, but he knew there was absolutely no way he could make this situation better for her. After a very quiet hour of driving, Aidan put his hand on her knee.

"Do you want to come to my house tonight?" he asked, hopefully.

Anna looked down at her lap for a minute, trying to decide if she wanted to go to his house. "I don't feel like myself. I'm so sad I can barely breathe. I want to be with you, but I worry about disappointing Mom, too. She's been stuck taking care of Harry for a week now and I'm not sure what to do."

"Anna, I don't want to push you, but I want to be able to take care of you if you'll let me. I go in at six tomorrow morning. Why don't you go in and relax if you can," he added when he saw the dirty look cloud her eyes. "Let me go in and take Harry for a good long walk so your mom can get a little rest as well. See if you can take a nap, then call me, okay?"

"That would be really kind of you, thanks," she said, her nose stinging with a new surge of tears. She gathered up the hospital grade pump that Aidan had rented while he grabbed her bags. Anna let him lead the way into the house so that Harry didn't bombard her. She was getting around really well, but she was incredibly sore and under strict instructions to take it easy while she healed.

Aidan braced himself, making certain Harry didn't jump up onto his hurt arm. "Hey, big boy, have you missed us?" he asked the frantic Poodle. Eadie and Ruthie were close on Harry's heels, ready to gather hugs and to pump Anna for information about how Benjamin was doing, and how she was handling the separation.

"Why don't you go on up, Anna, I'll fill the ladies in on the latest and then take Harry for a walk," he suggested.

Anna nodded in reply and kissed each woman on the cheek before heading for her room.

"My God, she looks so broken," Eadie said, big tears in her eyes.

Ruthie was speechless, which never happened.

"It's awful, Eadie. It's just an awful feeling to drive away without him. We know he's safer there than with us right now, it's just sad though," Aidan explained. He shrugged his shoulders, nothing more to say.

"She's strong, honey. She's going to be okay," Eadie said, squaring her shoulders. "And Aidan, you're strong and you're going to be okay, too," she decided.

Aidan nodded in agreement. "Eadie, I asked Anna to marry me today. Again," he clarified.

Eadie smiled broadly and Ruthie clasped her hands to her heart.

"She agreed, but she's tired. She's so tired and scared," Aidan said. "I want to care for her if she'll let me. I want her to know she can really lean on me.

"I'm so thankful you two found each other," Eadie said, pulling Aidan into a hug. "Both my girls have found wonderful partners to spend their lives with. That's what

Walt and I dreamed of for them," she said, her voice catching on the emotion. "God, I miss that man. He'd have had a fit over another grandson," she said.

Ruthie put her arm around Eadie's waist. "He sure would've, sis. He was a good man and loved his family. And you," she said, giving Eadie a squeeze as she patted away her tears.

"I'm going to take Harry, here, for a walk, then I'll get out of your hair. I've asked Anna if she'd like to stay over tonight, but I'm not sure she's up to it. I have to go in at six tomorrow morning, so if she comes over, would either of you be able to pick her up when she's ready and take her to the hospital?"

"Oh that's right," Ruthie said, "she can't drive for a few weeks, can she?"

"No driving for two weeks, no heavy lifting, no laundry, no handling the wild man, here," he said, gesturing to Harry. "Would it be better if I brought Harry home with me?" he asked, not minding at all. He and the dog got along just fine.

"No way, kid. Get your own dog," Ruthie said. "Plus, when you're not at work you'll likely be at the hospital. Eadie will be happy to shuttle Anna around when you're working, and I'm happy taking care of that handsome fella."

"Okay, sounds like we've got a pretty good system in place already then," he said, thankful that Anna had such a good family.

"I'll take him out, then I'm going to head over to check in on Sorcha to see if I can do anything for her.

"Aidan," Eadie said quietly.

"Yes, ma'am?"

"Don't forget to take care of you, too. You're in this up to your elbows, and you've had your own trauma on top of your family's," she said.

"Yes, ma'am," he answered soberly. Maybe she was right. He was bone-tired and his arm ached terribly. Maybe he'd call Finn or Lochlan to see if they could check in on Sorcha, if they hadn't already. That was one of the benefits of a huge family, he thought. Someone was always available to pitch in.

Anna left her bed only long enough to pump, shower, and sit up to eat the food that Eadie had brought up. She hadn't realized a person could be as tired as she felt. She was sick about not being at the hospital with Benjamin, but several of her nurses, including Sarah, had reminded her that she had to keep her own energy up. She was encouraged by the NICU nurses to call anytime she wanted to get updates on his feedings, oxygen levels and weights, and typically called every four hours when she pumped. Anna decided to get a little journal to note the details in, so that she didn't forget anything.

She texted Aidan that she was too exhausted to come over but that she loved him. Anna surrendered to the motherly attention that Eadie was all too happy to lavish on her, and tried not to feel too guilty with every minute that passed.

THOUGH SHE CONTINUOUSLY felt fear that the other shoe was about to drop, Anna found that each visit to the NICU during the following week brought a new sense of relief. Benjamin's oxygen level was able to be reduced each day and his feedings were going better. Her mother had been happy to take her to the hospital every day, and she had soaked up as many minutes of Kangaroo Care as she could. While Aidan was able to drift off into a nap while he held his son, Anna couldn't tear her eyes off him long enough to rest. The nurses would snuggle the baby to her chest, cover them with two warm blankets and then would pass Anna a little hand mirror. No matter what his angle, she was able to see his beautiful little face.

Each day, Anna and Eadie went to Robertsville and stayed until Anna could tell her mother was getting tired. One more week and she'd be able to drive herself without worrying about exhausting her mother. Jesse was still working full-time but was on deck to help a few days next week. Anna couldn't wait to get some time with her. She had lived away for so long, it had sometimes been six months to a year between face-to-face visits with her sister. Now that they were in the same town, if they went a few days between visits, they each got a little cagey. They had each gained a deepened sense of gratitude for family after the loss of their father. The truth that each day was a gift resonated a little more strongly than it did before.

The hour drive to Robertsville seemed like torture, but the walk from the parking lot to the NICU doors was a special kind of hell. The closer she got, the more erratic her heartbeat. Her need to see her baby was desperate.

After scrubbing up, Anna was finally able to breathe easily once she saw her son. Today there was a new surprise. Benjamin was dressed in a pair of too-big preemie footie pajamas. Anna couldn't contain herself, she laughed at the sight of him.

Her laugh bubbled up from the tips of her toes. It was a monumental relief to see her son in something that looked like a full-term baby would wear. The clothes somehow made him look like less of a "feeder and a grower" and more like a typical baby.

"That's a sound I like to hear," Alex said, standing beside Anna. "How are you, Grandma?" she asked Eadie. "Is our patient here behaving at home like she should?"

"Yes, she's doing great," Eadie beamed.

Anna handed over the bottles of milk that she had pumped during the night, Alex clucking approval on her walk to the fridge. It was funny what a sense of pride Anna had in each little bottle. She might not have been able to do much, but at least that was going according to plan.

They cooed over Benjamin and positioned their chairs so they could see him as they waited for Alex to hand him over, wires and all. Eadie pulled out her yarn so that she could keep busy, happily working away at more little hats than Benjamin would ever be able to wear. She had already started giving bags of them to the nurse on duty so they could be distributed to the other babies as needed.

Alex entered their area and started getting Benjamin out of his now unheated incubator. "He's doing a great job maintaining his temperature so far, so this is going well. We put him in his new jammies this morning after his bath, right before his head scan."

"He had another already?" Anna asked, fearful of what it might mean.

"Yes, he'll get one once a week, just to be sure he's still doing well. Keep in mind, Anna, that even if there's a brain bleed, it's par for the course for preemies, usually."

Anna nodded in response, not feeling comfortable with it at all. There was a lot about preemies that scared the living hell out of her.

"When do we get the results back?"

"It'll be today sometime; it just depends on how backed up they are."

There was really nothing to argue, it was what it was, Anna guessed.

The day passed like ones before it. Eadie and Anna watched Benjamin's every move and assisted with diaper changes, temp checks, and feedings. They were as involved as they were allowed to be. Anna's phone beeped and she saw Aidan had sent a message. He would be there in an hour and wondered if he could pick anything up for them.

Anna could see that Eadie was dragging. "Mom, do you want to go ahead and go home? I can tell you're tired. Aidan will be here in an hour or so. I can get a ride home with him."

"Kid, I think I'll take you up on it. I'm worn out today," she said, gathering up her things.

Anna thanked her mother and walked her to her car, enjoying the chance to stretch her legs. Anna could already feel some of the bloating coming off, but it was driving her crazy to be so sedentary. When she arrived back at Benjamin's bed, she asked yet again if the scan results had come in. Still no news.

THE SHIFT CHANGE happened at six as it did each day, and Anna waited anxiously wondering which nurse she'd be assigned. Yet another hour passed and still no news.

"Can you tell me please if Benjamin's brain scan has come back in yet?" she asked the new nurse.

"Let me go check, I'll be right back," she said, going back to the hall to see if anyone had any news.

She returned and nonchalantly said, "Yes, it came in about an hour ago, the scan was clean. He's fine, no bleeds."

The mix of relief and anxiety hit Anna like a ton of bricks. She'd held it together pretty well so far, despite the tremendous fear she'd been fighting. The never-ending alarms jolted her nerves so badly that she jumped whether it was Benjamin's monitor alarming or that of another baby. The crushing pressure that she had been under surfaced suddenly, and Anna was in the throes of a panic attack.

"My God, you people," she said quietly, her breath

coming in gasps. "You people have no idea what it's like to wait for that news! I've been waiting all day, scared out of my mind!" she said, her voice breaking on her sobs.

Kathy, the charge nurse, walked through the halls. The volume of Anna's voice caught her attention and she flew into Benjamin's space and took over. "Let's get Mom sat down and get her some ice water," she said, directing Benjamin's nurse.

"Okay, Anna, take a deep breath," she encouraged.

"I'm okay," Anna said, fighting for her breath. "I've been waiting all day to find out if he had a bleed, asking every hour for an update and I've had no news. Finally, I get news and find out it's been in for an hour!"

"Alright, honey, I'll find out what happened. We have a lot of kids getting scans today, it just took too long," she said, placing a cold washcloth on Anna's neck.

Anna couldn't even bring herself to feel badly about her tirade. How much is a person expected to be able to take for God's sake.

When Aidan arrived, she was calmed down and holding Benjamin.

"There's my beautiful family," he said, reaching down to kiss each of them on the forehead.

"Look who's wearing PJs," she said, holding their son out for Aidan to see.

"Look at that! He looks so different with clothes on," Aidan said proudly.

She smiled. "He does, doesn't he? It's so precious."

Aidan nodded, pulling his chair close to Anna's.

"We got good news today," she shared, "no brain bleeds."

"Thank God, those scans scare me to death," he said.

"Me too," she answered, deciding to share the story of her meltdown later.

They stayed for an hour or so before Aidan needed to leave. He had to be back at the mines at six again the next morning, and the drive after a ten-hour shift was a long one.

"Will you stay with me tonight?" Aidan asked, slipping his arm around Anna's shoulders as they walked through the hospital to the truck.

"I'd love to. I'd hoped you'd ask, honestly. I packed a bag," she said, nodding at the backpack he was carrying. "I even packed my pump," she said with a faux-seductive voice.

"Aw, you evil temptress," he teased. "Good. I've missed holding you."

"I've missed it too," she answered.

They were both exhausted, but the events of the day gave them plenty to talk over on the drive home. Aidan had a lot to share about being back underground, finally. Anna recounted her meltdown to him. He reached over with his hand on her knee and gave her a squeeze. Not for the first time, Anna noted how affectionate he was. She was glad about that. Benjamin would need to see that it was a part of being a good man. She wanted him to have a model to show that it's more than brains and brawn. It's about tenderness and touch as well.

Aidan was so happy to have Anna back in his home, he realized, as he carried in her things. It had been too long since she'd been there. The little place seemed happier with her around. They practically raced to get ready for bed and into the covers. Anna still felt very much not herself, but she was all too happy to get back into his arms.

He pulled her close, thankful to feel her against him. It would be several more weeks until they could be together again, but God she felt good. They lay together with her head on his chest. She turned her face up toward his, and it was the only invitation he needed to kiss her lips.

Aidan brushed her hair back from her face and cradled her jaw in his hands gently. The scrape of his evening beard felt so strange and wonderful to her skin. She had probably never felt less sexy in her life, but even still, he made her feel special.

He turned on his side and his hand roamed down her arm. Anna was all too aware of her new curves and with each kiss that grew a little deeper, she wondered if he, too, was curious about her new body. As Aidan's palm cupped her breast, she felt his body respond against hers, and she felt hers respond as well, just not in a sexy way.

Her milk let down and no breast pad was going to hold it. She moaned, and he moaned, misinterpreting the sound against his lips. As she backed her head up, he followed, lost in the sensation. When she pulled away and laughed as she stepped her way into the bathroom, he groaned.

"I know those aren't permanent, but I like them. A lot," he said. "A lot."

Anna laughed. "I know! How could you not? I'm straight as an arrow, but they turn me on!"

"Amen to that," he said under his breath.

She came back to bed with a sleepy smile. "Okay, Tiger. You'd better get to sleep. Your five o'clock alarm is going to come early.

"Yes, ma'am," he answered dutifully. Anna set her alarm so that she would get up when she needed to pump and call to check on Benjamin. Getting up every four hours was exhausting, but she considered it prep work for what she'd be dealing with when the baby came home. It wasn't sexy at all, but she still loved sleeping next to Aidan. She felt like it was where she belonged.

JESSE HAD CHAUFFEUR duty on the weekends. Missing a day at the hospital wasn't an option for Anna, even if she had to hitchhike to get there. Jesse showed up with a decaf caramel latte and a bagel as big as Anna's head. "I hit the new coffee shop in town. Pretty amazing, right?" she said at Anna's groan.

"I haven't had a latte in eight months," Anna answered blissfully.

"Say it, I'm the best sister."

"You're the best sister."

THEY RODE IN silence, enjoying their breakfast. Finally, Anna couldn't take it anymore and had to tell Jesse about the boob-grab incident.

"Oh man, that brings back memories. It was different

the third time around, but the first two times, I thought I was going to have to fight Drake off with a stick when my boobs were huge," she said, suddenly gasping.

"I can't believe I didn't tell you this," Jesse said.

"What?" Anna asked, eyes huge.

"He's dating again," Jesse said, "can you believe it?"

"Wait, I thought Drake was dating that lady he cheated on you with," Anna asked, confused.

"Nah, she dumped him when her cat turned up dead," Jesse winced, not loving that particular memory. "She was afraid Cole was going to show up with a voodoo doll and really screw him up," Jesse joked, feeling only slightly bad about the whole scenario. Of course her super sexy fling would turn out to have a dark side.

"Oh, speaking of Cole, what happened to him?" Anna asked.

Jesse winced. "Oh, he's still around. I saw him at the grocery store last week, talk about awkward."

"No!" Anna said, eyes as wide as saucers.

"Yes. It's hard to act normal around someone that wore your legs like a scarf," Jesse answered.

Anna grabbed her belly, "Oh God, Jesse, quit. I feel like my guts are going to spray out all over your car."

"Oops, sorry. I'll try to remember that.

"How did Cole act? What did you say?" Anna asked, nearly blushing on Jesse's behalf. Jesse and Cole had had an incredibly brief, incredibly intense whirlwind of a relationship while she and Levi were on the outs. Cole was mysterious, sexy, and more than a little bat-crap crazy.

"What a shame he was a nut," Anna said. I've got about five friends I can think of off the top of my head back in Colorado that would snatch him up in a heartbeat. My God, from what I remember, he was sexy."

Jesse sighed heavily. "Yes, yes he was. A very talented, slightly misguided, big-dicked son of a gun."

Anna clutched her belly once more and glared at Jesse.

"Sorry," she said, fanning her hands at her sister. "Keep your guts where they are, please. Anyway, you had asked about Drake," she said, getting back to business. Michael mentioned last month that Drake had told him that he is seeing one of the teachers from the kids' former school. Actually, Michael's favorite English teacher."

"Hmm, weird. How do you feel about it?" Anna asked, looking at Jesse.

She lifted a shoulder in a shrug. "I don't really feel any particular way about it, I guess," she answered. "What I do know, though, is that Michael adored that teacher. She was nice, funny, attractive," Jesse said. "I met her a few times during parent-teacher conferences and I got along well with her. She's a widow, no kids. It could turn out great. No extra drama for my kids and frankly, that's really all I'm worried about."

"Makes sense then. One question though," Anna said. "If she's so nice and normal, what the heck is she doing dating Drake?"

Jesse laughed despite herself. "Good question! Although,

if you remember, Drake could be very charming when he wanted to be. He's been pretty pleasant lately on the phone. He hasn't been horrible during our pick-ups and drop-offs with the boys. Maybe this lady is good for him.

"That could be a good thing," Anna said.

When Anna and Jesse arrived at the NICU they were surprised to see Benjamin's incubator missing. A tremendous surge of panic passed through Anna, jolting her so badly that she had to sit down. Jesse saw that Anna was safely tucked in a chair before tracking down the charge nurse.

Relief was written on her face when she got back to Anna.

"He's fine," she said. "He's fine, Sis. He's getting a chest x-ray and he'll be brought right back up," Jesse said, wrapping Anna in a hug.

Anna felt numb and wondered if she'd ever been so scared in all her life. She had immediately jumped to the worst conclusion. She was trying to piece back together her sanity when a familiar nurse pushing a bed came to Benjamin's area. "Hey," she said to Anna. "Look who's getting his big boy bed," she said.

Anna couldn't believe her eyes. The nurse was pushing an open-sided crib for Benjamin instead of an incubator. He was on day two of maintaining his body temperature and had done really well with it. He was being moved to an open crib. The nurse explained that things could change if he didn't tolerate the open air well, but for now this was the plan.

The nurse showed Anna how to work the side-rails while another nurse brought Benjamin back to his area in his incubator. Anna and Jesse quickly washed up and made themselves ready to hold the baby.

"Well, I'm dying to ask, but trying not to be pushy… what are the wedding plans?" Jesse asked.

Anna adjusted Benjamin's blankets so that she could peer at his face. "Little Man is ideally going to be released mid-December, so we'll wait until then. It'll just be something quiet and small."

Jesse nodded. "I get it. After what all you've been through, quiet and small sounds nice."

"Maybe we'll have something just for family at the little chapel at church. Nothing very fancy, just the family."

"Even his family?" Jesse sneered, making Anna laugh out loud and startle Benjamin.

"Yes, even his family," Anna answered. She had made the mistake of telling Jesse about the horrible thing Aidan's father had said, and Jesse would probably never forgive him.

"Cathleen called that night, Jesse. She apologized for Ira and I just felt awful for her. She said he hadn't meant what he had said to come out so ugly. In his generation, that's what it was called when a child was born outside of marriage," Anna said with a half-hearted shrug.

"Cathleen can say what she likes," Jesse said dismissively, "but I still think Ira sounds like a horse's ass."

"Yup," Anna agreed, "but we're going to chalk this up

to the first of many foot-in-mouth episodes," she said to Benjamin. "You'd better have my perfect genes instead of your father's" she said sarcastically, making Jesse laugh.

JESSE WAS QUIET on the long drive home, secretly happy that Anna fell asleep. She needed the time alone to think about what might be the perfect wedding gift to give to Aidan and Anna. Jesse had a plan forming in her mind and would have to do some major investigating. She'd also need some renovation help and muscle. Jesse smiled to herself thinking how much she'd like to see Levi in a tool belt. Suddenly she didn't need to have the heat on quite so high in the vehicle. That man definitely had her number.

# Twenty-Six

THE WEEK PASSED WITH MORE good news. Benjamin was officially on room or open air. His heart rate drops had drastically reduced and his cannula was off more than it was on at the end of the week. The team decided it was time to take him off it since he managed to pull it into his mouth more than he had it in his nose. Anna was so excited about his progress, but didn't allow herself to focus on when they might bring him home. She was afraid if she wished too hard for it to happen that she'd somehow jinx herself. She also knew that she'd hear the apnea and bradycardia alarms buzzing loudly in her memory for the rest of her life, no matter what was going on with her son or how old he was. At home she even jerked when the dryer buzzer went off to let her know a load of laundry was complete.

Anna continually worked to focus on being in the

moment instead of planning ahead, a never-ending struggle. She closed her eyes in the recliner, thankful to have warm little Benjamin nestled against her. Every sound he made, every little wiggle made her fall more and more in love. His little eyes tracked her, his fingers grasped hers and his nuzzling had turned into short bursts of nursing. His head was covered with a fine, coppery-blond fuzz; Anna thought for certain he would be a redhead. She cupped his little head and admired her handsome little son.

The weather was supposed to turn bad in the early evening, so Anna let Eadie know she'd be ready to leave soon. She put Benjamin back to bed in his crib and as was her habit, stayed until he drifted off to sleep. There were days she stood beside his crib patting his little back for what felt like ages, bone-tired but thrilled to have a baby's back to pat. She knew how close she had come to losing him. Each day she watched other families come and go, their babies at every point on the spectrum. There were tiny two-pounders that alarmed every few minutes, their mothers and fathers wild-eyed with dark, dark circles under their eyes. There were "feeders and growers" like her Benjamin, babies that came early and might've had a rough start but were really just there to gain weight and get better at eating and growing. Anna whispered silent prayers for every family she saw pass by.

THAT EVENING, ANNA had gotten home much earlier than normal. The sleet started to fall, and Anna settled in at

Aidan's house. She knew he would be home within the hour and was pleased to have had time to cook supper for him. The kitchen smelled delicious and she had built a fire in the fireplace. His house was always tidy, but it made her happy to actually catch him with a load of laundry to do. Anna felt a little like they were playing house, but she liked it. She had settled into a chair to put her feet up and drink some tea when the phone rang.

"This is Tara, Benjamin's nurse for the evening, everything is fine," she said as Anna's heart began to race. "I was calling to let you know that we're really low on his milk supply," Tara said.

Anna sputtered into the phone, "But I brought eight more bottles today when I arrived."

"We've checked both refrigerators, and there aren't any more bottles. I'm sorry."

"Can you check again, please? I live an hour away and know that I brought eight bottles when I visited this morning," Anna said, a mix of panic and impatience building in her chest.

"Yes, I'll check again. I'm going to put you on hold, please," Tara said. As she waited, Anna mentally calculated the risk of driving back to the hospital despite the sleet. She was two days from being officially released to drive, but had snuck and driven a few blocks to Aidan's house. She couldn't ask her mother to take her, Aidan wasn't off from work yet, and he'd be exhausted if he was home. Jesse was at a ballgame, and Anna didn't want to horn in on more of her family time. She'd have to drive herself.

"I'm sorry, Anna, but there's nothing here," the nurse explained.

"I can't imagine how that can be. I brought in eight, five-ounce bottles this morning, but if you can't find it, you can't find it. I'll be there in around an hour," Anna said, trying to walk the fine line between pissed off and polite.

She turned off the oven, and left a note for Aidan explaining the rest of the cooking instructions and letting him know where she was. Next, Anna sent him a text but knew he wouldn't be able to get it until he was above-ground. She tried not to think about her family's reaction and hoped she could be back safe and sound before anyone knew what she'd done.

Anna packed up a bag of bottles that she had stored in the refrigerator as well as her coat and bag. The roads were already slick, but she didn't know what her choices were. Benjamin was finally doing so well with his feedings that she didn't want to chance him being switched to formula and screwing up his tummy. Every day they went without a heart rate drop or belly incident was one more step out the door, she reasoned.

The sleet hammered against her car and the wind pushed against her progress for the majority of the drive. There were two times she was the only car trudging along as other cars pulled to the side of the road with their hazard lights flashing, waiting for the onslaught to let up. Anna gritted her teeth each time she was passed by a semi. *It's like they think they're invincible*, she thought, trying to stay positive.

The hour-long drive took two hours. Anna pulled into the hospital parking lot as her phone rang.

"What do you think you're doing," Aidan hissed into the phone.

Anna's entire body had been in edge during her drive. She was like one enormous tensed muscle, and frankly, she wasn't receptive to his tone.

"I'm delivering milk, Aidan," she snapped, wincing at the pain in her middle. Who would've thought a person used their torso so much while driving. Every time she turned to check her blind spots, her incision ached.

He paused for a minute, wanting to avoid making her do anything but pay attention to the road. "Are you using hands-free for the phone," he asked in a calm voice.

She rolled her eyes. "Yes. It's sleeting to beat the band out here. I'm being careful," she said.

He sighed. "That's all I want, Anna. It scared me to death to find your text when I got to my phone," Aidan said. "What the heck happened to make you get out right now," he asked, his anger easing a little.

As Anna told the story, he felt his anger building again. *What happened to the bottles? Did they get lost? Dumped? Given to another baby?  How does that even happen?* he wondered. His heart ached seeing how hard she was working to take care of their son in the only way she could. More than that, it killed him watching her wage a battle with herself at every moment, working to stay positive rather than dwell on the bitter disappointment that Benjamin came early and had to be in the NICU. He was grateful as hell that they had access to a top notch NICU. During his service, he'd been dropped into countries before where people didn't even have access to clean water, let alone a hospital that could support premature babies.

It scared him to death to think about her being alone at night, driving in the ice. "Where are you now, babe?" he asked, trying to suppress his fear and the way a mind can wander to the what ifs.

"I just pulled into the parking lot. It's been slow-moving on the highway. I think I'll just go ahead and stay over tonight. I'm not getting back out into this mess."

"Sounds like a good plan," he said. "Okay then, be safe. Love you, Anna."

"Love you, too. Night," she said, a small smile teasing her lips as she disconnected the call.

Anna thought she'd take her chance and check in with Sorcha. As she thought the call was going to go to voicemail, Sorcha answered, breathless.

"Hello?" she gasped into the phone.

"Sorcha, are you alright? Now an okay time?"

"Oh God bless, it's as good as any. Whew," she said, trying to catch her breath.

"What the heck is going on?" Anna couldn't wait to hear the explanation. No matter what it was, she could always count on Sorcha to tell a good story. It had been that way since they were kids. She was always the best person in the world to get in deep trouble with, if anything, for the bullcrap story she'd try to feed their parents.

"Evan got to come home today. I'd like to say it's amazing to have him home, but mainly it's like I have the world's bitchiest toddler in my house. The poor son-of-a-bitch can't even get on the toilet by himself yet. We've been married for many years now and I've seen him all kinds of naked during that time. I have not, mind you, ever had to witness bathroom time. We have boundaries," she said, muttering "Jesus" under her breath.

"Sorcha," Anna laughed.

"I'm serious. I've been wiping asses for two years now with Clara, and all I can say is thank you Lord that I don't have to go there. I'd have to get a divorce."

Anna couldn't help herself, she laughed hard and winced, her stomach still tender to have a good laugh.

"I finally got him tucked into bed a little bit ago. I had let Clara stay up way too late because she was over the moon excited for Daddy to be home. That backfired tremendously," she hissed into the phone.

"Clara and I were painting little Christmas trees for the grandmas while Evan was in the bathroom for nine hours. He called for help and when I came back to the kitchen, Clara was covered in green paint up to her armpits. It's like she had become the Hulk," she said, giving in to a little laughter.

"Now, I'm about to chug a big glass of wine and clean the green paint out of the tub and the floorboards and of course the grain of the table that for some reason I didn't think to protect with the tarp I usually use.

And then, I might just chug another and go the hell to

sleep. It ought to be great until Evan has to pee or something," she said, stopping for a breath.

"Hey, why are you calling me so late?" Sorcha said. "You sound like you're in the car."

Anna told her about the lost milk. Sorcha's reply was so salty that Anna actually blushed. She nodded along in agreement. "I know, I can't believe it either. I'm just going to find a place to sleep there. There's a couch close to his area. I may just crash there if I can get away with it. It's slicker than snot out here. I'm not about to drive home in this. I'm here now, Sorch. I'll check in in a few days."

"Sounds good," she answered. "Love you, Anna. Pat the baby for me," Sorcha said tiredly into the phone.

"Will do, love you too." Anna resolved to keep a positive outlook instead when she delivered the bag of milk. The usual sense of panic kicked in as she parked the vehicle in the parking garage. It's like her heart was on a string to Benjamin's and it pulled harder and harder the closer she was to him. After she stopped at the big sinks by the NICU door, she rounded the corner to his area.

Anna stopped in her tracks, the tenderness of what she saw rooted her to the ground. One of her favorite NICU nurses was holding her son, close and cuddled in tight, rocking him side to side in that natural way that mothers and people who genuinely love babies naturally do.

Her irritation fled looking at that scene. The woman who comforted her son when she wasn't there, and did so with tremendous love, wouldn't have dragged her out onto an icy road without reason. If the milk was lost, it was lost. It was disappointing, but what was she going to do about it? At least it allowed her to catch this little scene, raising her comfort level with the nurses by leaps and bounds.

Anna cleared her throat as she got close to Benjamin's bed so as not to startle the nurse.

Nora turned her head and smiled in greeting. "Hey, what are you doing here so late?" she asked, her surprise evident in her pretty young face.

"I got a call that you guys didn't have the milk I brought in this morning," Anna answered, setting down her bags to take a closer look at Benjamin.

"Anna, we've got at least four more bottles in the refrigerator. I just saw them myself," she said with confusion. "Let me get you settled in with this little nugget and I'll go find out what's going on."

Anna was so exhausted from the drive that she didn't even want to argue about it. She sat down in the recliner and sighed contentedly as Benjamin was lowered into her arms. Nora added two warm blankets and offered to bring Anna some water when she got back.

A few minutes passed and Anna dozed off. When she awoke, Nora was quick to sit beside her. She offered a big cup of ice water like a peace offering. "Anna, I'm so sorry." She winced. "I feel so terrible that you got back out in this god-awful weather. The day nurse had put your milk in a different refrigerator than we usually store it in because we were running out of room. We had it in a different hallway and she forgot to note it in the system.

Anna heaved a sigh and looked down at Benjamin's sleeping face. "I'm not going to lie, the drive freaked me out, but it was worth it to hold him longer." She gazed down at that little face and noticed the baby had the shape of Aidan's eyes and eyebrows – or what would be eyebrows. Right now they were just little spaces above his eyes that turned really white when he filled his pants or cried when he was upset or mad.

"Look at him, Nora. He's a doll baby."

"He really is," the nurse agreed. "You guys are going to do really well when you get him home.

"When do you think that will be?"

"It's hard to tell, and we're not supposed to predict it even, because that's setting your hopes up for something that might change," she said, placing her hand on Anna's shoulder. "At this stage though, he's a little over five pounds. He's stopped having heart rate drops, which is awesome. He has to go at least 24 hours without one before he can go home. If he has one, the clock restarts. Know what I mean?"

Anna nodded and sent up a quick prayer for those heart rate drops to stay away.

"Really, all we're waiting on now is for Benjamin to start taking all his feedings by breast or bottle and then we can remove his ng tube."

"That sounds like heaven. I'd love to see that little face without tubes and tape."

"It's a good face," Nora agreed.

"I think he's going to look a lot like his daddy," Anna added.

"I hope that's a good thing," a deep voice said behind her.

Anna jerked her head around to see Aidan standing beside her chair.

"What are you doing here?" she asked, eyes as round as saucers.

"I missed my family," he said, placing a kiss to her lips and one to Benjamin's little head.

"I got on the road right after we talked," he explained, shrugging his shoulder a little. "I didn't want to be without you tonight."

"Here you go," Nora said, returning to their area with a second recliner. She positioned it beside Anna's and made herself busy checking monitors.

Aidan sat down into the chair and kicked off his shoes. Anna couldn't help but smile at how remarkably comfortable he was in his own skin. He watched her for a while as she attempted to nurse and then bottle feed and burp the baby.

"You look beautiful right now," Aidan said, smiling sleepily at Anna.

"What? You're sleep deprived," she said, dismissing his compliment.

"I'm serious. You're as beautiful right now as you've ever been. You're exhausted, you've got who-knows-what down the front of your shirt, but you're beautiful."

Anna changed Benjamin's diaper and placed him on his father's chest. She tucked a receiving blanket around the baby and sat beside them. "Thank you," Anna said, placing her hand on Aidan's arm. "You look pretty beautiful yourself right now," she said, relaxing back into the recliner.

They cat-napped through most of the night like that, between quiet visits from the nurse to check on Benjamin. At 4 AM, Aidan woke to leave for work. His alarm silently vibrated, bringing with it morning, stiff necks, and dark circles as well as a deeper appreciation for one another.

Anna knew she needed to get home and get some rest. After a few more hours with Benjamin, giving him a bath, dressing him in his clothes and caring for him as much as she was allowed, she started her drive back home.

She was on autopilot driving home, so she jerked a little when her phone rang. She was fighting sleep and needed a little conversation.

"Hello?" she answered, wondering what Jesse was doing calling in the middle of the day.

"Hey, Sis, you busy?"

"Just driving," she said before launching into the breastmilk mix-up, the icy drive, and Aidan's surprise visit.

"Oh, Anna, he's a keeper," Jesse said, a smile evident in her voice. "He missed his family," she said, her voice wistful. "Have you given any more thought to your wedding?" Jesse asked, attempting nonchalance but failing.

"No, Jess, not until the baby comes home.

Jesse made the obligatory listening noises but she wasn't fooling Anna. "What are you up to, Sis?"

"Well, I'm not really up to anything, just thinking

ahead. I know you mentioned you'd like to be married sooner than later, and if Benjamin keeps doing so well he might be coming home in just a few weeks, right?"

"Yes," Anna said, a sense of panic building in her chest. "I hadn't really thought about it like that. Holy crap. I need to get his room in order at Aidan's, now that it's going to be, well, our house."

"Now she's with me," Jesse said. "That puts us at early- to mid-December. I know it'll be mainly family, but we need to think of timing for those that would like to attend.

"Oh my God," Anna said. "I don't know that I have the brainpower to put together a wedding, big or small right now."

"That's where I can help. You know this stuff is right up my alley, Anna."

"When I get home I can call the church to see if the pastor will let us use the small chapel rather than the sanctuary, and find out when she's avail…"

"I'll do it! I'll call her and take care of everything," Jesse interrupted.

Anna wrinkled her forehead, wondering what Jesse was doing.

"Okay. You're on. The trouble is, I want Benjamin to be there, and right now that's still only speculation."

"I get it, Anna. I'll find out when the pastor is available and let her know all about the situation. I know you're kind of in a fog right now, but I think you ought to know that Mom called out some kind of prayer warrior Batman signal.

There are people and churches from all over Southern Illinois praying for my little nephew," Jesse said.

Tears stung Anna's eyes and nose. "Jesse, don't make me cry. I'm so tired and have at least half an hour more to go," Anna said, swiping the wetness off her face.

"Alright, sorry. Didn't mean to make you cry," she consoled. "One more thing, let's talk about Benjamin's nursery. Do you have any idea what you're wanting for your place? Mom's chomping at the bit to set up a nursery at her house and I wondered if you wanted me to help with that as well."

"Jesse, that would be amazing. Thank you so much. I thought I had more time to pick this stuff out. At this point, I'll just be thrilled to have it purchased by the time Benjamin is ready to come home.

"I'll do you one better. I'll get it purchased and between Mom and me, we'll have it washed and ready for the little fella when he comes home. Sound good?" Jesse answered. Anna could practically hear the smile on her sister's face.

"Sounds good," Anna answered, thankful.

"Should we talk about a baby shower? Or a wedding shower?" Jesse asked.

"I think for now we should focus on getting the baby healthy and home and getting me and Aidan married. That's enough major life change for one month, agreed?"

"Agreed. I'm on it," Jesse promised.

"Oh my God," Anna said, suddenly feeling deflated.

"What?"

"A dress. I don't have a dress," Anna nearly moaned.

"I've got this," Jesse answered. "Get some rest, Sis," she said, hanging up the phone.

Anna looked out at the frozen scenery around her and decided that for a typical control freak, she was totally fine handing this over to Jesse. Anna was particular, but there was nobody in her world as detailed and efficient as Jesse. She was going to trust her sister and focus on Aidan and Benjamin.

# *Twenty-Seven*

OVER THE NEXT MONTH AIDAN VISITED the hospital at least two nights a week and one on the weekends. His hours were relentless, which Anna knew was a part of his job. She knew he'd be switching shifts soon, and for now she was just thankful to get time with him in the evenings.

He was so attentive and tender with her that she couldn't wait to spend her life with him. He was already a pretty amazing father. He held Benjamin like he was made of porcelain. The nurses had injected as much normalcy as they could into their routines, even allowing parents to bathe their preemies in little tubs with washcloths. While Anna's hands shook with nervousness when she bathed him in the little gray tub, Aidan's hands were completely steady.

Anna told herself it's because of his practice with Clara, but she had to accept that he was a calmer person than she was, end of story. She nearly let herself feel envious of that, but decided to thank her lucky stars they were even together to begin with. If she was going to get her dander up over something, it was going to be over something more than envy over his steady hands with the baby.

On her drive home, she got a call from a number she didn't recognize. Anna barely turned the radio down when she answered the phone. It was probably a wrong number anyway.

"Hello?" she answered, thumb poised above the disconnect button.

"Anna?" the man's voice questioned.

She flicked off the radio. "This is Anna speaking."

The voice on the other end of the phone sighed. "Anna, it's Ira. May we talk?" he asked, his voice gruff. Anna's stomach turned a little at the sound of his voice. She had tried to take Cathleen at her word about Ira's meaning, but still, she couldn't help but feel angry at Ira's choice of words when he had visited Ben for the first time.

"Anna," he paused, trying to piece together the right words, "I'd like to apologize. I am so sorry for the way I worded my question about your marriage and my grandson."

She felt frozen, fairly certain that Ira Doherty had probably never apologized to another human in his life. Anna was still plenty pissed, but decided for Aidan's sake to take the high road. There was enough worry in their family right now as it was. "It definitely caught me off guard, Ira, but we want to put it behind us," she said, wishing the call would hurry up and get over with.

He sighed into the phone. "Honestly, the word just kind of fell out of my mouth," he said, a half-laugh on his lips. "You'll notice that happens sometimes."

It was Anna's turn to laugh. "I've figured that out. I practically grew up in your house, don't forget."

"I know, kid, I know. That's something else I wanted to talk about with you while I've got you without an audience for a minute. We're a pretty traditional family, Anna. I think Sorcha calls it close minded, whatever that means," he said, his voice trailing off.

Anna froze, wondering what could possibly come next. This was the most she had ever heard Ira speak at one time.

"What I'm trying to say, is that Cathleen and I are so glad it's you. We've wanted Aidan to find a girl and settle down for a long time. Things may have come about in a little different fashion than we would have planned on, but people can like it or lump it. We're happy to have you in our family, and we can't wait to love that baby," he said, his voice thickening with emotion.

Anna couldn't help it, tears flooded her eyes. The loud and gruff Ira Doherty had just given her his blessing. She sniffed noisily and unladylike, wiping her nose on her sleeve. "Ira, thank you. I think we're all going to be just fine."

"Cathleen and I would like to bring something by tonight, if you guys will be home."

"Sure, Aidan should be home by seven or so tonight," she answered, mind reeling.

"Alright, we'll be by then," he said, ending the call.

What a strange call. Emotion, apologizes, more words

than she'd ever heard Ira string together at a time. This life as a Doherty was going to be messy, she thought with a smile. Anna could imagine Cathleen pacing back and forth outside the room where Ira was talking, trying to listen and at the same time feeling guilty for eavesdropping.

AIDAN HAD JUST taken off his coat and boots in the mudroom when the doorbell rang. He closed his eyes, wishing whoever that was would just go away. He was bone tired from his shift and ready to spend some time with Anna. Although she'd been working to make herself feel at home there, she still felt a little like a visitor. He sniffed the air appreciatively, picking up the scent of Italian beef. She passed by the hallway in a blur and waved to him on her rush to the door.

"Hey! I didn't hear you come in, I've got it," she said, throwing open the door.

Aidan walked into the hallway and watched with surprise as his father and mother came in the house balancing something big between them. He closed the distance to take the end his mother was struggling with. When they settled it on the floor, Cathleen removed the blanket that had covered the delivery. Aidan immediately recognized the crib his family had used for all five children.

Anna's hand went to her mouth and she looked at Cathleen. Cathleen was looking at Aidan with big, happy tears in her eyes.

"Mom, thank you," he said, pulling her into a hug.

Anna delighted in watching Cathleen's face. She saw her melt into her son's hug, then bat his hug away so that she could turn to Anna.

"You're welcome, honey. Anna, I hope this is okay with you. I couldn't decide if it was better to ask, but then it would ruin the surprise," she said, her face showing that she plainly hoped Anna was okay with the gift.

Anna wrapped Cathleen into a big hug. "Cathleen, it's beautiful and so special. Thank you," she said. Next, she turned to Ira with a hug. "Thank you, Ira."

"We had it refinished," Cathleen said shyly. "It had been in the attic for over twenty years. I couldn't stand to part with it even though I felt silly over it."

Ira shifted his weight from foot to foot. "It wasn't silly, Cath, we had a lot of memories with that crib. Five kids. Hell, you can still see the teeth marks from one of them,"

"Finn," Cathleen and Aidan said at the same time. Everyone laughed, and the remaining tension left the room.

"Thanks, Pop," Aidan said, pulling his father into an embrace. Ira patted his back hard a few times and pulled away.

Anna thanked her lucky stars that Aidan was so much more comfortable with affection and sharing his thoughts than his father.

"Can we put it someplace out of the way?" Cathleen asked. "You probably haven't even had time to get the room ready, have you, Son?" she asked as Aidan shook his head.

"Good news on that front," Anna said. "Jesse volunteered

to help put it together, if we were okay with it," she asked, waiting for Aidan's reply.

"That's fine with me. I'm not particular," he said. "I'll just be thrilled to get the little guy home."

"Great, I was relieved too. Jesse's got an eye for that kind of thing, and honestly I'd rather spend my time at the hospital than picking out sheets."

"That's right, sweetie. Family is here to help. Thank God you're both home so we all get to be with you all through this."

"That being said, it smells like dinner is on the table, Cathleen. Let's get out of here so the kids can eat and rest," Ira said. "Five o'clock comes early, doesn't it, Son."

Aidan nodded in agreement. Ira had retired from the mines and knew all about it. He had worked for thirty years in the coal mines and spent his days tinkering in his garage, avoiding conversation. Aidan had the feeling his mother was thankful that Ira had his own hobbies. After having him gone for thirty years, she would have a tough time adjusting to stepping over him in the house. With a pang, he thought of Eadie and how she'd give anything to have Walt to step over at home. Their parents' relationships were different, but each a good example in their own ways. Aidan put his arm around Anna as they walked his parents to their car.

He rubbed his hands up and down her arms to warm her on their way back into the house.

"What a beautiful gift," she said, snapping a picture. "I'm going to send this to Jesse after dinner, she's going to love it."

"Yes, it's pretty cool," he admitted. "Now for supper. It smells great and I'm starving," he said, happily taking the cups from Anna's hands to help finish setting the table. He wasn't sure what happened between them, but he was thankful there wasn't any weirdness between his father and Anna. He had been worrying himself sick over how that would pan out.

He watched Anna over dinner and felt his heart grow full with thankfulness. She was like fire to him. He thought she was beautiful to watch, never the same twice and could always make him hot. She could also piss him off quicker than anyone he knew, but he wanted to love and take care of her for the rest of his life anyway.

They settled into bed and he held her body close beside him, reveling in the feel of her. She wiggled around a little and he knew it would be just a few minutes before she scooted away from him. Anna seemed to alternate quickly between hot and cold in bed. He tried to wait it out to see how long it would be tonight.

It was the same each night she'd stayed with him. She started off close and within minutes, out popped her feet from the covers.

"Hormones," she hissed in a whisper.

He leaned over her as she flopped onto her back. "You'll line out eventually," he said. "or so I've heard," he added quickly as her nostrils flared at him. "I know, I know, I'm just a man, what do I know," Aidan said, placing a kiss against her neck. His hand splayed on her belly. He felt her tense;

she hadn't accepted that her body would take more than just a few weeks to bounce back to pre-baby condition. He moved his hand slowly away from the area which made her uncomfortable and instead moved them to a place where he was very comfortable.

Aidan marveled over the ways a baby changed a body. To him, all of it was beautiful. As his fingers touched and teased her, he heard her breathing change and felt a familiar thrill move through his body. His hand found her breast and gently cupped it, working to control his own breathing. *Just a few more weeks*, he thought, missing her body.

Desire burned through Anna as she tried to decide what it was she wanted, and how best to give him what he wanted. They hadn't been able to touch much during the first several weeks, but she was finally feeling a little more like herself, despite feeling like a furnace most of the time. She liked the way her new body seemed to excite him, no matter how temporary the changes were.

Anna rolled to her side, reaching out for him. Her arms wrapped around him and she enjoyed the feel of his lips against her skin. Her hand moved down his shoulder, tenderly down his arm, avoiding where his injury had been. She smiled as she felt him shiver, his kisses pausing. She could almost hear his thoughts, begging for what he hoped she was about to do.

She teased at his boxers, first at the waist, dipping a finger below the waistband, moving around from back to front. Slowly she moved her hands around, feeling his muscled glutes, his strong thighs and eventually, to the opening where she found him, straining to find her.

Anna took him in her hand, finding the weight of him as pleasing as he found her breasts. Her fingers moved against him, velvety soft and hard, the perfect embodiment of the word contrast. They weren't together the way they wanted to be, but it was as close as they could be in the moment. Anna drifted to sleep in his arms and slept like the dead.

"Good morning, Anna," Dr. Moore said, entering Benjamin's area.

"Morning," she said, smiling. Over the last month, Dr. Moore had quickly become her favorite neonatologist. There were a pair of them that checked on the babies each day. One was clearly brilliant but lacked in social skills. Dr. Moore, however, was incredibly personable. He looked a little like a lumberjack, Anna thought. He had a neatly trimmed beard and wore a plaid shirt and suspenders – a stark contrast to the other doctor who looked like he was a sport coat away from a fancy dinner party. Anna would take a less-polished appearance and good bedside manner over a dry personality any day.

Dr. Moore sat down on a swivel chair across from Anna. "Benjamin is doing great, Anna. He's steadily gaining weight now. He's taking all his feedings by bottle or breast and has been for four days now. No heart rate drops at all in five days," he said smiling.

Anna's heart was racing and pounding in her ears. She was afraid to breathe, afraid to disturb the direction of the conversation.

Dr. Moore stared at her with a half-smile. Anna finally realized he was waiting her out. He wanted to make sure she was soaking in what he was saying.

"Yes, sir, he's doing well," she said, rubbing the pad of her thumb against his little cheek. She looked back into the doctor's eyes, wondering if she was smiling as stupidly as she felt like she was.

"We're ready to talk about going home now," he said.

Anna's heart nearly exploded with joy and fear. Home. Away from the nurses and the people that actually knew how to take care of a baby. "Home," she repeated, attempting to gather her senses.

"Yes. Are things all ready at your house, all settled?" Dr. Moore asked, as Anna realized how much time of his she was taking with her lack of conversational skills. She gave her head a quick shake.

"Pretty much. My sister is setting up his room so that I can be here. My husband, uh, fiancé, uh... Aidan," she stumbled over her words. "We're getting married soon, you know, things just happened crazily out of order, and we...." She stopped, realizing she was having the worst case of verbal diarrhea that she'd ever had in her entire life.

Dr. Moore's eyes were bugged out, waiting for her to finish her answer.

"Sorry, I'm a little nervous," she said.

He patted her knee. "It's okay," he said. "Believe it or not, this is usually the way it goes. You spend weeks and weeks waiting for this moment, and then when it comes, it hits you like a ton of bricks."

All Anna could do was nod her head in agreement.

"Okay then, if all goes as planned and this little fella doesn't throw us any surprises, you should be taking him home tomorrow. Your nurse will go through the discharge process with you today and talk you through the car seat test so that you know the drill. It's an ordeal, but you finally get your boy home," he said, standing to leave.

Anna couldn't hold it in. She stood with Benjamin in her arms and hugged the doctor the best she could.

She sat back down and stared into Benjamin's little face. "You're coming home, buddy." Later, after Anna settled Benjamin into his crib and watched him until he fell asleep, her fingers flew to her phone. Though he wouldn't get to see the message until hours later, she couldn't wait for him to know that Benjamin would be discharged tomorrow.

The 'red alert' message went to Jesse, Eadie, Sorcha, and Cathleen next. Anna's phone dinged with messages the whole drive home, but she was too busy thinking of things she needed to do to answer. Her mind bounced around from task to task, to a dreamy state, to fears she was afraid to chase down their spooky little rabbit holes. *We're going to be fine*, she thought to herself, her new little mantra.

# Twenty-Eight

ANNA STARED AHEAD AT AIDAN, trying to decide if she was annoyed or pleased. How was it possible for him to drive so maddeningly slow, she wondered? He always drove with such a lead foot, but he was understandably nervous. She expected him to meet somewhere in the middle and drive like maybe a normal human being. Instead, she glanced at her side mirror to see a line of at least six cars stacked behind them. It was going to be a long drive home on the mostly two-lane road.

From her seat, she had a perfect view of Benjamin. "Your father is driving like a snail," she said, whispering to the baby.

"Hmm?" he said, half-turning around. "Everything okay?" he asked.

"Everything is fine," she said, checking for the 100th time that Benjamin's little blue snot-sucker syringe was tucked beneath his little elbow in the car seat. Thankfully the crisp and cold December day was clear of snow and ice.

JESSE, CATHLEEN, AND EADIE were all hard at work to make their homecoming very welcoming. Cathleen was cooking up a storm to feed the troops while Eadie packed Anna's things at her house. Like the master-magician she was, Jesse had managed to install a complete nursery in the space of a few days. She'd even enlisted the help of her kids. She shopped online at a store in a neighboring city and then sent her two oldest sons, Michael and Luke, after the goods. Levi, her husband, was assigned to hauling over the boxes of things that Eadie was busy packing so that Anna could be fully moved in. Jesse worked to unpack what Levi hauled over as Ryan, Jesse's youngest, painted Benjamin's room the lightest shade of gray. The room had a slightly beachy, nautical feeling, or at least it would by the time Jesse was finished with it.

Hannah and James each had an important job as well. They were in charge of folding the baby laundry that Jesse ferried in from the dryer. Jesse couldn't help but get choked up, watching the family work together like a well-oiled machine.

Levi walked into the house and saw her standing in the doorway, lovingly watching his children as they sorted and folded little blankets and onesies, socks and gowns. "Doing okay, babe?" he asked, snaking his arm around her. Levi knew

Jesse was exhausted, but he also knew she kind of thrived on pulling off something amazing in a short amount of time. She was a worrier, and she talked a lot. A lot. But, she had a heart for family and loved showing her love. That was worth occasionally tired ears, he decided, pulling her in close.

"We could do this too, you know," he said, tilting his head toward the nursery with a devilish smile on his face.

She frowned at him. "What are you talking about?"

He answered by holding his hips against her and wiggling his eyebrows. He pulled her into the hallway, away from the eyes of his nine-year-old twins.

Jesse laughed. "You have to be out of your mind," she said, putting her cold nose against his neck, making him shiver.

"Come on, doesn't it sound like fun?" he asked. "The sleepless nights, the reflux, the poopy diapers?"

"You have definitely lost your mind," she answered. "We already have to drive a Suburban to fit us all in the same vehicle.

"You had that when you moved home, you can't blame it on me," he said, sneaking his hand up the waist of her flannel shirt.

She leaned her head back and took his face in her hands. "Are you seriously asking?" she said, her face screwed up in the most confusing expression he had ever seen on her. We'd be a hundred by the time a baby graduated high school," she said, shaking her head. "No, no way. Definitely not," Jesse replied, pushing against his chest.

"But we could pretend," he said, swatting her on the butt.

"We could practice, you mean?" she clarified, nodding her head in agreement.

"Yes, lots of practice," he said.

Jesse smiled slowly and took a step toward him. She gave him a kiss that curled his toes and pulled away, inches from his mouth. "Get back to work," she whispered.

Levi moaned as if tortured. "Yes, ma'am," he grumbled, heading back to the driveway and awaiting boxes.

The cozy house glowed brightly as the new little family pulled into the driveway. They put the car in park and Aidan grinned back at Anna. "We don't have to go in, you know," he said.

Anna exhaled. She couldn't believe how lucky they were to have help, and at the same time, couldn't wait for everyone to leave so they could feel what it was like to be a little family of three.

"That house is bursting with people," Anna said, looking at the shadows crossing before the windows.

"It is. I think we have enough gas to make it out here for at least another hour," he said conspiratorially.

She sighed. "We are awful people," she said.

"We are," he answered. "But we have each other."

"And this guy," she said, scooping Benjamin up from his car seat. Aidan opened the door to help her out while he handled their bags with one strong arm.

"Let's go meet your family, Benjamin," he said, shepherding his family to their front door.

THE NEXT FEW hours were a circus of hand-washing as family came and went out the front door, with the grandparents taking their turns holding their grandson. Ruthie stayed at Eadie's home to keep Harry company, her gift for the evening. The cousins understood they could look but not touch the baby until Anna deemed them all germ-free enough to take the risk. She had been made well aware of the risk of RSV, and thankfully her family understood. Anna found a way to pull each child aside over the evening to thank them for their hard work in making their home ready.

Long glances were exchanged throughout the evening as Anna and Aidan waited for their home to empty of people a few at a time. Thankfully, everyone seemed to sense how exhausted they were and filtered out pretty quickly after the supper dishes were cleaned up and leftovers stored away, enough to keep them stocked up for the next few days.

Aidan took the baby so that Anna could go take a bubble bath. She soaked and scrubbed, feeling the tension of the last five weeks course through her body. She whispered a prayer for God to teach her from the experience. Her own theory had been that life is never perfect, and that bad or scary things would come and go. Her job was to learn lessons where she could and try hard not to expect answers to the 'why' questions.

When she came back into the living room, she found Aidan asleep in his chair with Benjamin snuggled in close.

He had been fed a bottle and changed into fresh pajamas. Anna placed a hand on his back and another on Aidan's shoulder. As he blinked awake, Anna took the baby and walked into the nursery, flicking off lights in the house as she went.

She sat down in the glider and closed her eyes, holding Benjamin close. Moonlight filtered through the curtains and Anna allowed herself to take stock of the moment. She knew it wouldn't always be peaceful. It would probably rarely be peaceful, but she had this one moment where everything seemed perfect. She listened as Aidan checked the locks on the doors and the water ran in the shower. After a little while, she placed Benjamin in his heirloom crib. Anna watched him sleep for a while and flicked on the baby monitor.

ONCE SHE MADE certain the other end of the monitor was turned on, she collapsed on the bed, asleep before Aidan even exited the shower. He made the rounds, double checking that the house was locked up tight and that the baby was fine, and finally, looked in on his sleeping soon-to-be wife. Life felt pretty good, he thought, smiling as he thought of the plans Jesse had shared with him after dinner. He had to give it to her, she was a pretty excellent schemer. Aidan couldn't wait to see Anna's face when she learned what they had in store for her.

JESSE ARRIVED THE next morning expecting to find a walking zombie and crabby baby. Aidan had to return to work that day, and Jesse was curious how Anna would handle flying solo without the nurses at hand. She had her invisible white-knight hat on and was ready to charge in and save the day.

Instead, she found her capable, only faintly zombie-like sister in the living room.

"Surprise! I brought food," she said, whipping out a package of doughnuts and setting a duffle bag down by the door.

"Yes," Anna whispered. "I'll make you some coffee," she said, handing Benjamin over to Jesse.

"Did you know a baby can wake up every two hours?" Anna asked, fake smiling.

"Yes, yes I did," Jesse said. "Did you keep Mommy up, you little stinker?" Jesse asked the baby. "His hair is going to be orange, isn't it?" Jesse asked.

"Oh yeah. Majorly orange," Anna answered.

Jesse smiled, adoring the tiny hands. While Anna puttered around the kitchen, she tried to decide how to proceed.

"Anna, I found something you might like to look at. Can you grab that bag by the door?

Anna retrieved the bag and set it down on the table. She opened it and pulled out a gown on a hanger.

"Jesse," she said reverently. "What did you find?"

"Mom and I were talking, and she remembered she still had her wedding dress."

"I remember seeing their pictures," she said. "Wow, I can't believe Mom kept it all these years. It still looks beautiful."

"Leave it to Mom. I think she has every original box, garment bag, and shoe box that everything she ever bought came in," Jesse said.

"Oh my God, the shoe boxes!" They laughed. When they were little, they used to sneak in the top of her closet and stack the boxes like bricks to make forts. Eadie's punishment for them sneaking into her closet was to make them put all the shoes back in the correct boxes. They had loved it and always managed to turn it into a game.

"I'm going to go try it on," Anna said, washing the doughnut off her hands. Guess I'd better kiss these goodbye." She smiled.

"Don't give me that crap. You just had a baby, give yourself a break," Jesse snapped.

"I know, I know," Anna said, taking the dress into her bedroom.

She looked down at the dress, impressed that Eadie had chosen it. It was made of an almost gauzy material, flowing into billowing sleeves capped at the wrist. The neckline was a deep v, but was designed to bare more chest bone than breast. With her newfound curves, Anna wasn't in any position to wear it open, but she imagined it could be fitted with a pretty lacy piece for modesty. The v closed a few inches before the empire waist, where it featured tiny little buttons that trailed all the way to the hem. Pockets were sewn into the sides, making the dress a vision of Bohemian romance.

Anna closed her eyes and visualized her mother's wedding pictures, with her nearly white blond hair topped with a baby's breath wreath. Anna was pleased with the fit and stepped out of the bedroom to show Jesse. The sun streamed through the windows and made a gorgeous vision of Anna's coppery-blond hair.

"It's perfect," Jesse said, smiling up at Anna. "Look, baby, it's perfect!" she said, pointing Benjamin toward his mother. "What do you think?" she asked Anna.

"I love it. Think these shoes will work?" she asked raising the hem to reveal buttery soft, cognac lace up boots.

"Those are pretty. Really though, you could wear combat boots under that and nobody would ever know," she said as Anna swished the hem around.

"True, it's plenty long enough," Anna agreed. "Jesse, I haven't made the first call to the pastor to check on dates." She sighed and then stopped, not missing the weird look that flashed on Jesse's face.

"No need, I'm taking care of it, remember?" Jesse asked, forcing her fake-smile. When she sensed Anna was going to press her, she kept talking.

"I called the church and the pastor is available this Saturday afternoon," Jesse said, waiting for Anna to comment one way or another.

"This Saturday?" she gasped, "There's no way I could be ready by then, Jesse. There's the license, the rings, the flowers, the…" she floundered, realizing that now that she had the dress, the groom and the family available, there wasn't really much else she actually needed to worry about gathering.

Jesse let her sputter for a minute until she found the moment to pounce. "If you can get him there, you can get a license at the County Clerk's office. I don't want to spoil the surprise, but the flowers and rings have already been taken care of, as well as the photographer."

"I'll have to talk with Aidan and make sure he's off work, Jesse. His schedule can change any time," Anna said, walking to the fridge where he kept his calendar.

"Anna, he's off work. Everything is set, and everyone is on board. Now we just need the bride," Jesse said, placing the baby in his little bassinet in the living room. "One more thing...look what else I found," she said, digging through her bag. She pulled out a little box and opened it. Inside was the sweetest little baby boy outfit that Anna had ever seen.

"Okay," she said, nodding at her sister. She pulled Jesse into a hug. "Let's get married," Anna said, smiling at Jesse.

"Let's get married," Jesse said, dancing around the room.

# Twenty-Nine

"I've got everything, dear. Don't worry," Eadie said, holding Benjamin in his carseat.

"You've got the snot sucker? And the car seat base is installed, right? The carseat snaps when you get fitted into the base. Want me to do it?" Anna asked, looking from Eadie to Jesse.

"I think she thinks this is your first time around, Eadie," Ruthie said, half-joking. Anna fought back the urge to give Ruthie a dirty look.

"Trust me, kid, I've got this. Let Jesse finish getting you ready, and we'll meet you at the church," Eadie said, giving her daughter a kiss. "You look beautiful, honey. See you soon," she said, carrying Benjamin like a born-grandmother.

"I know *she's* not new at this, but I am," Anna said under her breath.

Jesse exhaled, calming her own nerves. "Take it easy, it's all going to be okay. It's a big day, and everyone is a little on-edge," she said, talking as much to herself as she was Anna.

"You've got the certificates?" Anna asked for the 100th time.

"Yes, for the love of God, I have everything we need," Jesse answered. Jesse had gotten five kids, herself, and one husband ready and out the door already. Now all she needed was for the bride to chill out a little bit and she might just pull this thing off. Levi had already taken all the kids to the church, all she had to do now was get Anna to the church.

She'd been working on this plan for weeks now, and this was the moment she was most excited about. She wrapped Anna up in a gorgeous, vintage green velvet coat that she had found online and practically shoved her out the door.

Anna climbed into the SUV and focused on taking calming breaths. *It's just a short ride to the church*, she thought, though she'd feel better when she had Benjamin within reach again. Jesse pulled out of the driveway and attempted to make small talk with Anna. When they drove right by the church they attended, she thought Anna's head was going to snap off her body.

"Jesse, where are you going?" she asked. "Why aren't there any cars at the church?"

"Just hold your horses, this will all make sense in a little while," Jesse said, turning to look at her sister. "I mean it. Don't ask me any more questions about where we're going. This is part of the fun," she said.

Anna squirmed in her chair and fidgeted with her purse. She had a horrible fear that she was going to have some sitcom, surprise birthday party-type experience. All she wanted was a quiet wedding with their families.

They drove out of town and Anna was completely stumped about where they were going until they took a turn off the highway. She turned in her seat to look at her sister. "What have you been up to, Jesse?" she asked.

"Nope, not a word," Jesse said, smiling so hard Anna thought her face was going to break.

After a few more miles and fairly tense turns up the ice-covered back roads, Jesse pulled into a familiar parking lot. They were at the old, closed-up church beside Copper Creek. But, instead of looking abandoned, the church was lit with candles glowing in the windows. There were cars in the parking lot and the once-forgotten church glowed with warmth and light.

Boughs of evergreen were draped along the entrance and the white wood of the building fairly shined against the backdrop of the setting sun. Anna's eyes welled up with tears and she grabbed Jesse by the neck to hug her.

"Sis, what have you done?" she said softly.

Jesse pulled her handkerchief out of her purse, handing one to Anna as well and took a deep breath. "Anna, when I think back on being a kid with you, this place is at the forefront of so many of our memories. No matter what else was going on in our lives, or how much bigger than you I thought I was, when we were here, this place was a great equalizer. We would play and holler and soak in the sunshine, no matter what the stage.

I can't think of this place without thinking of family. If Dad were here, he would think you look so beautiful," she said, her face crumpling with tears. "He'd walk you down the aisle and be so happy to do it. Levi is honored to do it, but I know it's not the same," Jesse said.

When Anna could speak, she thanked Jesse. "This is so special, and I'm thankful that you put it together. And I'm thankful that Levi is walking me down the aisle. I hope Aidan and I, and you and Levi, are as happy as Mom and Dad were.

"We will be, and so will you, Sis. Let's get in there now before we freeze, okay?" she said. "We've got it all warmed up in there, but we might want to get in and out all the same."

Anna nodded, wondering how Jesse was able to pull together heating a hundred-year-old church as well as getting the windows fixed. As they got closer to the door, Levi opened up and extended a hand to Jesse, and then to Anna.

"You look beautiful, kid," he said.

"Thank you," she said, smiling with surprise. The church had heaters in all four corners of the room. There were evergreen boughs draped on the inside of the pews, with candles perched on holders lined up and down the aisle. The wood floors gleamed with polish, and a piano had been brought in somehow. Anna nodded hello to her pastor and their church's pianist. Filling the dozen or so pews were her and Aidan's families. At the front of the church she saw her mother and Ruthie snuggling Benjamin. Cathleen and Ira were on the other front pew, smiling back at her. Jesse's children and stepchildren, as well as all of Aidan's brothers and sisters were crowded in the pew. Sorcha stood at the front of the church in a beautiful, dark green silk gown, and Evan was opposite her in a wheelchair, looking handsome in a suit.

Anna shot Sorcha a look, to which she answered with a shrug. Now Anna realized why Sorcha hadn't taken any of her calls this week. She was terrible at keeping secrets. Jesse took Anna's coat, tucked it in a little closet and produced from a side table a beautiful red rose bouquet. It was accented with ivy and white stephanotis flowers, waxy and delicate.

Jesse adjusted Anna's hair and gave her a kiss on the cheek. "I love you, Anna."

"I love you too, Jesse."

Jesse walked ahead of Anna in a deep purple gown, taking a seat next to Ruthie and Eadie on the front pew. The pianist started the *Wedding March* as Aidan entered through a side door at the front of the church. He stepped into place and looked toward her, his eyes locking on hers.

Her breath caught in her chest as Levi extended his elbow. She gratefully accepted and he patted her hand and began the slow walk down the aisle. With each step, Anna inhaled the fresh smell of the boughs and lost herself in Aidan's eyes.

At the altar, the pastor smiled at Anna and Levi. "Who

gives this woman?" she asked. "Her mother, her sister and I," he said, beyond honored to participate in the ceremony. He placed Anna's hand in Aidan's and clasped the other man in a hug. "Welcome to the family," he said quietly before taking his seat beside Jesse.

When Aidan smiled at Anna, her heart melted. There he stood, big, strong, and stubborn. Anna knew in her heart that Aidan was going to be an excellent husband. He was sure to be a challenge; he was stubborn as a mule. He had some demons, but she knew she wasn't exactly a walk in the park, either. What she was certain about though, was that he loved her and she loved him, and they both loved that little baby. She smiled thinking about the night it all started so many years ago. Who would've thought one night in a tree house could lead to all of this.

## *The End*

Made in the USA
Middletown, DE
03 January 2023